PROTECTING PIPER

A WAVERLY WILDCATS NOVEL

JENNIFER BONDS

Protecting Piper: A Waverly Wildcats Novel

Cover Art & Design by Cover Ever After
ISBN (Amazon): 978-1-953794-13-0
ISBN (B&N): 978-1-953794-28-4
ISBN (Ingram): 978-1-953794-32-1
First Edition 2023

www.jenniferbonds.com

Hello, Gorgeous.
This one's for you.

1

PIPER

DaddyDom: That's right, Baby Girl. Show me what you've got.

The words scroll across my screen and I hold up not one, but two dresses.

"I can't decide which one to wear." A sultry smile curves my lips and I bat my lashes at the camera. "Can you help me choose?"

The responses come fast and furious, the screen lighting up like the Vegas strip.

"Ah, ah, ah." I spread my arms wide, giving my fans a full body shot as I dangle a fire engine red halter from my fingertips. "To vote for the red dress, send me a rose. If you prefer the black dress,"—I twist the hanger playfully—"send me a diamond."

Emojis flood the screen, but all I see are dollar signs as I scan the replies.

"Oh, it looks like Geoffrey prefers the black one." I hold the dress in front of me, sliding the fabric suggestively over my bare thigh. "The LBD is a classic and it *would* show off my stems."

Not that it matters. I'm not trying to impress anyone. Not in real life, anyway.

"Do we have any leg guys in the house?"

There's a flurry of activity on-screen and I widen my eyes as a bouquet of roses appears.

"Five roses from *GoodTimeGuy*. Thanks, baby." I stare into the camera lens, as if I'm speaking directly to him, and murmur, "I admire a man who knows what he wants."

Especially when he's willing to pay for it.

"I've always loved the color red and my tits look *ah-maz-ing* in this dress."

JustJosh: Don't sell yourself short, Queen. It's your tits that make the dress, not the other way around.

"You're too sweet, Josh. I've missed chatting with you. We should do a private session soon."

There's another burst of activity and the emojis shift from ice blue diamonds to scarlet roses.

"It's going to be a close one," I purr, drawing my elbows in to bolster my cleavage. "We'll just give it another second or two so you can cast those last-minute votes. You know I love it when my guys give me a helping hand."

As does my tuition bill.

SmoothOperator: I'll give you a hand any time you need it, day or night.

I make a mental note to send him a DM. Personal attention is key in this business and it's easier to upgrade existing subscribers than to generate new ones.

The flood of emojis slow to a trickle, but it's just as well because I'm pressed for time.

"It looks like we've got a winner!" I toss the black dress on the bed and hold the red one against my body, using my free hand to smooth the fabric over my curves. I do a slow turn, giving my viewers one last look at the lacy black thong that reveals every juicy dimple on my bare ass.

Always leave them wanting more.

"Thanks, guys. I hate to cut this short, but I'll be back tomorrow night with fresh content, and trust me, you don't want to miss it. In the meantime, don't have too much fun without me."

I blow the camera a kiss and sign off just as my phone vibrates with an incoming call.

Shit. What time is it?

My gaze slides to the clock on the nightstand. Ten-oh-one glows on its face, the hostile red numbers giving *you're late* vibes.

Fuuuck.

I scramble to grab the phone and swipe accept.

"Don't even think about blowing me off," Jenna says by way of greeting. "It's your birthday and dammit, we are celebrating whether you like it or not."

The corner of my mouth hitches skyward. "You and I have very different ideas of what that entails."

Mine includes a big ass slice of lemon cake with no less than three layers of cream cheese frosting. Jenna's includes loud music, Greek Row, and handsy dudes with questionable judgment.

"Where are you?" she asks, suspicion coloring her words. "Because I'm standing out front of Sig Chi and you're nowhere in sight."

That's because I was shaking my ass for money on the internet.

"Sorry. I had some work to finish up, and I lost track of time."

Jenna is my best friend, but even she doesn't know about my side hustle. No one does.

She sighs. "You're still at home, aren't you?"

Busted.

"Yes, but I'm almost ready." I slip the red dress off the hanger. *Multitasking for the win.* If it weren't for my fans, I'd still be trying to figure out what to wear. "I'll be there in ten. Fifteen at the latest."

"*Giiirl.* How are you gonna be late on your own birthday?"

I snort, because she's one to talk. Jenna and I bonded over our mutual tardiness when we were forced to take Sociology of the Family at 8 a.m. freshman year. The prof took immense pleasure in humiliating late arrivals, which was just wrong because...*sociology.* Three years later and we're still tight, bound by tedious lesson plans and a love of iced coffee.

"How much homework can you have, anyway?" she asks, the raucous sounds of the party carrying through the line. "Classes just started."

"The sooner I get off the phone, the sooner I'll get out the door," I tease, dodging her question as I shimmy into the halter, careful not to snag the fabric on my sky-high heels. "Go get your drink on. I'll find you when I get there."

Hell, she'll probably have a better time without me.

Greek Row isn't my scene. I'd rather spend my Saturday night curled up with a good book and a bottle of cheap wine, which is just one of the reasons I don't have many friends in College Park. But between work and school, who has time for a social life?

Besides, I can socialize after I graduate.

"Fine, but you better text me the instant you arrive," Jenna orders. "The girls can't wait to see you!"

I roll my eyes and disconnect. '*The girls*' probably don't give a damn whether I show up or not. Jenna is a sweetheart, but her roommates are toxic AF. The last time I hung out with them, Kylie—Or maybe it's Rylee?—goaded Jenna into doing way too many tequila shots. Then, when she could hardly stand, they ditched her to go dancing at another bar. *Dancing.* Like leaving her behind, blitzed out of her mind, wasn't a big *fuck you* to girl code.

God only knows what would have happened if I hadn't been there to take her home.

All's well that ends well.

Banishing the memory, I duck into the closet and grab a tiny black clutch that can be worn crossbody.

My phone vibrates and I don't need caller ID to know it's Jenna. The girl has zero chill, which is number nineteen on the list of reasons I love her.

I stuff the phone in my bag, touch up my lipstick, and head out.

It's humid as hell when I step onto the sidewalk in front of my apartment building—*yay global warming*—and I can feel my hair frizz, one golden strand after another curling as it sucks up the moisture in the air.

A tiny voice in the back of my head begs me to spring for an Uber, but it's not happening. I work too damn hard to blow cash needlessly, especially this early in the semester.

Halfway down University Drive, my cell vibrates again.

This time, I fish it out of my purse, expecting to see Jenna's name, but when I glance at the screen, my stomach drops.

Nora.

I should've expected this, but... It wouldn't be the first time my mother forgot my birthday, and honestly, it's better that way.

For me.

I draw a steadying breath, filling my lungs with hot, sticky air, and steel my resolve as I swipe to reveal the full message.

Nora: Happy birthday, baby. Twenty-two and fully grown! Do you think you could send your mama some cash? I'm a little light this week and food prices are insane.

Jesus Christ. The woman has no shame. She couldn't even be bothered to type a separate message for the cash grab.

Typical.

Red-hot fury bubbles up from the pit of my stomach. Six months of radio silence and now this? A birthday text wrapped in manipulation and guilt?

Talk about the gift that keeps on giving.

My pace quickens and I blow right past one ivy covered building after the next, fueled by outrage and indignation.

The implication that she won't be able to eat this week unless I send cash is just too much, especially when we both know she'll spend whatever I send on booze and cigarettes.

Do not engage.

Anything short of a promise to send money will end in a fight and I'm not about to ruin this night by arguing with a selfish, bitter—

Letting her live rent free in your head is the definition of engaging.

Right. I'll just leave her on read.

I'm about to lock the phone when another message pops up.

Nora: Don't ignore me, Piper Reynolds. I brought you into this world.

You little ingrate is unspoken, but heavily implied.

Maybe she's learning self-control at the ripe old age of forty-two.

Or not. Three little dots appear on the screen and I brace for impact.

Nora: I know you read my message.

Do. Not. Engage.

I huff out a breath, reaching for calm as I round the corner onto Greek Row.

Waverly University is known for its picturesque quad and

impressive stonework, but this is a whole other level of extra. Elegant mansions line the street, some brick, some colonial, all massive. I've been here before, but only in passing. I've never actually set foot in any of these houses, but there's no way they can be as nice on the inside as they are on the outside. Not with hundreds of drunk students lining their halls and...puking in the yard.

A guy in a pink polo hurls into an azalea bush as his buddies cheer him on from the front porch of ATO.

Gross.

I avert my gaze, giving silent thanks the puker isn't partying at Sig Chi. They probably have their own messy drunks, but watching someone else toss their cookies doesn't exactly make me want to pound a beer.

My phone buzzes in my hand and I silently debate the merits of blocking my mother before I break down and read the message.

Nora: Don't be stingy. I see the pictures on your Instagram.

Nora: You clearly aren't hurting for grocery money.

The thinly veiled dig at my weight is so on brand it barely registers. The woman has been tearing me down all my life, but after years of guilt and shame, I've finally learned to appreciate my body.

Without it, I wouldn't be able to dance, attend college, teach.

Pay for the much-needed therapy required to undo years of childhood trauma.

So fuck diet culture, fat shaming assholes, and body dysmorphia.

I'm a fine ass woman with banging curves and tonight I'm going to shake it off like the Queen of Pop herself.

I toss my hair over my shoulder, lift my chin, and strut like I'm working the damn catwalk.

Me-ow.

A few heads turn my way as I approach Sig Chi, but my eyes are fixed straight ahead. The frat house, a brick behemoth with a wide front porch and thick white columns, would put Times Square to shame. Lights glow in every window and the pulse of music drifts from the open front door, the thumping bass a siren song for bad decisions.

There are people everywhere. On the porch. In the grass. On the freaking roof.

What have I gotten myself into?

Sweat beads along my brow and I silently curse myself for agreeing to a night on Greek Row. After all, it's *my* birthday. If I'd said I wanted to hit the Diner or catch a movie, Jenna would've agreed.

But no, I had to slip back into my people pleasing ways because she's crushing on some frat bro who probably goes by Tripp, only wears Lacoste, and isn't worth a second of her time.

You could always text her and say you aren't feeling well.

Yeah, right. She'd see right through my bullshit.

It's fine. I'll have a few drinks and then I can duck out and—

The heel of my stiletto slips between the cracks in the sidewalk and I careen forward, arms flailing.

"Sonofabitch!"

I manage to avoid face-planting on the sidewalk—*Go me!* —but the victory is short-lived. My stupid freaking heel is wedged in that crack like a thong that's two sizes too small.

Because *of course* it is.

"You've got to be kidding me." I bend over, ass on full display as I wrestle with my shoe. "Is this karma? Am I being punished for being late? Because if so, I'm pretty sure birthday rules apply. Like, you get a free pass or whatever."

Aaand...now I'm talking to myself.

I let out a string of curses that would make a barfly blush and jerk my foot so hard the strap of my shoe cuts off circulation to my toes.

Spoiler alert: the little fucker doesn't budge.

"Happy birthday to me." I sigh and wipe the sweat from my brow. "First Nora, now this?"

At least the night can't get any worse.

2

BRADY

GREEK ROW IS A MADHOUSE. The treelined street may look stately and conservative by the light of day, but when the sun sets, all bets are off. It's practically a mecca for students looking to get wasted and have a good time. Thanks to today's win over Idaho, the crowds are even more intense than usual as my boys and I make our way down the block.

"This is going to be a shit show," Reid says, narrowing his eyes as we approach Sig Chi.

"Or it's going to be the greatest night of our lives," Coop shoots back with his usual swagger. "Loud music, cold beer, gorgeous women. What more could you ask for?"

Reid, ever the pragmatist, just shakes his head.

It's not too late to bail.

"Don't even think about it." Parker claps me on the back, as if reading my mind. "Tonight, we're celebrating."

"Fuckin' right we are," Smith chimes in.

I scoff. "Since when do y'all need an excuse to party?"

"Since never." Parker shrugs. "But it sure as hell beats the alternative."

No kidding. Today's game was too close for comfort, but

we pulled out the W, which means we get to party and Coach will look the other way as long as no one gets arrested. Saturday night is the only time the guys and I can cut loose during football season because Sunday is our day off.

No workouts, no practice, no games.

"One down, eleven to go!" Coop crows, fist bumping a guy who stumbles past in a blue and white Wildcat jersey.

"Don't get cocky," Reid warns. "We still have miles to go."

Not to mention a grueling schedule and a brand-new kicker. Kennedy performed well today, but time will tell how she holds up under the pressure of being thrust into the spotlight.

"Thanks for the reminder, Debbie Downer." Coop turns his trademark smirk my way and I brace for impact. "You're starting to sound like Vaughn."

"You say that like it's a bad thing." I roll my eyes, but the fact is, if Cooper DeLaurentis wasn't busting my balls, he wouldn't be Cooper DeLaurentis.

"One anti-fun mountain man is more than enough in my book." He slings an arm around Reid's shoulders, as if oblivious to the oppressive heat that's got me sweating like a sinner in church. "For the record, if you two grow matching beards, I'm staging an intervention."

"Uh, oh," Parker taunts in a sing-song voice. "Someone's jelly."

"Not in this lifetime." Coop gestures to his face, which bears a strong resemblance to the god of thunder. "You think I want to hide this jawline under a fuckin' bird nest?"

My middle finger shoots up reflexively. "Relax, Princess. One day you'll hit puberty and then you'll be able to grow a beard of your own, just like a *real* man."

"Screw you. If that thing gets any bigger, it won't fit through the door."

"Funny," I deadpan. "I was going to say the same thing about your head."

The rest of the guys howl with laughter and I silently curse my new beard.

It's hot and itchy and I only grew it because they kept ragging on my baby face. Now I'm stuck with it, at least until the jokes cool down. No way am I going to give Coop the pleasure of thinking I couldn't handle a little shit talk.

I'd never hear the end of it.

Imagine how they'd react if they knew you were a virgin.

A shudder ripples down my spine.

My boys are my home away from home—the family I chose—but that doesn't mean they won't give me a hard time.

It's what brothers do.

"Now this," Coop says, turning left onto the sidewalk that leads up to the Sig house, "is what I call a party."

Like every other frat on Greek Row, the Sig Chi celebration has spread outside. Partygoers spill onto the porch and drunk couples dot the lawn, stumbling around as they grope one another in the dark. The music is loud, the vibe chaotic, the inhibitions low.

So, basically my worst nightmare.

The thing is, I get tongue tied around women and all the PDA at these frat parties makes me twitch. Maybe I'm old-fashioned or maybe it's the lack of experience, but shouldn't intimacy should be...well, intimate? Just the thought of all those probing stares is enough to spike my blood pressure.

Reid's eyes lock on mine, and I turn away.

With the expectations of Wildcat Nation at an all-time high, our captain has enough on his plate without worrying about me. Besides, I've been to dozens of these ragers over the years. One more isn't going to kill me.

I follow the guys up the walk, but pull up short when I spot a woman bent over at the waist, wrestling with her shoe.

"Stupid motherfucking piece of shit—"

The words spew from her mouth exorcist style as she struggles for balance, her tiny red dress inching skyward, threatening to expose her backside.

Whatever she says next is drowned out by the rushing in my ears.

Before I can make a conscious decision, my feet are moving, my stride chewing up the distance between us. "Need a hand?"

Her body stiffens, and she pauses her tirade for just a beat. "Nope."

She tugs on the shiny black heel, which is buried between two slabs of concrete, but it doesn't yield.

"I really think—"

"It's all good," she says, face masked by a curtain of shiny blonde hair. "I've got this totally under control."

Her voice is low and husky, soothing despite the rebuff.

"All right, but my mama taught me to step up when I see a woman in distress."

She straightens, tossing those blonde waves over her shoulder, and my mouth goes bone dry as I stare into the face of the most beautiful woman I've ever seen. My brain kicks into overdrive, searing every gorgeous detail into memory: dewy golden skin, full crimson lips, high cheekbones, and eyes like summer skies in West Virginia.

Perfection.

"I can take care of myself, thank you very much." She plants her hands on her hips and my gaze follows, devouring her luscious curves before returning to her eyes, which are nearly level with my own. At 6'6, that *never* happens. "You can go now."

I clear my throat, searching for something to say, but come up empty.

And this is why you're single.

If Coop were here, he'd have no problem coming up with something witty, but charm must've skipped a generation in my family because I've got nothing.

No, that's not true. I've got something better than pretty words: action.

"Uh, let me just..." Flames lick my cheeks and I curse my useless tongue. "I can probably..."

Screw it.

I squat down to release the shoe just as the blonde jerks her knee up.

The heel of the patent leather torture device snaps off and she drives her knee into my gut. Air bursts from my lungs and I fold like an accordion, pain radiating from the point of impact as I drop to my knees. The sudden movement must throw her off balance too because her nails dig into the rigid muscles of my shoulders and before I know it, my face is buried between her thighs.

They're soft and warm and... *Holy shit.*

My face is in her...

In her...

Vagina.

Fuck.

Fuckfuckfuck.

What am I supposed to do now? What's protocol for burying your face in a stranger's lady bits? Do I give her a compliment? Apologize and throw myself at her mercy?

For starters, try removing your face from her vag before things get awkward.

This cannot be happening. If I get tagged for sexual harassment, Coach is going to kill me.

For a long moment, we stand frozen, neither of us moving.

Then, as if by silent agreement, we spring apart.

"I'm so sorry. I didn't mean to…" I trail off, face a five-alarm blaze as I gesture to her nether regions.

"It's fine." She sighs and glances down at her broken heel, which is protruding from the sidewalk like a fence post. "That's what I get for buying cheap shoes."

I wouldn't know a designer label if it bit me in the ass, but I nod, letting fast fashion take one for the team.

"Well, as delightful as this has been," she says, shifting her weight, "I think this is my sign to call it a night."

She turns to go, gait awkward and uneven, and I leap into action, pulling my phone from my pocket.

"Wait. Let me get you an Uber."

It's the least I can do after— *Nope.* Not even going there.

I pull up the app and I'm punching in the request when she turns—unsteadily—on her good heel.

"It's just a few blocks. I'm not going to waste money on a car service."

"My treat," I say automatically, noting the driver is only two minutes away. "I won't be able to sleep tonight without knowing you got home safe and sound."

"I'm a big girl. I think I can manage on my own."

Until some drunk creep tries to hit on you…

Yeah, that's not happening.

"I can't, in good conscience, let you walk home alone."

My mother would have my hide. Besides, I'd never forgive myself if something happened to her. College Park isn't exactly crime central, but I'm not about to risk her safety on some half-baked statistic. I don't know a damn thing about her. Hell, I don't even know her name. But I know with every fiber of my being that I want to protect her from harm.

"Right." She laughs, the low timbre as smooth as scotch. "Because it's not in your nature to ignore a damsel in distress."

Relief floods my chest. Now we're getting somewhere. "Exactly."

"Oh my God." She rolls those cerulean eyes skyward. "I can't even."

"You can't even what?"

I've completely lost the thread of the conversation.

"Are you serious right now?" She studies me, brow furrowed. "Jesus, you are."

"I...have no idea what you're talking about."

"It's just an expression of speech." The corner of her mouth twitches and, damn, what I wouldn't give to see her smile. "This whole boy next door routine may work on other women, but I'm no damsel and I'm hardly in distress."

"The Uber will be here any minute." I glance down at her busted shoe. "You can't walk home in those things. You'll break your ankle."

She shrugs. "I can always go barefoot."

"The hell you can." Just the thought of it makes my stomach clench. "Do you have any idea what kind of crap is littering this street?"

She arches a brow and I dive on the silent challenge.

"Rocks. Rusty nails. Broken bottles." I tick them off on my fingers for emphasis. "Hepatitis B."

She snorts. "Pretty sure that's an STI."

"Exactly."

It wouldn't be the first time some douchebro tossed a used condom by the wayside.

Before she can lob another protest my way, a dark Toyota Corolla glides to the curb, an Uber decal displayed on the windshield.

Thank Christ. If it had taken any longer, she really would have tried to walk home barefoot.

I confirm the driver and license plate match the details in the app and then I open the rear door. "No point walking when there's a perfectly good car right here."

Indecision flares in her eyes and I watch, transfixed, as she worries her bottom lip, teeth sinking into the tender flesh.

"It's the least I can do." I step away from the car to give her space. My size makes people edgy and the last thing I want to do is scare this girl. "No strings."

She nods, a quick, decisive jerk of the chin. "What the hell."

I avert my gaze as she climbs into the back seat and just as I'm about to close the door, she looks up at me from under her lashes, a brilliant smile lighting her face. "Thanks."

"Anytime." At least, that's what I try to say, but she's so damn pretty when she smiles that my tongue gets twisted in knots and it comes out sounding like Klingon.

She pulls the door shut and I watch as the car pulls away from the curb.

It's only as the red glow of the taillights grow smaller that I realize I didn't even get her name.

3

PIPER

WORST BIRTHDAY EVER.

Worst birthday ever.

The Uber driver, a Black woman who can't be much older than me, types my address into the GPS as I text Jenna. She's going to kill me for bailing, but what choice do I have? It's not like I can strut around in one four-inch heel all night.

My legs are strong, but they're not that strong.

I press send and relax into the headrest, letting my eyes drift shut as the car pulls away from the curb.

The night wasn't a total bust.

Ha. It'll take more than one well-mannered stranger to restore my faith in men.

Says the woman who left her knight in shining armor in the dust.

I did not leave him in the dust. There was a sidewalk.

And it's early. Chances are, he's staying to party.

Or...he just used his last ten bucks to get you an Uber.

Doubtful. Waverly's an expensive school. Most of the students are solidly middle-class, if not affluent. Besides, it's not like I asked him for a ride. *He's* the one who insisted on being all chivalrous.

So that makes it okay for you to behave like an entitled asshole?
Yes. *No.*
"Ugh."
"Everything okay back there?" the driver asks, voice laced with concern.

My eyes snap open and maybe it's guilt or maybe it's curiosity, but I twist in my seat, peering out the back window.

Sure enough, my sexy savior is making his way down the street, hands shoved into the pockets of his jeans.

"Can you pull over?"

The driver complies and I roll down my window. When he catches up, I call out to him. "Need a lift?"

Surprise transforms his rugged features, but it's quickly replaced by a shy smile. And damn if my ovaries don't come to attention. "You don't mind sharing?"

There's a dirty joke on the tip of my tongue, but I bite it back. "You're the one paying. That means you get to use the service, too."

"I didn't want to come off like an entitled creep." *Be still my heart.* He rakes his fingers through his inky black hair and *wow.* His hands are the size of dinner plates.

You know what they say about guys with big hands...
I slam the door on that line of thinking.
Yes, he has a drool worthy smile.
Yes, he seems genuinely charming.
No, I am not interested.
I shove the car door open. "Come on, Galahad, get in."

He squeezes into the back with me—no small feat since he's an actual freaking giant—and rattles off his address to the driver.

"Okay if I drop you first?" she asks, gaze finding mine in the rearview mirror. "Your place is closer."

"Works for me."

"Y'all can drop me first," Galahad drawls, his low gravel sending me. "If you don't want me to see where you live, I mean."

I turn to face him and it's all I can do not to laugh. The poor guy is folded like origami. The top of his head is pressed to the ceiling despite the fact that he's ducking, and he has to sit sideways because his legs are way too long for the cramped backseat.

Who even is this man?

He shifts awkwardly, and I realize he's still waiting for an answer.

"It's fine," I say, waving off his concern.

My building has great security and with over two hundred apartments, it's nothing if not anonymous.

We ride in silence for a few blocks, the only sound the steady beat of R&B pulsing from the stereo. College Park passes in a blur, giving me ample time to study the walking contradiction beside me.

The guy is proof you can't judge a book by its cover.

Despite his size—which is intimidating as hell—he's soft-spoken, compassionate, and apparently self-aware.

I'm a tall woman at 5'10, and even I was intimidated when I looked up to find him towering over me on Greek Row. His height is staggering, yes, but he's also muscular, with broad shoulders and a barrel chest that suggests regular workouts. He's fit, but not ripped, and there's a softness to him that's easy to miss if you don't look too closely.

It's not just physical, it's in his eyes as well.

They're gentle. Warm. Reassuring.

A woman could lose herself in those whiskey-colored irises.

And don't even get me started on his body art. I'm a sucker for a good tattoo and his left arm is inked wrist to shirtsleeve with roses, and nestled between the shadowed blossoms is an intricate compass that points north.

Does it hold special meaning for him?

I part my lips to ask, but the driver cuts me off.

"Here we are," she says, rolling to a stop in front of my building.

I glance up at the high-rise, and when I turn back to Galahad, he's already climbing out of the car.

No surprise there.

The man has proven he's got impeccable—if not antiquated—manners. Dumping a woman at the curb probably isn't his style.

He jogs around the car and before I know it, he's opening my door.

Damn. No guy has ever opened a door for me on a date.

This isn't a date.

Whatever. It's still a nice gesture.

I slide out of the car, praying I don't accidentally flash him the goods.

The goods he had his nose buried in ten minutes ago?

My entire body heats at the memory of his beard scraping my thighs and it's all I can do not to fan myself as I straighten.

"Thanks again for the ride."

"It was no problem." He offers me that shy smile again and it nearly undoes me. I don't know what it is about this guy, but it's like the universe is testing my resolve. "I'm Brady Vaughn, by the way."

Brady.

The name is traditional, yet reserved, just like the man before me.

It suits him.

"And you are?"

I weigh the question. I'm not in the habit of giving my

name to strangers, but he gave me a lift and despite his size, he seems harmless enough, like a giant teddy bear.

So do all serial killers before they chop you into little pieces.

Yeah, but how many of them use Uber?

Brady clears his throat and I throw caution to the wind.

"I'm Piper."

"It's nice to meet you, Piper." He extends his hand and when I take it, his calloused fingers envelop my own. His grip is firm, his touch feather light, and when our palms brush, lightning sparks between us, shooting straight up my arm and into my chest, where it warms me from the inside out. "Well." He releases my hand. "Now that we've been properly introduced, maybe I could take you out sometime?"

"You want to take me out?" Because yes, despite the warmth flooding my body, my brain is light-years behind. "Like a date?"

The words escape before I can stop them, but in my defense, I so didn't see this coming. There was no flirting in the car. No witty banter. No accidentally bumping my knee with his, which is actually pretty freaking awesome because despite being smashed in the backseat of a compact sedan, he didn't even try to manspread.

"Yes." Brady's ruddy cheeks flush scarlet behind his thick beard. "I'd like to take you on a date, Piper."

"Oh." Alarm bells clang in my head as I meet his hooded Jack Daniel's eyes. "That's really sweet, but—"

"You already have a boyfriend." Disappointment flickers across his face and he throws those massive hands up in self-defense. "I should've known. It was stupid of me to think a gorgeous woman like you would be single."

Gorgeous? Did he just call me gorgeous?

So not the point, Piper.

Right.

"It's not that," I say, trying to soften the blow. "It's just that I don't date."

It's too risky with my X-rated side hustle. If the College of Education—or worse, a prospective employer—found out I was camming, I'd lose everything I've worked so hard to achieve.

Public schools are liberal, but they're not *that* liberal.

So, yeah, even though Brady Vaughn seems like the perfect man—an assessment my ovaries wholeheartedly support—dating is a risk I can't afford to take.

"You don't date?" Brady echoes, perplexed. "Ever?"

I shrug. "No time. Between work and school, I'm spread pretty thin."

The only reason Jenna and I remain tight is because she refused to let me cut her out when I started camming. She didn't know why I was pulling back from our friendship sophomore year, but with her usual grit and determination, she just kept chipping away at my defenses until I caved.

Still, I'm careful to keep my work secret because I don't want to put her in an awkward situation.

"How about coffee, then?" Hope shines in his eyes and something in my chest loosens. "No one's too busy for coffee."

True, but... If things go well, next time he'll want to have dinner. Maybe watch a movie. Then what?

Then you'll have to break it off before he finds out you're a cam girl.

No, it's better to not start anything at all. No point wasting my time or his.

"I'm sorry." I step away and give him a little finger wave as I make my retreat. "You seem like a great guy, but I just can't."

I turn on my broken heel and this time, I don't look back.

The elevator ride up to my apartment is endless and by the

time I lock the door behind me, I'm ready to put this entire night into a black hole.

Well, maybe not the *entire* night.

Meeting Brady was...refreshing.

Wrong time, wrong place.

It's the story of my life. With a sigh, I unbuckle my shoes and drop what's left of them into the kitchen trashcan.

Maybe if we'd met a year from now, things could have been different. But we didn't and they aren't. There's no point dwelling on what might have been, even if it's the first time I've ever been tempted to break my no dating rule.

I pad down the hall to my bedroom, flipping light switches as I go.

The thing about living alone is, it's lonely.

Fortunately, I'm no stranger to solitude. My mother wasn't around much growing up and I learned early that light and sound make great companions, especially when the darkness creeps in.

I pull up my music app, choose a playlist, and drop my phone in the docking station next to the bed. It's just after eleven. If I crash now, I can get an early start tomorrow, but between my mother's texts and the tension with Brady, I'm too revved up to sleep.

Normally I'd have a glass of wine to help me relax, but I don't drink when I'm in my feelings. I've seen the damage it can do, and I vowed long ago not to venture down that path.

All dressed up and nowhere to go.

Fuck it. I grab my laptop from the foot of the bed and flip the screen up.

No way am I going to waste this look feeling sorry for myself. My hair and makeup are already done, I might as well get a head start on this week's content.

I log into Fangirl and scroll through my messages.

Most are inane comments on my last livestream, but members can also send requests for personalized content. It's one of the more lucrative aspects of Fangirl and a great way to supplement my subscription income.

I read through the requests, searching for something that doesn't require a lot of prep work.

PediFiend: Hey CurvyGirl, I've been thinking about those smooth, sexy feet of yours. Can I get my monthly pics early? Dying to see your fall colors.

I glance down at my toenails, which are painted the same shade of emerald green he requested last month, and make a mental note to schedule a pedicure.

CrushingIt: How do you feel about crush vids? I'd love to see you get those pretty feet messy with a box of fat, juicy beetles. They'd squish so nice under those big beautiful heels of yours. (Bare feet required.)

I shudder at the prospect of live insects crawling on my skin, but my gaze shifts automatically to the dollar sign in the upper right corner of the message.

Two hundred dollars? To step on some bugs?

My stomach lurches.

Nope.

No way. Can't do it.

Don't yuck someone else's yum.

It's a fundamental rule of camming. You have to be adventurous to make it in this business, but that doesn't mean accepting every offer that comes across your dashboard. If you're not into a kink, viewers will know, and nothing kills the vibe faster than an unenthusiastic performance.

I keep scrolling and pause, curiosity piqued, when I see the words *alien cock*.

SpaceCowboy: How do you feel about alien cock? I'm looking to expand my private collection and I'd love to see you ride a big blue tentacle, tits bouncing as you impregnate yourself with alien eggs and lay them for my viewing pleasure.

That's a thing? How did I not know about this?

I run to Etsy, and sure enough, there are listings for all kinds of fantasy dildos. There's a jellyfish. Dragons. Monsters. Alien ovipositors with silicone eggs.

Oh, and you can custom order in your favorite color.

Damn. I need to up my game.

And do some Kegels.

So much for making personalized content.

I close the laptop and scan the room, confirming there are no identifying items on display. Nothing's changed since I filmed earlier, but there's no such thing as being too cautious. The last thing I need is a stray Waverly sweatshirt showing up in one of my videos.

Mistakes like that lead to exposure.

I grab a pair of red heels from my closet and, as I slip them on, Brady Vaughn comes loping into my thoughts.

What would your knight in shining armor think if he could see you now?

The poor guy would probably be scandalized.

I'm not ashamed of the work I do, but the world is full of people who look down on sex workers. People who equate sexual health—sexual empowerment—with depravity. People who would never allow a sex worker, or even a former sex worker, to teach their children in the classroom.

I don't know if Brady is one of those people, but he definitely gives sweet and naïve.

I'll bet just the word *sex* makes him blush.

Who knew guys like that still existed?

More importantly, why do I care? It's not like I'm ever going to see him again.

Not outside of my fantasies, anyway.

Inside them.... I can savor every sexy inch of the bearded giant.

Arousal slams into me like a tsunami and my nipples pucker at the thought of Brady's full lips on my skin, his thick cock buried between my soft thighs. My pussy clenches, aching to be filled, and a whimper bursts from my lips.

This need—my desire for Brady—is a ravenous creature that won't be denied.

I grab my favorite vibrator from the nightstand and power up my camera, a sultry smile fixed firmly in place.

It's playtime.

4

BRADY

"Same time next week?"

Marty nods and I squeeze his shoulder before rising to my feet. He tears into the care package I delivered, my presence all but forgotten as he unwraps a sandwich.

Who's going to look out for him when you're gone?

Guilt tears at my conscience and my scalp begins to tingle, but I can't afford to let it weigh me down. There's still plenty of time to figure it out. To convince Marty the local shelter is worth another go. To help him get back on his feet.

Just because he's down on his luck now, doesn't mean he can't turn things around.

I shove my hands into the pockets of my gym shorts and make my way down College Ave, scanning every passing face for Piper's gorgeous smile. I come up empty.

Again.

It's been two weeks—two weeks of pulse-pounding anticipation—and all I have to show for my efforts is disappointment.

It's frustrating as hell, but I haven't given up hope.

Our paths crossed once. There's nothing to stop them from crossing again.

The familiar scent of grilled cinnamon stickies invades my nostrils and my stomach growls. One look at the line snaking out of the Diner is all it takes to kill my appetite.

So much for breakfast.

I duck my head and cross the street, praying I haven't been spotted.

It's a statistical improbability for someone my size, but a guy can hope.

Don't get me wrong. I appreciate the fans and all the support the team gets, but I'd rather not spend my day off breaking down plays and fielding questions about next week's matchup against Iowa.

My cell vibrates and I pull the device from my pocket, swiping accept as I bring it to my ear. "Hey, Gran."

"Have you found my future granddaughter-in-law yet?" she demands, getting right to the point.

It's the second time in as many weeks she's called to ask this question.

You're the dumbass who told her about Piper.

Yeah, well, if I'd known then what I know now, I probably would've kept the story to myself.

Bullshit.

I've never been good at keeping things from Gran, even when I was little. Once, when I was eight, I accidentally drove my grandfather's tractor through her flower garden. I swore up and down it must've been wild deer, but she wasn't buying.

So, yeah. One look at my face on video chat and she'd have known something was up.

"I'm not getting any younger," she announces when I don't answer.

"You're only sixty-two." I press up against the window of an organic food store, allowing a woman with a stroller to pass. "I think we've got time."

"And I think you should've gotten her number."

No kidding, but I was so damn nervous I totally fumbled the play.

"What can I say? It was a rookie mistake." One I won't repeat if the universe gives me a second chance. "Besides, aren't you the one who always says what's meant to be, will be?"

My grandparents fell in love at first sight. It was the same for my parents, though my father turned out to be a cheating bastard.

You win some, you lose some.

I don't know if Piper and I are meant to be, but I'm damn sure going to find out. I was drawn to her in a way I've never been drawn to a woman before, and it wasn't just her looks. It was the way she stood her ground. Found humor in a crappy situation.

The way she reminded you of the two most important women in your life.

"You still have to put in the work." Gran laughs quietly. "Did you know your grandfather brought me flowers every day for a month when we started dating? It was part of his charm offensive."

My chest tightens at the mention of my grandfather. He was a good man and if he hadn't died in a farming accident ten years ago, I have no doubt he'd be at her side recounting every detail of their courtship.

"I'll be sure to send Piper flowers," I promise. "*If* I ever find her."

"Honestly, Brady. It's like you're not even trying." She sighs and I imagine her sitting in her porch rocker, sipping her coffee. "It's been two weeks."

Two long, torturous weeks.

"How hard can it be to find one woman?" she asks breezily.

Seriously?

"There are forty thousand students on campus, half of which are women. Plus, you've got professors, administrators, coaches—"

"Prince Charming didn't give up on his true love," she interjects, ignoring my extremely valid protest as she compares me to a prick who couldn't even remember his woman's face. "And he had to search every home in the kingdom."

I chuckle in spite of myself. "That's called stalking, and it's against the law."

"That didn't stop your grandfather." She pauses, as if weighing her next words. "I suppose it's a different time. Don't get arrested, sweetheart. Your mother would be so disappointed."

She's not the only one.

"You can relax, Gran. I—"

Holy shit.

I freeze, unable to believe my eyes.

Piper.

I'd know her delectable body anywhere. It's the first thing I think about when I wake up in the morning and the last thing I see before I fall asleep at night.

I open my mouth to call out, but I'm at a loss for words. I've spent weeks searching for this woman, and in all that time, I didn't once consider what I'd say when I found her.

Dumbass.

No point dwelling on past mistakes. What I need right now is a plan. She's thirty yards out and closing in fast.

What would Parker do in this situation?

He definitely wouldn't panic.

No, he'd be cool. Collected. In control.

Fuck. Why am I like this? I talk to women all the time in class. This is no different. So what if Piper is gorgeous and magnetic and totally out of my league?

She slows and my stomach sinks when she opens a shop door and disappears inside.

This is your chance, asshole. Don't blow it.

"Gran, I've got to go. I'll call you later."

We disconnect and I hurry to catch up with Piper. When I reach Flex, I don't think twice about entering. If this is where Piper's at, it's where I need to be, too. The lobby is light and airy, muted shades of gray and white filling the open space. There's a small reception desk to the right of the door and behind it, a dark-haired woman speaks into a headset. She holds up a finger to indicate she'll be right with me. I nod and turn to the wide corridor that extends to the rear of the building.

There's a flash of blonde hair as Piper turns right at the end of the hall.

Determination flares in my gut and when the receptionist turns her back, I slip down the corridor.

I pass a yoga studio and an aerial studio, both of which are dark, but visible through a wall of plate-glass windows. My expectations are non-existent when I reach the last room, which is probably a good thing because nothing could have prepared me for what I see when I look through the viewing pane.

Surprise washes over me as I take in the large space. It's brightly lit and there are a dozen women—including Piper—stuffing their belongings into cubbies at one end of the studio. But it's not the cubbies or the women that steal my breath.

It's the silver poles that extend floor to ceiling throughout the room.

They're...stripper poles.

What the hell?

I watch dumbstruck as the women fan out, chatting and stretching, but I only have eyes for Piper.

Her hair is pulled up in a sleek ponytail and she's stripped down to a black bra and a pair of strappy black booty shorts that show off her long legs and voluptuous curves.

She looks incredible.

I can't tear my eyes off her as she crosses the room, joining a petite brunette in the back row. She hasn't spotted me yet, but that's okay. I enjoy watching.

Because that doesn't sound creepy at all.

What's the point of having an observation window if you can't use it?

To my left, someone clears their throat. "Can I help you?"

My muscles tense and I slowly turn to face a slender Asian woman. Like Piper, she's wearing booty shorts, but her arms are crossed in a way that suggests I'm dangerously close to being kicked out.

Way to go, asshole. She probably thinks you're a perv.

"It's not what it looks like."

The corner of her mouth twitches. "Are you interested in joining the class?

"I... Uh." *Say something. Anything.* "I was curious."

"Don't be embarrassed." She nods to the studio, her posture relaxing. "Pole is a great workout. It will help you increase strength, flexibility, and cardiovascular health. It can also spice things up in the bedroom."

Heat stings my face and I silently pray the floor will swallow me whole.

This is what you get for obsessing over a woman you barely know.

I'd like to know her. That's the whole point of this stupid exercise.

"I think maybe I'm in the wrong place." I rub the back of my neck. Like my face, it's scorching hot. "I should go."

"Nonsense." She offers me an indulgent smile. "At least come in and try a free class before you decide. Some of my best students over the years have been men."

I have no idea if she's bullshitting me right now, but even if she's serious, I doubt her best students have been three-hundred-pound linemen with dad bods.

It's just one class.

And it could be my only chance to talk to Piper.

You're either in or you're out. Which is it?

"You think those poles will hold my weight?"

"Absolutely. There are no weight limits for pole. I'm Mai, by the way." She offers her hand and I shake it, prepared to go all in. "Now let's go introduce you to your new favorite sport."

I follow Mai into the studio and while she takes up her position at the front of the class, I head to the cubbies to dump my socks and shoes. My size fifteen sneakers are way too large for the bin, so I put them on top of the shelf. They hang over the edge, but at least no one will trip on them.

When I turn around, there are thirteen pairs of eyes tracking my every move.

I'm no stranger to public scrutiny—I play D1 football, after all—but it's still unnerving. I force a smile and make my way to the back row, pretending not to notice the curious stares.

It doesn't matter.

I'm not here for them. I'm here for Piper.

And Piper? She doesn't look thrilled to see me.

Her eyes narrow as I take up my position at the pole next to hers.

"Oh, no you don't." She shakes her head, ponytail swinging. "That pole is taken."

I make a show of looking around, buying time as I consider my response. I could do what she expects, stammer an apology and move along. Or I could man the fuck up because getting to know her is going to require conversation. Yes, I'm probably going to stumble over my words, and there's a ninety percent chance I'm going to screw this up, but I won't know if I don't try.

"The pole looks available to me." I give her what I hope is a disarming smile. "Mai said I could take any open spot."

Piper plants her hands on her hips and Jesus Christ, how am I supposed to concentrate on making actual words when she's practically naked?

"What are you doing here? You're not even in this class."

I inhale slowly, making sure my tongue is in working order before I reply. "I'm thinking about joining."

"Really?" She scrunches her nose and it's goddamn adorable. "So it's a total coincidence that two weeks after you asked me out, you just happen to show up in my pole class?"

She's been counting the weeks.

It's an unexpected, but encouraging development.

"What can I say?" I shrug. "Fate works in mysterious ways."

Her reply comes lightning fast. "I don't believe in fate."

"Then I guess it's a good thing I've got enough faith for the both of us."

Clearly, I'm going to need it.

Mai leads the class through a series of stretches and though I'm not what you'd call limber, I manage. Most of the class seems to have forgotten my presence, but I can feel Piper's gaze on me as Mai demonstrates the proper technique for gripping the pole.

The demonstration is entirely for my benefit and I try to

pay attention, but it's hard to concentrate with Piper mere feet away, the sweet scent of her floral perfume overtaking my senses.

"Okay," Mai says, grabbing the pole at head height. "We're going to start off today with a simple wrap-around move. Remember to keep your wrists straight ladies and gentleman."

I press the palm of my right hand into the pole and curl my fingers around the cool metal.

The pole is bolted to the floor and feels sturdy, but I'm still not convinced it can hold my weight. Apprehension must show on my face, because Piper murmurs a warning.

"I don't know why you're here, but if you're not serious about pole, you should leave now. This class is no joke, Brady."

Brady.

The sound of my name on her lips is music to my ears. I couldn't leave now, even if I wanted to.

Which I don't.

"Don't worry about me, darlin'. I'm as serious as a heart attack."

If I have to make a fool of myself to get this woman's attention, so be it. My pride is a small price to pay for the pleasure of her company.

"Suit yourself." She spins effortlessly around the pole and I watch in awe as she ends the graceful move with a deep arch of her back. Her ponytail sweeps the floor and in one fluid motion, she returns to an upright position. Her eyes meet mine and she throws out one final warning. "Just try to keep up."

5

———

PIPER

WHAT THE ACTUAL hell is Brady Vaughn doing in my pole class?

Forget the fact that he just called me darlin' in that seductive rasp of his. It can't be a coincidence, and, real talk, there isn't a single thing about him that screams pole life.

Pole is for everyone.

Okay, yes. That's true. Our class is comprised of college students and mothers and even one grandma, but still...

Jenna, who's stationed to my left, shoots me a look that clearly asks, *Is that Uber guy?*

I nod and leave it at that, because what can I possibly say?

I'm sure as hell not going to admit I've been fantasizing about Brady since my birthday, or reveal that when I need a little stress relief, it's fantasy Brady who delivers the Big O.

Jenna wouldn't understand.

Hell, she'd tell me to go for it. But how can I when even the simple act of dating puts me at risk of exposure, puts everything I've worked so hard for on the line?

No, the only way I can safely be with Brady is in my head. That's just how it has to be.

Mai leads us through a series of simple moves designed to warm up our bodies, and I do my best to focus on my movements and not on the man beside me.

Mai does a four count, and I roll my hips, dropping it low. I bring it back up and rotate around the pole, so it's behind my left arm as I execute two body rolls, hips moving suggestively. Then I spin around onto my knees, spread them wide, and do two more body rolls, this time thrusting my hips toward the pole.

The moves are basic, but they still require strength and control.

I pop my booty as I transition to an upright position and maybe it's my imagination, but I feel Brady's eyes on me as I dance.

Nerves prickle my skin as I execute a reverse sunwheel, and I nearly lose my grip on the pole.

Get it together, Piper.

I do these moves on Fangirl all the time. There's no reason to feel self-conscious, but tell that to my stupid brain.

It's not the same.

It really isn't. Camming is a job, and though I've got an audience, I'm detached from the viewers. There's a certain level of separation, even when I'm giving the illusion there isn't.

But here and now? There's no divide.

Brady Vaughn is right next to me in the flesh. The big, sexy, bearded flesh.

And the guy is struggling.

His first attempt to circle the pole is a complete disaster. He barely moves and I cringe when he nearly face-plants on the hardwood floor.

He's gripping the pole too tightly, not giving himself the

freedom to move fluidly. It's a common mistake for beginners, one I learned to avoid after weeks of aching fingers.

"This is harder than it looks," he grumbles, cheeks flushing.

I press my lips together, hiding a smile as I continue to mirror Mai's moves, which get progressively more challenging.

As I fly around the pole, I catch glimpses of Brady. It's a good thing I'm paying attention because when he attempts to whip his leg out for a pirouette, he nearly kicks me in the ribs.

I release my grip on the pole and just manage to dodge his incoming foot.

Our poles are six feet apart, but his arms and legs are crazy long.

"I'm so sorry." He releases his pole and rakes his fingers through his hair, flustered. "Are you okay?"

"I'm fine." I give him a once-over, which I immediately regret because his thin athletic shorts leave little to the imagination. *Who needs gray sweatpants season when you've got this view?* "Just try not to fully extend next time."

"No full extension. Got it." He grins, revealing a dimple in his right cheek, and my traitorous little heart flutters. "How long have you been dancing?"

"A few years."

Two, to be exact.

"Well, you're incredible." His eyes widen, and when he speaks, I swear there's actual awe in his voice. "I've never seen anyone move like that before."

Pride fills my chest and though I know he's probably just flattering me, it's nice to have my hard work recognized by someone other than my instructor. You have to be strong to pole dance, and mastering the long lines that make the moves look graceful requires dedication and endless repetition.

"Let's try that one more time!" Mai calls, making a beeline for Brady.

I force myself to turn my back on him and Jenna's eyes are nearly bugging out of her head as she mouths, "What the hell?"

What the hell indeed.

I shrug and throw myself back into the warmup routine. Beside me, Mai walks Brady through the steps, one by one. By the time the second track on the playlist ends, he can successfully complete a wraparound. It's clumsy and awkward, but he doesn't kick anyone, so I guess it's progress.

Mai tells Brady to continue working on the basic warmup moves and returns to the front of the studio, where she demonstrates a twisted grip Ayesha with a dismount kick. We've been training the move for weeks, and because I have a pole in my bedroom at home, I've nearly mastered it. Inverted moves are among my favorites, but they require tremendous flexibility and, of course, strength.

I position my right foot at the base of the pole and slip into a side straddle, extending my left foot toward the ceiling and hooking my heel around the upper part of the pole. It took me ages to get to a full split, and I have to stretch several times a week to maintain it, but it's worth the effort because it opens up so many additional tricks and gives them a more graceful appearance.

I adjust my grip on the pole and push up with my right foot, transitioning to inverted D before splitting and lowering my legs. I hold the position for a count of three and finish with a handspring.

"Damn!" Jenna pulls a face. "How the hell do you make that look so easy?"

"Practice."

She sighs. "I could practice until I'm covered in pole kisses and I still wouldn't look that good."

"Bullshit." Jenna's a talented dancer. There isn't a single move she can't master.

"What's a pole kiss?" Brady asks, wiping his hands on his gym shorts.

Jenna and I exchange a knowing look. "You'll find out soon enough."

The unsightly bruises are a rite of passage when you start poling.

"Well, doesn't that sound ominous."

"You could always quit while you still have your dignity," I suggest, only half kidding.

Pole requires focus and Brady's presence in this studio is a distraction I don't need.

"I don't have it in me to quit." My stomach flips at the intensity of his words, and when his gaze locks on mine, I know he means them. "When I set my mind to something, I always see it through."

I swallow past the lump in my throat. "Then I guess it's a good thing you're just sampling the class."

"Who says I was talking about the class?"

My mouth goes dry and I silently curse my past self. How did I mistake this man for a teddy bear when he's so clearly a grizzly?

"Okay." Jenna nods, grinning like a hyena. "I see what's happening here."

How is that possible when I don't have a freaking clue what's going on right now?

"I like him." She nudges me. "I'm Jenna, by the way."

"It's nice to meet you, Jenna." Brady extends a hand and she shakes it, her tiny fingers disappearing in his meaty grip.

"Ditto." She turns that sly grin my way and then gestures

to her pole. "I'd better get back to it if I'm ever going to be as good as Piper."

He chuckles. "That makes two of us."

Hallelujah.

If he keeps looking at me like that, my panties are going to go up in flames.

We practice for another forty minutes and Mai makes the rounds, offering feedback on technique and position. When she gets to Brady, she insists he stretch up on his toes like he's wearing high heels.

"You must learn to display your muscles to your best advantage."

To his credit, he does it without complaint and it's all I can do not to laugh as the gentle giant tiptoes around the pole, the insane muscles in his calves rippling with each step.

"That's a good start." Mai gestures to me. "Look at Piper. Her toes are always pointed and she has beautiful lines."

The last thing I want is Brady studying my lines.

Just ignore him. Pretend you're alone in your room. Just you and the camera.

If only it were that easy...

My breath hitches, but I keep going. The routine is one I'm choreographing for showcase day. It's the one day a year where each student gets to perform for a live audience, and since I'm graduating in the spring, I'm determined to take my performance to the next level.

I've been working on it for months, posting short clips for my subscribers, and so far, the feedback has been fantastic.

Of course, I'm usually wearing a thong when I do it, so it's possible they just like seeing my bare ass.

I try to lose myself in the tricky combinations, but it's impossible with Brady's heated stare searing my flesh. Our eyes meet as I arch into a seahorse and desire flares behind his whiskey irises, sparking an unexpected yearning low in my belly.

I've never done a live strip tease, but this must be what it feels like.

Seductive. Intimate. Voyeuristic.

Your darkest desires laid bare.

My panties grow damp as I work the pole, and I give silent thanks for the thin barrier between my pussy and booty shorts. I could never show my face here again if I leaked through my clothes.

When I finish the routine, there's a round of applause, and I know before looking that it's Brady. A few heads turn our way, but I ignore them, unable to tear my eyes from the man who made me wet with a mere look.

That was no mere look.

Facts. That was a smoldering *I want to fuck your brains out* look if I've ever seen one.

"Nice job, Piper." Mai gives me a perfunctory smile. "Your routine is coming along nicely." She turns to Brady and pats his ridiculously large biceps. "If you stick with us, that could be you in a few months."

I stiffen, praying he'll tell her the class isn't for him, but whatever he says is lost to my ears as Jenna appears at my side.

"Want to grab a smoothie?" She releases her hair from its ponytail and shakes it out. "I missed breakfast and I'm starving."

"Sounds good to me."

I'd say yes to just about anything right now if it meant distancing myself from Brady. I need time to clear my head... and my hormones.

We grab our stuff from the cubbies and I slip Waverly sweats on over my pole gear. I'm stepping into my flip-flops when Brady approaches.

"Did I hear you say you're going for smoothies?" He flashes a boyish smile and rubs the back of his neck, laying the charm on thick. "I don't want to be that guy, but would you mind if I join you? I missed breakfast."

Is he serious right now? Because that's a big hell no for me.

I'm about to tell him as much when Jenna smiles and chirps, "The more, the merrier!"

6

———

BRADY

THE LOOK on Piper's face is priceless when I invite myself to join them for smoothies.

It's the kind of thing Coop would do, and while I wouldn't normally pull such an arrogant move, I warned her. I'm no quitter. Now that I've found her, I'm not about to let this opportunity slip through my fingers.

Piper huffs out a breath, looking like she's about to blow a gasket as we exit Flex, but it's all good. I can play the long game. Especially since I already know how it's going to end.

"So, what made you decide to try pole?" Jenna asks, grinning as she leads us down College Ave. "In case you didn't notice, there's a distinct lack of penises in the class."

Heat floods my cheeks and her smile widens.

"My, uh…" I clear my throat. I managed to get through the damn class while sporting a Piper-inspired semi. Surely I can get through this conversation. "Coach Collins thought it would improve my footwork."

Yeah-fuckin'-right.

Coach would have my balls in a sling if he caught wind of

this. Sunday is supposed to be a rest day, not a *break-your-ankle-pole-dancing-and-screw-the-team-over* day.

"You play football? What position?"

I shove my hands in the pockets of my shorts. "Left tackle."

"Did you hear that, Pipes?" She hooks her arm through Piper's. "He plays football." She turns back to me. "Wait. Left tackle is the blindside, like in that movie, right?"

"It depends on whether the quarterback is right or left-handed, but in this case, yeah. Reid's right-handed, so it's my job to provide protection."

She cocks her head thoughtfully, but there's mischief in her eyes. "So would you say you're the strong, protective type, then?"

Piper shoots her a WTF look and I can't suppress the chuckle that escapes my lips.

"I guess you could say that."

After all, I've been taking care of my mom and grandma for the last ten years.

"My older brother played football. He made me promise to never, under any circumstances, date a player. He says you're all man-whores." Piper snickers and Jenna hastily adds, "No offense."

"None taken."

Though I doubt this conversation is doing me any favors with Piper.

"Fortunately," Jenna continues, flashing me a knowing grin. "Piper is an only child, so she's free to date all the man-whores she wants."

Jesus Christ. This woman is the female version of Coop.

Imagine the hell they'd raise if they ever met.

I shudder at the prospect.

"I don't have time to date one man-whore, let alone man-whores plural." Piper gives her friend a pointed look. "I came to Waverly for the academics, not the social scene."

"Can't you do both?" I cringe the instant the words are out of my mouth, and I make an awkward attempt at clarification. "Not the man-whore part, but the social part."

Because hell no, I don't want Piper playing the field with some fuckboy who doesn't deserve her time or attention.

She shrugs. "Not with my schedule."

Damn if I can't relate. During football season, my schedule is brutal. Most days, I'm up at five and I don't crash until midnight with conditioning, team meetings, classes, practice, and study hall crammed in. But I'm not trying to make this conversation about myself. "What's your major?"

"Elementary Education."

Talk about a selfless gig.

Long hours, low pay, not nearly enough respect. The woman is a saint.

"We're both education majors." She gestures to Jenna, who's double-timing it to match our long strides. "It's how we met."

I slow my pace and Piper does the same.

"What about you?" Jenna asks. "What are you studying besides playbooks?"

"I'm an agribusiness major."

"Like farming?" Her brow furrows. "I thought all you jock types studied communications and sports marketing. You know, easy stuff."

She's kidding, but it's a common misconception. Despite being a certified himbo, Coop is one of the smartest guys I know, and Reid makes the Dean's List every semester. Parker and I aren't exactly slouches either. Coach wouldn't allow it. He runs a tight program and he expects the best from his athletes on and off the field.

"I'm here to get an education, same as you." I shrug. "Football is just a means to an end."

Jenna rolls her eyes. "Says the guy who will probably graduate wearing a CFP championship ring."

"I try not to get caught up in the hype."

We're 3-0, but it's still early. Anything could happen, so there's no point looking beyond next week's game. Not when we've still got the entire season ahead of us.

"It must be a lot of pressure," Piper says, toying with the end of her ponytail as we approach the smoothie bar. "Having all of Wildcat Nation expecting you to deliver a national title."

"It is, but you get used to it after a while."

She scrunches her nose. "I don't think I'd ever get used to it."

"Don't get me wrong, I still get stressed before a big game, but at the end of the day, it is just a game." She looks doubtful and I dig deep, searching for the right words. "Back home, on my family's farm, the stakes are much higher when you're delivering a breech calf or caring for a horse with colic. It's not about winning or losing, it's about life or death. It gives you perspective."

I respect the guys who live and breathe the game, the ones who want to go pro, but that will never be me.

"You live on a farm?" She smiles, her lips forming a Cupid's bow, and my pulse quickens. "Why am I not surprised?"

"What can I say? I'm a simple guy." I step in front of her and open the door to the restaurant, holding it wide. "What you see is what you get."

Maybe it's my imagination, but I swear her cheeks flush as she steps inside.

We order our smoothies and the girls grab a table while I pay the bill. It seems like the right thing to do given I invited myself along on this little adventure. They're whispering as I shove my wallet back in my pocket, but their faces give nothing away.

For all I know, they could be plotting to ditch me.

Shit. I never should have asked to join their smoothie run. Crashing two events in one day is probably bad form.

Should've quit while you were ahead, asshole.

Yeah, right. At no point in that pole class was I ahead. If anything, I probably dug myself into a deeper hole. Not only did I make a complete fool of myself trying to do the most basic maneuvers, I couldn't tear my eyes from Piper. She caught me gawking more than once. Though, to be fair, her gaze lingered on me when she performed her final routine of the day.

And that routine?

It was fucking hot. When she arched her back against the pole, her breasts straining against the tiny sports bra, I nearly came on the spot.

"Come on, Brady." The sound of my name rips me from my thoughts, and I look over to find Jenna patting the empty chair next to her. *They got a table for three.* That has to be a good sign, right? "I've never met a real-life farmer and I want to know all the things."

I grab my strawberry-banana smoothie off the counter, relishing the ice-cold contrast to my heated flesh, and then I take the empty chair, attempting to fold my legs under the world's smallest table.

Christ. Who designed these things? It's like they were made for munchkins.

"So, what kind of farm do you have?" Jenna asks, swirling her straw around in her cup.

"Our major crops are wheat, hay, and corn, but we also raise cattle and we've got a small orchard where we grow apples." She stares at me, clearly unimpressed. "My grandma also keeps chickens, goats, and a few sheep."

"Your grandma has her own petting zoo?" Piper snarks, grinning ear to ear as she lifts her smoothie to her mouth.

I chuckle, because I've never thought of it that way, but it's an apt description. "I guess you could say that."

"Do you have baby chicks?" Jenna bounces in her seat, clearly excited by the prospect. "Please tell me you have chicks."

"As a matter of fact, we do."

I pull out my phone and bring up pictures of the peeps that hatched this past spring.

"*Ohmygod*," Jenna squeals, holding the phone between herself and Piper as she swipes through the pics. "That's the cutest freaking thing I've ever seen."

Screw cute. My attention is fixed on Piper as she wraps those cherry red lips around her straw and sucks.

Fuuuck.

I definitely should not be thinking about how it would feel to have those lips wrapped around my cock, but everything about this woman makes me hard. I crave her in a way I've never craved anyone before.

So, yeah. We're sitting in a smoothie bar wearing the same sweaty clothes we wore to work out, and it's erotic as hell.

Piper's blue eyes find mine across the table and when her pupils blow wide, I'm certain she knows *exactly* what I'm thinking.

The tension between us grows palpable and the urge to kiss her, to feel her soft lips against mine, is nearly overwhelming.

Jenna clears her throat, shattering the moment.

Piper slowly lowers her cup to the table, and when she

speaks, her voice is unsteady. "The chicks are adorable. Do you keep pictures of all the farm animals on your phone?"

"Of course. I can't be seen playing favorites."

"So you admit you have favorites?"

Hell yeah, I do. Some of those chickens are vicious little fuckers when they're hungry. Or tired. Or you look at them the wrong way.

"I plead the fifth."

She makes a *tsking* noise and shakes her head slowly. "I didn't peg you for the sort of person who takes the easy way out, Brady."

Fuck me.

The way she says my name sends blood rushing straight to my cock.

"I like to choose my battles."

She quirks a brow. "Are we at war?"

"I should hope not." I lean forward, shoving my smoothie aside. *It's now or never.* "I'm still hoping to take you on a proper date."

Her smile evaporates and it's a kick to the balls. "I told you; I don't have time to date."

"Make time."

I want to respect her boundaries, and I'm not the kind of guy who can't take no for an answer, but...*she counted the weeks.*

That has to mean something.

"For what it's worth." Jenna slides my phone across the table. "I definitely think you two should go on a date. Your chemistry is..." She makes a show of fanning herself and turns to Piper. "Besides, do you have any idea what a scarcity of decent guys there is on campus? As someone who's dated her share of pricks, I can assure you most of them are only interested in sex, sports, and themselves." She glances my way. "One for three is practically a unicorn."

It's not exactly a glowing endorsement, but I'm in no position to argue, so I focus on Piper.

"What do you say, Piper? Are you ready to give me a shot?"

"No." She climbs to her feet, the corner of her mouth twitching, and Jenna follows her lead. "I won't change my mind, so I suggest you find someone who's actually interested in dating."

It isn't the reply I was hoping for, but it's not unexpected. Piper is going to make me work for it, but if there's one thing I'm not afraid of, it's hard work.

Jenna sighs. "Will we see you in class next week?"

Damn, right.

"I'll be there next Sunday," I promise, holding Piper's stare. "And I'll keep coming back until you give me a fair shot."

7

PIPER

WHO WANTS TO TAKE—LET alone teach—a three-hour pre-student teaching seminar on Friday afternoons? It's torture.

Which is pretty on brand for Dr. Barnes.

If I wasn't desperate to score one of her famous recommendation letters, there's no way I'd have signed up for this course.

It could be worse.

True. She could've scheduled it for 8 a.m.

I shudder at the thought and sip my iced coffee as I settle back in my chair. The cold brew goes down smoothly, the caffeine providing a much-needed boost to my system.

My classmates file in, Jenna bringing up the rear with her dark hair piled on top of her head in a messy bun.

She slides into the seat next to me and I pass her an iced coffee.

"You're a lifesaver." She grins as she raises the oversized cup to her lips. "I'm about to drop."

"Late night?" I ask, pulling my laptop from my bag.

"Long day, and it's only half over." She turns to face me,

eyes narrowed. "Barnes should give us credit just for showing up."

"It's a pass/fail class. All you have to do is turn in your notes and Barnes will pass you."

Probably.

The woman is a hardass, but she's fair.

"Easy for you to say. She's your advisor, *and* she loves you."

Love is a gross exaggeration, but I keep that to myself since Jenna's advisor blew off their last meeting. The guy is a massive douche—the kind who gives tenure a bad name—but Jenna refuses to request a new advisor. She hasn't said it aloud, but I think she's worried about retaliation. With our student teaching assignments pending, I can't blame her.

The door opens and Dr. Barnes strides in, her no-nonsense heels tap-tap-tapping the linoleum floor as she crosses the auditorium. Her silver braids are pinned up in a sleek bun and though it's eighty degrees outside, she's wearing a blazer.

The woman is stone cold.

Facts. In the three years she's been advising me, I haven't seen her so much as break a sweat. She never gets flustered, never loses her temper, and she for damn sure doesn't accept excuses, which is probably why her recommendation letters carry so much weight.

I admire and fear her in equal measure.

Dr. Barnes places her bag on the podium and pulls out a laptop before acknowledging the class. "Today we'll be discussing performance expectations for student teaching."

The quiet hum of shifting bags and shuffling papers fills the room as Dr. Barnes gestures for the teaching assistant to connect her laptop to the overhead projector.

"You'd think someone who's been teaching for forty years would be a bit more tech savvy," Jenna muses. "Then again," she adds, wiggling her brows, "if Mike McConnell was my TA, I'd probably let him play with my device, too."

Eww. "Don't be gross."

"What?" She bats her lashes, feigning innocence. "I'm just saying he's cute. Plus, he's got a great ass."

I study the TA as he searches for the correct adapter.

He's tall and slim with dark curls, midnight eyes, and an air of confidence that occasionally crosses the line to arrogance.

I shrug. "He's not my type."

"What exactly is your type? Thicc and awkward with eyes like Jack Daniels?"

"No." *Yes.* "I don't even have a type."

Growing up, I had a front-row seat to the revolving door of shitty boyfriends my mother brought home. You could say the experience soured me on relationships. I went on a few dates freshman year, but love and romance have never been a priority.

You can't miss what you never had.

"Bullshit." Jenna crosses her arms. "Brady is clearly your type, and he's struggled through *three* pole classes for you. No other guy would do that. Why not just admit you're into him and put the poor guy out of his misery?"

Because admitting I'm attracted to him also means acknowledging that I've seriously considered breaking my no dating rule.

What can I say? I'm weak.

And you want to know if the reality of the man will live up to the fantasy.

Guilty.

When I don't answer, Jenna continues, unfazed by the one-sided conversation. "He's clearly not going to give up, and I've seen you watching him during class."

"The guy is six and a half feet tall. It's impossible to miss him."

Brady is determined. I'll give him that. Two weeks ago, the football team had an away game in Iowa and though they must've gotten home late Saturday night, he was waiting when I arrived at the studio Sunday morning, that irresistible smile peeking out from behind his beard.

"The way he looks at you during class?" Jenna gives me the side-eye. "It's a wonder you haven't combusted."

She's not wrong. I was so turned on by the time I left the studio last week that I went straight home to masturbate.

"I'm just saying, if a guy looked at me that way, I'd consider myself a lucky bitch and screw his brains out."

If only it were that simple.

Yes, Brady is sweet and considerate and totally into me, but I've worked too hard to risk my education or my career on a quick lay.

If he was looking for a quick lay, he'd go to Greek Row.

My pulse skitters, but I refuse to acknowledge the truth my body already knows. Brady won't quit until he breaks through my defenses...and my heart is already bracing for impact.

I'm saved from giving it any further thought when Dr. Barnes speaks. "Student teaching assignments for spring semester will be finalized in the next few weeks. We will do our best to take your requests into account, but there are no guarantees for placement."

"If I don't get Lancaster, I'm going to be big mad," Jenna whispers. "I want to sleep in my own bed and eat my weight in home-cooked meals before I officially reach adult status."

Now who's a lucky bitch?

"What about you?" She nudges me with her elbow. "What's your first choice?"

"I don't really have a preference." *As long as it's not home.*

There's nothing for me in New Kensington. Maybe there never was.

I'm *proud* of the person I've become at Waverly—strong, independent, confident—and now that I've broken the cycle, I won't go back.

Not for my mother, not for anyone.

"As you embark on this next leg of your educational journey," Dr. Barnes continues, scanning the room somberly, "it's important to remember that while you are in the field, you are representing Waverly University. It is my expectation that you conduct yourselves with proper decorum."

IE- Don't get caught stripping online.

If I had a dollar for every time Barnes gave this speech—or some variation of it—I wouldn't need to bare it all on camera to pay my exorbitant tuition bill.

"You will be working with young, impressionable minds." Dr. Barnes' eyes settle on me and my stomach drops. If she knew what I did with my new alien dildo last night, she'd probably stroke out. "Everything you say and do will leave a mark. If you screw up, your advisor will hear about it."

Just the thought of getting a disciplinary call from Dr. Barnes sends a shiver racing up my spine.

She's the kind of instructor who believes there is no separation between the teacher and the job. As far as she's concerned, we're on duty 24/7. There is no down time, even in the privacy of our own homes.

"My advice is to conduct yourself at all times—in school, after hours, on social media—as if you are being watched. Because if you fail your assignment, you may find yourself in need of an alternative career path."

The words prick at my skin, a silent warning, but I shake them off.

Dr. Barnes isn't one for subtleties. If she knew about my

Fangirl channel, I'd have already been disciplined. The speech is just another reminder of what I stand to lose if I get caught.

Barnes continues lecturing, but my attention is on the TA as he distributes pre-student teaching info guides. He's quick and efficient, all business as he moves from one aisle to the next. I can see why Barnes chose him to assist her. They're practically a matched set.

He stops at our row, counting out the correct number of packets, and when he hands them to me, our eyes meet. For a beat, he says nothing. Does nothing. Just stares down at me, face a blank slate.

"Thanks." I take an envelope off the stack and pass the rest to Jenna.

He nods and moves on, oblivious as my bestie twists around in her seat.

"Quit staring at his ass," I hiss. "You're going to get us both in trouble. And whatever happened to Tripp?"

"Tripp?"

"You know, the frat guy you were crushing on?"

"I'm keeping my options open." She pretends to study her nails. "I'm young and single. It's perfectly natural to be attracted to more than one sexy, intelligent man."

"Agreed, but banging your TA is a recipe for disaster." She smirks, as if I've just issued a challenge. "Don't say I didn't warn you."

Because any instructor—official or otherwise—who's open to sleeping with one of his students is shady AF.

8

———

BRADY

I HITCH my bag up on my shoulder and jog up the steps to the football building. It's Friday afternoon and we've got our last practice before the Nebraska game tomorrow. We're 5-0, and the buzz surrounding a championship run has reached a fever pitch.

It's all anyone wants to talk about, even in the agricultural college.

Case in point, I'm running late because I stayed after class to ask a question about the homework assignment in Supply Chain Management and the prof turned what should have been a five-minute conversation into a thirty minute one, grilling me about the team's prospects.

Ironically enough, the only respite to be found is in the pole studio.

No one there gives a damn if I play ball. They're more interested in whether I can complete a chair spin without injuring myself.

I can't.

That shit is harder than it looks and after three weeks of

classes, I'm no closer to mastering the move than I am scoring a date with Piper.

It's frustrating as hell.

I push through the glass doors at the front of the building and sigh in relief when the temperature drops ten degrees. Sunlight streams through the windows, glinting off the dated plaques and trophies that serve as a constant reminder of Waverly's fifteen-year drought.

One day—one problem—at a time.

When I reach the locker room, my roommates are already dressed.

"It's about time." Parker glances at the overhead clock. "I was starting to think you were going to have us all running laps today."

It's Coach's go-to punishment, one I'm careful to avoid.

"When have I ever been late to practice?" *That would be never.* I drop my bag on the floor in front of my locker. "I was tied up."

"Tied up?" Coop gives me a once-over as I strip down, his gaze lingering on the massive bruise discoloring my thigh. "I didn't think you went for the kinky shit, Vaughn. I figured you were straight vanilla."

I give him the finger and open my locker. "Don't you have some biceps curls to do?"

The last thing I want to discuss with Coop—or anyone else, for that matter—is my non-existent sex life. I've hooked up with girls before, but it's been a while, and I've never gone the whole way. Maybe it's stupid, but I guess I just want it to be special.

"Forget biceps curls," Reid says, tucking his helmet under his arm. "He should be reviewing the playbook."

Parker winces, and I can't say I blame him.

Coach just added two new plays and though we've been

practicing them for days, he won't call them during a game until we prove we've got them on lock.

"Relax, ye of little faith. I'm more than just a pretty face." Coop smirks and closes his locker. "I've got a mind like a steel trap."

"Too bad it's not connected to your mouth," Parker quips, throwing a balled-up towel at him.

Coop feigns indignation and they file out as I suit up.

Twenty minutes later, I'm on the field running plays with the offensive line as the coaching staff shouts directions from the sideline.

Although it's early October, it's unseasonably hot and sweat drips from my brow, stinging my eyes.

"Get your ass back in position, DeLaurentis!" Coach Collins brandishes his clipboard like a weapon, giving *fuck around and find out* vibes. The guy is old school and though rumor has it the university required him to take sensitivity training, it hasn't exactly taken. "You pull that shit tomorrow and you'll be running wind sprints 'til you puke!"

"Is it me or is Coach extra bitchy today?" Coop asks, taking his sweet time getting back to the line.

Parker shrugs, pads bobbing. "Maybe the old man is feeling the pressure."

Aren't we all?

"No way." Reid takes his place behind the center. "Coach has nerves of steel."

Coop smirks. "His clipboard would suggest otherwise."

"If you don't get moving,"—I give him a shove—"you're going to be seeing it up close and personal."

Our head coach has never actually hit anyone with the clipboard, but it's just a matter of time until it goes flying. The man is solid, but he's loud, unpredictable, and he scares the shit out of me.

Not that I'd ever admit it.

After all, I'm twice his size.

We run the play again and this time, Reid completes the pass to Coop, who runs it down the field, leaving our defenders panting in his wake.

By the fourth rep, I'm in the zone.

Set. Snap. Lunge.

I plow into the defensive end, planting my palms on his chest. He grunts at the loss of momentum and I latch onto his pads, curling my fingers into the chest protector for optimal leverage.

The poor bastard doesn't stand a chance.

I'm in complete control as I rotate our bodies, buying Reid the time he needs to find a receiver.

The ball rockets downfield and we line up to do it all over.

Set. Snap. Lunge.

Our defense is good, but our offense is better. Most of us have been playing together since freshman year, and if we play tomorrow the way we've been playing, we're going to roll the Cornhuskers on their home turf.

Will Piper be watching?

Does it matter?

Despite three excruciating weeks of pole, I'm no closer to scoring a date with her than I was the night we met.

I don't know how much longer I can go on like this. Watching her flip and twirl in those goddamn booty shorts with her ass cheeks hanging out is torture. Not only do I have to take a cold shower before class, I have to jerk off at least twice to avoid getting a stiffy in the middle of class.

There has to be something—

Fuck.

A hard mass slams into my shoulder, the crash of pads yanking me back to the present.

I barely keep my feet under me as I dig in my cleats and push back, but it's too late. The defensive end slips right past and strips Reid of the ball. It bounces once and a defensive tackle dives on top of it, making the recovery.

Double fuck.

Chaos erupts on the field as the D celebrates.

The way they're carrying on, you'd think it was their first turnover.

"Vaughn!" I snap to attention as Coach Walker strides across the field, a look of concern etched on his face. "You okay, son?"

I remove my helmet and drag the back of my hand across my forehead. "I'm good, coach."

"Then do you mind telling me what the hell just happened?" The offensive line coach plants his hands on his hips and gives me a quick once-over. "Because it looked like you were on another planet."

Might as well have been.

"Sorry, sir. I was distracted."

At the worst possible time.

"Distracted?" He glances at Reid and then back at me, mouth tight. "Do you plan to be distracted tomorrow, or can I count on you to do your damn job and protect your quarterback?"

I'm left tackle. Protecting Reid's blindside is my sole priority on the field.

If this had been an actual game, he'd be picking turf out of his facemask right now.

Shame burns my cheeks. Coach Walker has been like a father to me from the moment I arrived at Waverly. The last thing I want to do is let him down when he's invested so much time and energy in my development. With his help, I've become better, faster, stronger. If it weren't for his guidance,

I'd have dropped out last year when things at home were tight.

You owe him.

I need to get my head in the game because, like everyone else on this team, Coach Walker is jonesing for a national championship, and I'll do whatever I can to help make it happen.

"You can count on me, coach."

"I know." He claps me on the arm, an easy grin sliding into place. "Those first few reps looked good. That's what I want to see from you tomorrow, understand?"

"Yes, sir."

His brows knit together, and he points to my forearm. "What happened there?"

I glance down at the ugly purple bruise. I can't tell him it's a pole kiss. Taking the class violates my scholarship terms, and he'd kick my ass for risking injury.

"I ran into a door. In the dark."

It's the worst excuse in the history of excuses, so it's no surprise when he presses me.

"Were you drinking?"

"No, sir."

His features go tight and he studies me for what feels like an eternity. I've never been one to overindulge in alcohol, and Coach Walker knows it. "You get anymore nasty bruises like that and we're going to need to look at your diet. You could have a vitamin deficiency."

The only deficiency I'm suffering is my pride, but I nod, giving silent thanks my uniform hides the worst of the damage.

Coach Walker jogs off the field and I take my place on the line of scrimmage.

"What's up?" Parker nudges me from his position to my right. "It's not like you to miss a block."

"It's nothing."

I'm careful to avoid an outright lie, but no way am I going to admit I was daydreaming about a woman.

"Bullshit." Coop's declaration carries down the line, and I don't have to look to know he's smirking. "Last time your face got that red, it was because a server at the Wildcat's Den slipped you her number."

"Oh, shit!" Parker croons. "I forgot all about Napkingate." He turns to me, a crooked grin plastered on his sweaty face. "Talk about a missed opportunity."

A month ago, I might have agreed with him, but now that I've met Piper? No way.

I'm about to say as much, but Coop beats me to the punch. "Missed opportunity is right. If our boy doesn't find a woman soon, he's gonna end up dating one of his cousins back in West Virginia."

"Screw you," I mutter, mentally giving him the finger. "My cousins don't even live in West Virginia. They live in Kentucky."

The asshole nearly keels over laughing.

"What's so funny?"

"Kentucky," he wheezes, still cackling like a twelve-year-old girl. "Jesus, Vaughn. You make it too fucking easy."

"You guys want to shut the hell up so we can run this play or what?" Reid's delivery is dry, but there's an undertone of amusement in his voice. "I don't know about you, but I'd like to win the game tomorrow."

Damn right I want to win the game.

For Coach Walker.

For my boys.

For myself.

I'm not giving up on Piper, but right now, I need to focus on the team. I can't—*won't*—be the weak link. Not when there are so many dreams, so many futures, on the line. I may not be playing for a draft spot, but some of these guys are, and I'm not going to dick them over because I'm distracted.

We have an opportunity to break Waverly's losing streak and put some respect on Big Ten football, our program, and on the hard work it's taken to get us to 5-0. Fortunately, I've always been good at compartmentalizing, at prioritizing challenges.

And you can bet your ass when we take the field tomorrow, the only thing on my mind will be football.

9

———

PIPER

I DUCK INTO FLEX, making a quick pit stop before I meet Jenna at the Wildcat's Den to watch the Waverly-Nebraska game.

The reception desk is empty and I speedwalk back the hall, hoping to catch Mai before she starts her evening class. When I enter the studio, she's on her phone, scrolling through play lists.

"Piper." Her smile is warm and welcoming. "What brings you in today?"

"I..." Nervous energy courses through my veins and I flex my fingers at my sides. "I wanted to see if I could transfer to another class."

Preferably one without Brady Vaughn in it.

"Transfer?" She frowns. "I'm sorry, but all of my other classes are full."

Damn.

I knew it was a long shot, but I'd hoped...

Disappointment must show on my face because Mai's brow creases, a wrinkle marring her smooth forehead. "You've been in the Sunday morning class for two years. Why the change now?" She narrows her eyes and her frown deepens.

"Is Brady harassing you? Because I don't tolerate that kind of behavior in my studio."

This is it. My out.

All I have to do is say yes and Mai will cancel his membership.

Guilt gnaws at my conscience like a rabid dog, the bite sharp and unexpected.

It was your class long before it was his.

Facts. He only signed up because of me. He probably doesn't even like pole.

"Piper?" Mai touches my arm, her fingertips featherlight against my skin. "This is a safe space. Whatever is bothering you, you can tell me."

I really can't. And I can't trash Brady's reputation, either. I won't be a person who throws out accusations for personal gain.

"No, it's nothing like that." I force a bright smile. "I was just thinking of changing my schedule ahead of student teaching next semester."

Mai's features relax, her relief clear. "I'll let you know if anything opens up, but I'm glad to hear there are no issues. Brady seems like one of the good ones. He brings a unique energy to the class."

That's one way of putting it.

We say our goodbyes and when I arrive at the Wildcat's Den ten minutes later, the bar is packed with Waverly fans decked out in blue and white team gear. It's so loud I can barely hear myself think, the hum of too many competing voices and wall-to-wall televisions reverberating through the large space. I squeeze through the crush of warm bodies, trying not to breathe too deeply.

I spot Jenna at a booth in the back, and my stomach dips when I realize her roommates are seated across the table.

Why did I ever let her talk me into this?

Because she's a good friend and it won't kill you to spend a few hours watching football.

No, but it will put a dent in my weekly earnings. Saturday nights are prime time for live streaming. There are plenty of lonely guys stuck at home looking to make a connection and they're willing to pay top dollar.

But since I still owe Jenna for the botched birthday celebration, football it is.

"Over here!" she shouts, waving when she spots me in the crowd.

I make my way over to the booth and slide in next to her.

"You're just in time." She grabs an empty glass from the end of the table and fills it from a half-full pitcher. "The game is about to start."

Kylie—or maybe it's Rylee—flashes a simpering smile. "It's been a while."

And yet, it still hasn't been long enough.

I nod in acknowledgement and take a sip of my beer.

"Okay, ladies. We need to catch Piper up because she hasn't been following the team."

Jenna's other roommate, Alexis, trails a bored finger through the condensation on the side of her glass. "Where's your school spirit? We're having such a great season."

We. Like she's the one out on the field losing blood, sweat, and tears on behalf of the university.

I shrug. "I've just never really been into sports."

"We're going to change that today." Jenna beams. "The Wildcats are 5-0 and the Cornhuskers' offense is on fire, so it should be a good game."

"Cornhuskers?"

"You know, like husking corn." Jenna's eyes twinkle with

mischief as she casually adds, "I know a certain farmer who could probably explain it better than me."

I roll my eyes. "Don't even start."

Surely we can go at least one day without discussing said farmer?

"He's number fifty-three, by the way."

Jenna explains the rules and I find myself sucked into the game. It's fast-paced and hard-hitting and though I don't understand all the calls, I know just enough to be outraged when the Waverly defense gets a penalty for roughing the passer.

A loud roar of protest fills the bar and when the Nebraska quarterback finally climbs to his feet, seemingly satisfied with the call, a guy at the next table shouts, "Fuck that ref!"

As if on cue, the crowd repeats the curse.

"This is intense." I survey the bar. "Are people always this invested in the game?"

"We bleed blue and white," Kylie/Rylee says, sounding like she'd offer her firstborn to the football gods in exchange for a winning season.

"This is nothing." Jenna laughs. "You need to go to a home game. Cheering our boys on with one hundred thousand screaming fans is almost as exhilarating as sex."

"You've never been to a home game?" Alexis curls her lip, not even trying to mask her disdain. She's usually better at hiding her dislike of me, and I can't help but wonder how much she's had to drink. "How is that even possible?"

Football is a BFD—big fucking deal—at Waverly, but I didn't grow up playing sports, let alone watching them. It never even occurred to that I might be in the minority.

"I'm a bookish girlie, but I'm starting to see the appeal of the game."

We chat some more and by the time Waverly's offense

takes the field at the end of the fourth quarter, I'm enraptured. The camera zooms in on the quarterback, and by default, Brady, who's at his side. He struts out wearing the tightest white pants I've ever seen and *holy shit.*

Is that his cock?

The long, thick ridge is clearly visible through his pants, and I know I shouldn't be looking, but tell that to my pussy. Desire pools low in my belly and I shift in my seat, desperate to relieve the growing ache between my legs.

The thin shorts he wears to class have nothing on those pants.

"Having second thoughts?" Jenna whispers with a knowing grin.

I swallow, striving for a calm I don't feel. "About what?"

"Don't play coy." She offers me a napkin. "You're practically drooling."

Wonderful. I've been caught objectifying the man.

Which is totally unfair. He has plenty of qualities I appreciate in a person. It's just that those qualities aren't currently on display.

I take the napkin, crumple it up, and throw it at her. "I am not drooling."

"Keep telling yourself that, sis." She leans forward, resting her chin in her hand. "I don't know why you keep turning him down. You've got chemistry for days, and he's clearly smitten with you. Make it make sense already."

That's the thing. I can't.

The fears I harbor aren't ones that can be shared.

"I told you—"

"Yeah, yeah, yeah." Jenna waves off my tired protest. "You're busy with school. Aren't we all?" She flicks her chin toward the nearest tv. "If he can find the time to squeeze in a date, so can you. Besides, how many times have you complained about being the tallest person in the room? With Brady, you can have the best of both worlds. You can wear heels to show off those gorgeous legs and still fit right under his arm. Plus, when was your last date? Freshman year?"

I nod, grudgingly.

"Look, I know you have trust issues because of the guys your mom dated, but not all men are like that. Some guys—the good ones—stick."

I wouldn't know. My father was long gone before I was born and the guys my mother dated weren't exactly shining examples of human decency.

"What are you two whispering about over there?" Kylie/Rylee asks, slurring her words.

Jenna grins. "I'm trying to convince Piper to go on a date with Brady Vaughn."

Alexis perks up. "Tell me more."

"The poor guy has been asking her out for weeks and she won't give him the time of day." Jenna makes a *sad face* to emphasize her point.

"No shit." Alexis actually looks impressed. "Is he going pro after graduation?"

I shake my head. "No. He's planning to join the family business."

"Bummer." She flops back in her chair. "Pro ballers make bank. If I had a shot at locking one of them down, you can bet your ass I'd take it."

Jesus. What a gold digger.

Jenna rolls her eyes and raises her glass like she's offering a toast. "Not all of us are looking for a man to take care of us financially."

"I'll drink to that." I clink my glass against hers and take a long pull on my beer as Jenna does the same.

"*Exaaaactly.*" Kylie/Rylee nods sagely. "Some of us just want to be taken care of in the bedroom."

"Oh my God!" Jenna snorts, beer spewing from her lips. "You can't say shit like that while my mouth is full."

"What?" Kylie/Rylee's unfocused gaze bounces between us. "I'm just telling it like it is. And, real talk, even though Vaughn is mid, I'll bet he's got a big dick. I mean, he has to, right? He's practically a giant."

Anger flares deep in my chest and my jaw nearly hits the table.

Where the hell does she get off talking about Brady like that?

"Preach." Alexis throws up her hands like she's in a freaking gospel choir before devolving into an earsplitting cackle. "Oh, my God. What if he has a tiny cock? That would be tragic, amirite?"

Fury, red-hot and molten, rips through my veins like wildfire.

Beside me, the color drains from Jenna's face.

When no one responds, Alexis adds, "But hey, if you're really into the rugged look, more power to you."

A loud roar goes up from the crowd and I stand, hands clenched at my sides.

"Excuse me," I bite out, nails digging into the palms of my hands. "I need to use the bathroom."

Otherwise, I'm going to throat punch someone.

"Waverly's new kicker is about to try for the game-winning field goal," Kylie/Rylee squeals, gesturing to the screen. "You can't go now."

How she can keep track of the game when she can't seem to control the shit coming out of her mouth is beyond me, but I have to get away from this table.

Now.

I turn on my heel, not bothering to respond.

In the bathroom, I splash cold water on my face, turning their hateful words over in my mind.

So what if Brady isn't traditionally handsome? I like the way he looks, big and burly, like a human grizzly. He's got an incredible smile; one he shares freely with everyone he meets. He's thoughtful, funny—even when he's not trying to be—and laid-back. Which is a nice counterpoint to my stressed-out ass. Most importantly, he doesn't play games.

With Brady, what you see really is what you get.

Any woman would be lucky to have him as a partner.

Because Brady will be a partner. He respects women, and he'd never try to silence or condescend. He'll lift the woman in his life up, treating her like a goddess.

It just can't be me.

The door swings open and Jenna slips in behind me, cheeks flushed.

"Ignore them," she says, the words more command than suggestion. "They're just jealous."

What they are is shit humans, but Jenna needs to come to the realization on her own.

She's a big girl and she can choose her own friends. The last thing I want to do is come off like a jealous asshole myself. I'm not that kind of person, one who needs every bit of her friend's time and attention.

I grab a paper towel from the dispenser and dry my face.

"I know you don't want to hear this, so it's the last time I'll bring it up, but I wish you'd stop fighting this thing between you." I open my mouth to protest and she holds up a hand. "Brady will not stop coming to pole until you agree to go on a date with him. Have you thought about how you're going to feel if he gets hurt in class?"

No. Why would I?

He's a grown ass man and he can make his own life choices.

"I know you, Pipes. You can tell yourself it's his choice, but if something happens, he could lose his scholarship and you're going to feel responsible. Then you're going to agonize over it, wondering if your stubbornness also cost the Wildcats their shot at a national title." She sighs and gestures to the door. "You saw what the fans were like out there. They're...*passionate*." Yeah, if by passionate she means scarily obsessed. "Have you seen the things they're saying online? About the woman they believe is responsible for the kicker breaking his leg?"

"No." I throw my paper towel in the trash and level my gaze at her. "I don't listen to gossip or read tabloid trash. If Brady wants to take unnecessary risks with his safety, that's not on me."

"Fair enough." Jenna opens the door to let me pass by. "I'm just trying to look out for you."

I appreciate it, I do. Jenna's heart is in the right place, but I refuse to take responsibility for Brady's actions, no matter how well-intentioned or flattering.

When we exit the bathroom, the atmosphere in the bar is subdued. The sounds of the game have been replaced with quiet rock and a number of the tables have cleared out.

What the hell?

I check the nearest tv and flinch when I see the final score.

Waverly's new kicker missed the field goal, and the Wildcats lost by three.

It sucks, but it's not the end of the world. It's like Brady said, it's just a game.

Still, I can't help wondering... *How will I feel if something happens to him?*

10

BRADY

"Watch your grip, Brady!"

At Mai's instruction, I instinctively loosen my hold on the pole and crash knees first to the floor.

"Don't quit your day job." Piper grins down at me from her own pole where she's dangling upside down, the long line of her body on full display.

Today she's wearing a turquoise garter bra—yes, I know what a garter bra is, thanks to being the only dude in the class—and a pair of matching booty shorts that are cinched along the center of her deliciously round ass.

"What do I have to do to convince you I'm not a quitter?"

Apparently an entire month of pole classes hasn't done the trick.

"You'll have to figure that out for yourself, big guy." She laughs and the low, husky sound goes straight to my cock.

Christ. Everything about this woman turns me on.

It's distracting as hell.

I subtly adjust myself and climb to my feet as she transitions, flipping right side up so she's gripping the pole between her thighs. They may be soft, but they're strong as hell. The combination is wildly attractive.

"Are you suggesting—"

Pain lances through my calf like a blade, and I grab my pole for support.

Fuuuck.

I can't remember the last time I had a charley horse, but it hurts like a motherfucker, the muscle spasming uncontrollably as I slide to the floor.

"Are you okay?" Piper drops from her pole and crouches next to me, her ponytail falling over her shoulder. "Where are you hurt?"

There's actual fear in her eyes and I hate that I was the one to put it there.

"I'm fine," I hiss, through clenched teeth. "Muscle. Cramp."

My calf spasms again and I press my lips together, swallowing the sounds of my agony.

Piper's brow furrows, and she sinks her teeth into her lower lip. "Where at?"

"Calf."

Without another word, she begins massaging the sore muscle, her fingers moving deftly over my skin. She digs into the muscle like she's done this a thousand times before. The relief is immediate.

"Everything okay back there?" At Mai's question, several heads swivel in our direction.

"We're good," Piper calls back, head lowered, eyes on her work. "Just a muscle cramp."

"Just?" I grunt. "I got hit by a three-hundred-pound lineman yesterday, and this is way worse."

She snorts, but her tone is gentle when she speaks. "You played a good game yesterday."

I know she's trying to distract me from the pain, but there's nothing casual about her statement.

"You watched the game? I thought you weren't into football."

That's what she told me two weeks ago, anyway.

She looks up at me from under her lashes and I catch the hint of a smile on her lips. "It was Jenna's idea."

No surprise there. Jenna's had my back since day one.

If only Piper would take her advice.

The woman is stubborn as fuck. I knew it from the moment we met, and honestly, it's a trait I admire. I like a woman who can think for herself and knows her own mind, even when I'm hoping to change it.

Another spasm strikes and I gasp, breath whistling through my teeth.

"It sucks that you guys lost," she says, continuing to work my calf. "Is it going to affect your chance at playing in the championship?"

It's the million-dollar question. One I can't easily answer.

"It's too early to tell. It'll depend on how we play the rest of the season."

"That makes sense." She nods, fingers moving up the back of my calf. "How many games are there?"

"Twelve in the regular season and if we perform well enough, one bowl game, followed by the championship."

We won't know for sure which teams are playing in the semi-finals until the bowl games are announced in December. College football isn't a straight bracket system and the championship teams are selected by committee.

"I'm no expert, but if I were a betting person, I'd guess this muscle cramp is the result of insufficient hydration." She glances up, giving me a pointed look. "You played three and a half grueling hours of football yesterday and now you're here, working your ass off in the studio when you should be at home recovering."

She's not wrong, but it's a flawed argument.

"If I didn't come to class, I wouldn't get to see you." Her fingers go still and I rest my hand on hers. Awareness sizzles along my skin and the urge to kiss her strikes hard and fast, though I can't act on it. "It's worth the risk. *You're* worth the risk."

Her breath hitches and it takes all my self-control not to pull her close and capture her mouth with my own.

"I—" She clears her throat and pulls her hand from mine. The loss of contact is jarring, but I force myself to relax. The last thing I want to do is spook her when I'm finally making progress. "You should call it a day."

"You're probably right." We climb to our feet and I thank her for the massage. The pain has completely abated and if I didn't know better, I'd say she's got the magic touch. "I'll see you next week."

"You can't be serious." She gestures to my leg. "You're doing too much, Brady. You're going to burn out. Or get hurt."

It's a possibility, one I made peace with when I signed my name on the class waiver.

"I could get hit by a bus tomorrow. There are no guarantees in life."

It's a lesson I learned the hard way when my grandfather passed.

Piper's eyes drift shut and she tips her head back, as if thinking. Then her head snaps up, and she meets my gaze head-on. "If I agree to get coffee, will you end this madness?"

Hope sparks in my chest. "Does this mean I've finally won you over?"

"No, I just don't want to see you get hurt."

It's a start.

I can work with that.

"In that case, how about lunch?"

She cocks a hip and plants her hand on it. "Don't push your luck."

"Wouldn't dream of it, darlin'." I step into her personal space, something I'm usually careful to avoid. "I'm just negotiating for better terms."

Her gorgeous blue eyes go wide and she huffs out a breath. "Fine. One lunch."

I'M STILL FLYING high from my victory with Piper when I hop on Facetime with my mom and Gran for Sunday dinner. It's a longstanding family tradition we've maintained, despite the distance that now separates us.

We aren't eating the same dish and we can't share a table, but it's more about the conversation than the food.

They pepper me with questions about my week as we eat, and when there's a lull in the conversation, I change the subject.

"Have you looked at the business plan?"

My mom refuses to discuss finances outright, but the farm is struggling, and has been for a while. I used my free time over the summer to build an agritourism proposal that would supplement the farm's current income, but so far, I haven't had much luck pitching the idea.

"It's on my desk." Mom flashes a tired smile. "I just haven't had time to look at it yet."

It's a brush off. The farm keeps her busy, but she's not too busy to read my report. It would take an hour at most.

"Mom—"

"You need to stop worrying about the farm," she says, like

it's as simple as flipping a switch. "That's my job. Your job is to focus on school and football."

"I can do both."

I spear a piece of chicken and shove it in my mouth, chewing aggressively. I've got everything under control. My grades are fine, and I'm playing the best ball of my life.

"That isn't the point," she says firmly. "You shouldn't have to."

Frustration wells up from the pit of my stomach. I don't know what it says about me that all the women in my life are infuriatingly stubborn and independent, but just once, it would be nice if they'd let me help carry the burden.

"I graduate in eight months. You have to let me take on more responsibility." *The sooner, the better.* Purple shadows line her eyes and several tendrils of hair have escaped her braid to hang limply around her face. "When was the last time you even had a day off?"

She waves a hand dismissively. "I can sleep when I'm dead."

My stomach hardens and I have to remind myself that she's only forty-two.

It's just a figure of speech.

"Enjoy the time you have left at school. Your grandmother and I have been running this farm since before you were born. We will continue to do so until it's time for you to take over."

That's half the problem. They're convinced Willow Bend can weather any storm. Maybe they're right, but the thought of losing the legacy our family has created over the last five generations is gutting.

"Brady Jameson Vaughn." Gran leans in close to the screen, eyes narrowed. "Why on earth do you have a bag of ice tied to your thigh?"

Mom straightens and now there are two pairs of narrowed eyes staring critically at my ice clad thigh.

I sigh and set my plate down on the bed, accepting defeat.

There's always next week.

"Sunday is supposed to be your day off," Mom says, not missing a beat. "Coach Collins better not be overworking you. If he is, I'll be giving the NCAA a call, right after I give that man a piece of my mind."

Mama bear mode activated.

Like mother, like son.

"Relax, Mom. The bruises aren't from football."

"Then what are they from?"

I scrub a hand over my face and mumble, "Dance class."

Mom's brows shoot up. "I'm sorry, did you say dance class?"

I nod and adjust the ice pack on my left thigh, hoping she'll drop it.

"I want to know more about this class." Gran chuckles. "What kind of dance class leaves a strapping young man like yourself in recovery?"

The kind I can't possibly tell them about.

I do not need my mom and grandmother picturing me twirling around a pole.

"It's, uh, modern dance." I shrug. "Turns out it requires different muscles than football."

"Show us your moves!" Gran orders, practically vibrating in her seat. "I need to see this."

Oh, hell no. That will *never* happen.

"Maybe next time. I'm still a little sore."

With any luck, they'll forget all about this conversation by next week.

"I'm sorry, can we just back up to the part where you joined a dance class?" My mother's face is a mask of confusion, but I can't exactly blame her. She knows the terms of my scholarship. Which mean she knows I'm prohibited from engaging in activities that might cause injury. "What were you thinking?"

"I... There's this girl—"

"I knew it!" Gran crows, punching her fist in the air. "You finally found her."

"I did." The grin that splits my face is impossible to suppress. "Her name is Piper, and we're having lunch on Thursday."

I don't mention that it's taken me weeks to secure even a casual date.

"Look out, Molly." Gran winks at my mom. "I see wedding bells in the future."

"Mom!" My mother's face pales and she shoots Gran a *simmer down* stare. "It's just a first date. Let's not rush things." She turns back to the camera. "Ignore your grandmother. Take your time getting to know Piper. The last thing you want to do is rush into a serious relationship."

Like she did.

She doesn't say it aloud, but she doesn't have to. My father was a piece of shit who walked out and left her alone with an infant. It would be more shocking if she didn't have regrets about her own whirlwind romance.

"It's not about rushing or taking your time," Gran argues, looking smug. "When you know, you know. The moment I met your father, I knew I was going to marry him."

Mom smiles and her eyes are soft as she turns to Gran. "I know, but it's a different time. Brady's got his whole life ahead of him."

They spend the next thirty minutes grilling me about Piper. I recount our first meeting and how I later spotted her walking down College Ave. Gran practically swoons, and though mom isn't as enthusiastic, it's clear she's happy to see me happy.

When we finally say our goodbyes, I'm ready to crash.

I'm just about to disconnect when Gran calls out to me.

"I'm going to add condoms to your next care package. Is there a brand you prefer?" *Fucking hell.* My face ignites and I'm too mortified to even stammer a response. "We don't want any little Brady's running around before you tie the knot, after all."

Kill. Me. Now.

11

———

PIPER

The heat wave has finally broken and a cool fall breeze whips at my back as I enter College Park Brewery, flustered and acutely aware I'm three minutes late for my lunch date with Brady.

It's only three minutes.

Three minutes that suggest I'm an entitled jerk who doesn't respect his time.

Dr. Barnes has kicked students out of her classroom for less.

This isn't a lecture.

No, it's a date, which is infinitely more terrifying. My stomach has been twisted in knots all morning, and I haven't been able to concentrate on a damn thing, as evidenced by the fact that I'm wearing two different shoes.

Two. Different. Shoes.

How the hell does that even happen?

I put so much effort into choosing the right clothes last night—jeans and a cobalt sweater that brings out my eyes—and yet my shoes were a total fail.

If you hadn't been running late, it wouldn't have happened.

Fine. Yes, I spent a little extra time on my hair and makeup this morning, but it wasn't vanity. It was strategy.

I need to be confident and in control during this date. If I'm not, Brady will slip past my defenses and then who knows what might happen?

A second date.

My pulse flutters and adrenaline floods my system, my body unable or unwilling to accept that this is a onetime thing, despite the fact that I've been chanting it like a mantra for the last four days.

The hostess smiles and after a quick exchange, she leads me to the back of the restaurant where Brady's seated in a quiet corner near the windows. His hooded eyes find mine the instant I enter the dining room and my belly gives a familiar tug.

It's ridiculous to be nervous. I know that cerebrally. The man has seen me twirling around a pole in booty shorts and not much else, but tell that to the swarm of butterflies that have taken up residence in my stomach.

Like me, he's dressed casually in jeans and a forest green button up that accentuates his broad shoulders, the fabric stretched taut over the sculpted muscles of his arms and chest.

Sweet baby Jesus. Brady gets hotter every time I see him.

I don't know how that's possible, but I am so screwed. There's was no way a single date will satisfy my desire for this man.

You're not here to slake your thirst. You're here to make sure he doesn't get hurt.

Right. Priorities.

Brady climbs to his feet, a relieved smile spreading across his face as we approach the table.

I thank the hostess and then it's just Brady and me. Alone.

"You came." His tone is light, but there's a vulnerability in his whiskey-colored eyes I rarely see in class.

"Of course." I laugh, nervous energy bubbling up from the pit of my stomach. "Can't have Waverly's star tackle getting hurt on my account."

Brady chuckles. "I'm no star, but my battered body thanks you, nonetheless."

He pulls out my chair—because he really is the last living gentleman—and I lower myself into it, basking in the crisp, outdoorsy scent of his cologne.

It should be a crime for a guy to smell so good.

Brady takes his seat across from me and I reach for my menu, unsure where we go from here. I don't know his dating history, but it's been a minute for me and I'm not even sure where to start.

"I've never been here before." He grabs his menu from the center of the table and opens it. "Have you?"

"No, but I've heard good things." *From Jenna.*

The instant she found out we were meeting at the brewery, she began stalking their social accounts and reviews.

Silence falls as we study the menus, but it's easy. There's no awkward tension and Brady isn't compelled to fill the silence.

I peek at him over the top of my menu. His beard is neatly trimmed and I'm pretty sure he's had a haircut since I last saw him, but there's no outward sign of nerves. The man is as cool as a cucumber while I'm freaking the fuck out.

Spectacular.

Clearly, I should've used the time I wasted on hair and makeup to do a few deep breathing exercises this morning.

A server approaches the table and I quickly make my drink selection.

She greets us both, introducing herself as Zoe, but then

her attention seems to fix on Brady. I listen, feeling like a third wheel, as she recites the daily specials.

Not a star, my ass.

She obviously recognizes him as a Waverly football player. It's in the way she arches her back, pushing her breasts out as she points to something in the menu, and in the way she holds eye contact just a little too long.

I've never been one for girl-on-girl drama, and I'm definitely not the jealous type, but come on. We're clearly on a date. So what if it's lunchtime?

"What can I get for you?" Zoe finally asks, flashing Brady a big, accommodating smile.

He turns to me, totally oblivious. "Ladies first."

"I'll have iced tea, please." I smile up at her, pretending she wasn't just flirting with my date.

Brady orders a lemonade and when Zoe sashays away, hips swinging, he doesn't seem to notice.

"You can't be real," I blurt out, shaking my head.

A wrinkle forms between his brows and he cocks his head to the side. "What do you mean?"

"No one is this genuinely nice. You're helpful, polite, you don't swear, and you're completely unaware of your own charm." I smirk. "You're like Captain America, bearded edition."

He laughs low and deep, the quiet rumble doing unholy things to my body.

"I can honestly say this is the first time anyone's compared me to a super hero. I think I like it." He rubs the back of his neck. "For the record, I do swear on occasion."

"Good. No one should be perfect."

After all, it's our flaws that make us human.

We chat about classes and when Zoe returns with our drinks, Brady once again insists I order first.

"I'll have the bacon cheeseburger and fries." I hand her my menu.

"Are you sure?" She opens the menu and flips it around to reveal the first page. "We've got some really great salads if you're in the mood for something lighter."

"If I was in the mood for a salad, I'd have ordered a salad." I meet her stare head-on. I've dealt with enough fatphobic assholes to know she isn't trying to be helpful, and I'm not about to let her shame me into changing my order.

"My girl wants a bacon cheeseburger," Brady drawls, the words rolling off his tongue. "That's what she's going to get."

Holy. Hell.

My ovaries nearly explode at the possessive way he says *my girl*. It doesn't matter if this is our first and last date. It's the hottest damn thing I've ever experienced.

The server grimaces when he doubles the order, and this time when she leaves the table, there's nothing suggestive about her movements.

"I think you scared her." I lean in to rest my forearms on the table. "We might have to pick up our own meals from the kitchen."

He grunts. Actually. Freaking. Grunts.

"I wasn't trying to scare her, but I didn't like the way she treated you."

"People suck." I shrug. "You just have to ignore it."

His nostrils flare with indignation. "I will never sit back and ignore it when someone disrespects you."

Could this man be more perfect?

Not likely.

"The world is full of fatphobic people. If I let them get to me, I'd never leave the house."

"You're fucking gorgeous, Piper." He reaches across the table, taking my hands in his. They're big and rough, but it feels like the most natural thing in the world when he touches me and I can't bring myself to pull away, even though I know I should. "Inside and out. Only a fool could miss it."

A slow flush creeps up the back of my neck, and for once, I'm the one who can't seem to find words.

"If you ask me, that server could stand to eat a cheeseburger or five."

Preach.

"So you like your women curvy?" I slip my hands from his and fold them in my lap as common-sense returns.

"If you don't already know the answer to that question, you haven't been paying attention." His gaze rakes over me—what he can see above the table anyway—leaving a trail of fire in its wake. "Your curves are perfect."

"Too bad the rest of the world isn't as open-minded." I'm not fishing for compliments, but men can be so oblivious to societal beauty standards and the impact they have on a woman's self-esteem. As if being born with a pretty face or maintaining a twenty-six-inch waist can determine a person's worth. "If I had a dollar for every time someone gave me a backhanded compliment, I wouldn't have to—"

I catch myself just in time.

This is why it's too dangerous to let people in.

All it would take is one stupid slip of the tongue and my secret wouldn't be my own anymore.

Brady frowns. "You wouldn't have to what?"

"Nothing." I force a smile and take a sip of my tea as I gather my thoughts. "I just mean that people can be insensitive. Like, they'll say 'You dance well for a big girl.' Or, 'If I had your cheekbones, I wouldn't have to watch my weight either.'"

"That's messed up."

"It is, but I love my curves and I refuse to be ashamed because they don't fit someone else's idea of beauty."

"The worst thing anyone's ever said about me is that I have a dad-bod, and that came from Coop."

I snort-laugh. "That's actually a compliment."

"Pretty sure he didn't mean it as one."

"Then the joke's on him because women love dad bods. They're good for cuddling." I arch a brow. "Next time, ask if he wants to snuggle."

Brady shakes his head. "I'm pretty sure Coop doesn't want to cuddle with the likes of me."

"Fair enough." I swirl the straw in my glass, thoughts drifting back to Zoe. "I'm confident in my body and I don't give a damn what our fatphobic server thinks, but I hate seeing women tear each other down. We already have to contend with the patriarchy and impossible Hollywood standards. We should use our energy to lift one another up."

"Agreed, but you're wrong about one thing." He pauses, letting his words hang in the air. "A real man knows beauty comes in all shapes and sizes, and he damn sure recognizes it when he sees it."

12

———

BRADY

"Are you a feminist, Brady?"

There's a challenge in Piper's eyes, but I'm ready for it.

My earlier nerves have faded and we're starting to vibe, the tension between us crackling like lightning.

"I was raised by two strong women. Not only did they teach me respect, they taught me to look for inner beauty." I chuckle. "It was an important lesson, because on the farm, no one cares what you look like, only if you've got the feed bucket."

Piper laughs, and it's a goddamn relief. My shoulders relax and the tension leaks from my body. As angry as I am about the server's mistreatment of her, I don't want it to ruin our date. It's taken us weeks to get to this point, and the idea of Piper backsliding, of her closing up on me, is unacceptable.

"I still can't believe you grew up on a farm." She scrunches her nose. "I thought farmers were a dying breed."

She's kidding, but the comment hits a little too close to home.

Put it in the box, asshole.

I can worry about finances later. Piper deserves my

undivided attention, and I'll be damned if I'm going to give her anything less.

"What about you?" I reach for my lemonade. Condensation slides down the side of the glass, providing a welcome relief. The temperature outside has finally broken, but when I'm in the presence of this woman, I always run hot. "Tell me something about yourself."

"What do you want to know?"

"Everything."

It's the most honest answer I can give.

She drums her fingers on the table, as if thinking. "Let's see, my favorite color is pink, but not light pink, bright pink. Think fuchsia. My full name is Piper Lilian Reynolds, which I probably shouldn't have told you, but I guess we're beyond stalking at this point." She pauses, flashing me a shit-eating grin. "I love to read, but only fiction. Romance is my favorite, especially the spicy kind."

"Spicy? Like they cook while they're falling in love? Gran watches those kinds of movies on Hallmark all the time."

Piper bursts out laughing, her howls suggesting they do not, in fact, cook while falling in love. Tears stream down her face, but I can't bring myself to be embarrassed. Not when she's beaming at me like I'm the funniest guy on the planet.

"The spice is the..." She covers her mouth with her hand, trying to stifle her giggles. "You know, the sexy bits."

Jesus Christ. Maybe I should just tattoo *virgin* on my forehead and get it over with.

Heat scalds my cheeks as the server appears with our burgers, and by the time we're settled, Piper's regained her composure.

"So." I pop a fry in my mouth, searching for a topic that won't make me look like a raging dumbass. "Have you always wanted to be a teacher?"

Piper nibbles on a fry, chewing thoughtfully. "Yes, and no."

She's quiet for a long time, but I don't push. I can be patient if that's what she needs.

"My childhood wasn't what you'd call stable." She offers me a wry smile. "I never knew my father and my mother was so wrapped up in her own life—in men and alcohol—that she barely knew I existed. When I started school, it was a relief to be somewhere people actually cared about what I was doing."

My chest tightens, a vice squeezing the air from my lungs. Because while I was raised with love and compassion, Piper knew only indifference and heartache.

Is it any wonder she's so guarded?

I can't imagine growing up like that. Can't imagine the emotional scars it would leave on a child.

"For a long time, I didn't believe I could rise above my circumstances. Then, in seventh grade, we read *The Giver* and my English teacher, Mrs. Monroe, had us write an essay on the book. A few days after we turned them in, she pulled me aside to tell me I'd scored the highest grade in the class. I was floored." A wistful smile takes hold and her eyes lose focus. "God, I still remember the feeling of exhilaration when she told me. I'd never been the best at anything before that moment."

It's hard to imagine a version of Piper who lacked poise and confidence, and though my fingers ache to reach for her, I hold back.

This story has a happy ending.

It must because the confident woman before me is nothing like the lost child she's just described.

"Anyway, Mrs. Monroe said if I kept up the good work, I could go to college one day and become a writer." She flashes a self-deprecating smile and pops a fry in her mouth. "She may have also used the word famous, but as you've probably guessed, I decided to forgo fame and fortune so I can teach."

I scoop up my burger. "Fame and fortune are overrated."

Her shoulders sag. "You think I'm being naïve."

"Not at all." I hold her gaze, willing her to hear the sincerity of my words. "It sounds like Mrs. Monroe inspired you and you want to pay it forward."

"Exactly." She grabs her own burger and takes a ravenous bite, chewing and swallowing before she continues. "If it weren't for all the teachers who encouraged me over the years, who helped me realize my full potential, I'm not sure I would've been able to see a way out. Now that I'm free, I want to be that light for another child floundering in the dark."

It's the most selfless thing I've ever heard.

"I don't know why I'm telling you all of this." She shifts and our knees brush, the heat of her body warm against my own. "I guess you're just easy to talk to."

I've always been a good listener, but it's more than that. We have a connection, even if she refuses to acknowledge it.

"You don't have to explain yourself, Piper. When I said I wanted to know everything about you, I meant it."

Her cheeks flush and she lowers her gaze.

"God, I'm so bad at this." She drops her burger onto the plate. "I'm totally dominating the conversation. What about you? What's your favorite color?"

"I'm a sucker for the clear, bright blue of a mid-summer sky. The kind that's so captivating you can't tear your eyes away from it, and you wouldn't want to, even if you could, because it makes you so damn happy."

If she realizes I'm describing her eyes, she doesn't let it show.

"Well, that was oddly specific. Let's see..."

She sweeps her tongue across her lower lip and my cock stiffens.

Christ.

The hold this woman has on me should be illegal.

"I already know you're shit at dancing, football is a means to an end, and you don't play favorites with the farm animals, at least not that you'll admit." She shoots me the side-eye and I smirk because we both know I have favorites. "What else are you passionate about? "

The obvious answer is sitting directly across from me, but since admitting it would likely have her calling for the check, I go with the safe answer.

"Willow Bend. The farm has been in my family for five generations and it's my life. I honestly can't imagine living anywhere else after graduation. Hell, if my mom and grandmother hadn't insisted on higher education, I'd be at home right now working the land with them."

Of course, then I never would've met Piper, so maybe they had the right idea after all.

She nods slowly. "So it's just the three of you?"

"Yeah." I shove my plate away. "My grandfather was killed in a farming accident when I was twelve, so it's just been me, mom and Gran for the last ten years."

"Oh, Brady." Her eyes soften, and she reaches for my hand, squeezing it gently. "I'm so sorry."

"It was tough at first." Talking about my grandfather never gets easier. Pops was the only father I've ever known, and he taught me everything I know about being a good man. "Farming is a challenging business in the best of times and stepping into his shoes wasn't easy, but I've done everything I can to lighten the load for my mom and Gran."

For all the good it's done lately.

"I'm sure they appreciate it, but you were just a boy. They couldn't expect that of you."

"No, I'm sure they didn't, but Pops did. He was old-fashioned that way." If I close my eyes, I can still see his pale, sweaty face as he whispered his last words. "He told me to take care of them, and that's what I've done."

The look of pity on her face is a gut punch, but I can't bring myself to regret sharing this piece of myself.

A half-smile lights Piper's face. "I suppose that explains your protective nature."

"I suppose it does, which reminds me..." I slide my placemat out from under my plate. It's a thin sheet of ivory paper featuring the brewery's logo and homemade brews in black print. "I didn't have time to stop after class, but I promised my grandmother I'd bring you flowers."

"Oh, you didn't—"

"I know I didn't have to." I fold the placemat in half. "But it's tradition."

She watches in silence as I deftly transform the sheet of paper with only my memory to guide me.

When I'm done, I offer it to her. "A lily just for you, Piper Lilian Reynolds."

"This is amazing!" Her eyes go wide and she laughs as she accepts the paper flower. "How did you do that?"

"There weren't any other kids around to play with while I was growing up, so I taught myself origami." I grin, recalling the long hours and endless paper cuts it took to master the basic shapes. "If you ever need paper animals for your classroom, I'm your guy."

Piper tips her head back and laughs, revealing the long column of her throat. "You, Brady Vaughn, are full of surprises."

"Darlin', you haven't seen anything yet."

13

PIPER

"Piper!" I freeze mid-stride, turning to the woman behind the front desk of the apartment building. I'm getting way too many packages if the staff recognizes me on sight. "I was just about to call you. You've got a delivery."

"Oh, can I just—"

"Let me run to the back and grab it," she says, cutting me off as she disappears into the small room where deliveries are stored.

Most days it's a convenient service, but today? Not so much.

I've got class with Dr. Barnes in thirty minutes and I cannot be late.

I rack my brain, trying to remember what I might have ordered and if it will fit in my backpack, but nothing comes to mind.

When she returns carrying a stunning arrangement of white lilies, my concern for punctuality goes right out the window.

Brady.

It has to be. No one else would send me flowers, especially lilies.

"Oh, wow." I cross the lobby to the front desk and when she places the arrangement on the counter, I inhale, savoring the sweet scent of the blossoms.

"They're lovely." The leasing agent flashes me a knowing grin as I grab the little envelope bearing my name. "Whoever sent these is a keeper."

No kidding.

My date with Brady was perfect. Or as perfect as a first date can be, and when we finally parted ways, the desire to wrap him in my arms was nearly impossible to resist.

And not just because he oozes sex appeal.

The raw emotion in his voice when he talked about losing his grandfather and becoming the man of the house at just twelve nearly broke me, but it also helped me understand him. Helped me understand the sharply honed protective instinct that drives him to shield those he cares about from harm.

I tear open the envelope and remove the card. The message is scrawled in small, uneven letters and I'm certain Brady wrote it himself. Because *of course* he'd physically go to the florist to place his order. He always goes the extra mile.

Piper,

I had a great time yesterday. I'd love to take you out again sometime.

Brady

P.S. I know you're a modern woman who can

buy herself flowers, but I hope these brighten your day anyway.

MY STOMACH FLIPS and a subtle tingle spreads throughout my body, warming me from head to toe. No one's ever sent me flowers before. It's so incredibly sweet, and so incredibly Brady.

If he were standing in front of me now, I don't think I'd be able to resist flinging myself into his arms and crushing my lips to his. The scene plays in my mind's eye and—

Shit. Am I swooning? Is that what this feeling is?

Yup, I'm totally screwed.

As much as I'd like to take Brady up on his offer of a second date, I can't. It wouldn't be fair. Not when I haven't been honest with him about my Fangirl channel.

Technically, you didn't lie.

Bullshit. A lie of omission is still a lie.

I've got a pretty good sense of Brady's values, and despite our sizzling chemistry, I doubt he'd be down to date an adult entertainer. Even if he was okay with it, it would be too risky.

Which is why our first date has to be our last.

Stay strong, sis.

I arrange for the leasing agent to hold the flowers until I get back from class. The smart move would be to trash them, but I can't bring myself to do it. They're beautiful and they smell amazing and just the sight of them reminds me of the thoughtful man who sent them.

So no, I can't continue seeing Brady, but I can keep the flowers.

I make the long trek across campus, arriving at the lecture hall with five minutes to spare.

"So, how was the date?" Jenna asks, practically bouncing in her seat as I drop down next to her.

"It was fine."

I can't bring myself to recount the details aloud. Not when doing so will make me fall just a little harder. It's already impossible to explain to Jenna why there's no future for Brady and me. Catching feelings won't make it any easier.

I begin to unpack my things and when I glance up, the TA is staring.

Shit. Am I having a wardrobe malfunction?

I glance down, but nothing appears to be amiss. My pants are zipped, I'm wearing a bra, and my boobs are safely inside my t-shirt, where they belong.

Maybe it's my hair? I quickly finger comb the windblown locks as Jenna twists in her seat to stare at me.

"Fine?" She narrows her eyes. "Salads are fine. Boxed wine is fine. Brady Vaughn is...something way better than fine."

"Very articulate." I smirk. "Are you going to use that descriptor in the classroom?"

Jenna sticks out her tongue because apparently, we're on the same maturity level as the kids we aspire to teach. "Have you talked to him since your date?"

"Nope."

I don't mention that he's texted a few times or that I haven't responded because I don't want to lead him on.

And yet you can't bring yourself to shut him down or block him.

I ignore the snarky little voice in my head.

Yes, I'm a mess. No, acknowledging it isn't the cure.

Which is why I don't tell her about the flowers either.

Jenna flops back in her chair. "You're hopeless."

"Well aware."

Dammit. Why is Mike McConnell staring at me? Did I forget to turn in my homework?

I grab my phone and check the outgoing mail, which confirms I submitted the last assignment. Still, I resubmit just to be on the safe side.

Classroom observations start next week, so it's not a great time to be rocking the boat or missing assignments. I'm scheduled to observe Tuesday afternoons at a local elementary school, and after meeting the teacher I'll be shadowing, I'm looking forward to getting started.

Observations are the last big hurdle before student teaching begins in the spring and then it's on to graduation. I've worked so hard to get here, but it's strange to think that next year, I'll be teaching in my own classroom.

Assuming I can find a job.

One step at a time.

It's how I've survived the last three years. It'll get me through this one, too.

Beside me, Jenna perks up. "You should come to the HoCo parade with me and the girls this weekend. I'll bet Brady would love to have you there cheering him on."

Yes, he would. And damn if I don't want it, too.

The yearning in my gut is so strong, it's almost painful. I want to be there. To see Brady in his game-day uniform. To cheer him on alongside the rest of Wildcat Nation, but... I don't want to lead him on or give him false hope. We agreed to one date and one date only. Brady will keep his word and withdraw from pole class. I need to be strong enough to do the same, even if it's a promise I made only to myself.

"Come on." Jenna nudges me. "It'll be fun."

Yeah, right. As much as I want to see Brady, spending time with Jenna's roommates is a big hell no for me. I still haven't recovered from our trip to the Wildcat's Den.

"I can't. Sorry." I offer her an apologetic smile. "I'm way behind on my reading assignments and I have a test in Intro to ASD that's going to be brutal."

All of which is true.

What I don't tell her is that I've also scheduled two live streams for Saturday and I need the money to make rent. I've scraped together a decent nest egg to help me get on my feet after graduation, but I can't afford to dip into it for everyday expenses.

"But it's homecoming!"

"I know. I suck. We'll hang out soon," I promise. "Just you and me."

"You work too much." Jenna sighs. "You keep this up and one day you're going to wake up to realize you missed out on the best things in life."

A smiling image of Brady flashes through my mind, and I can't help but wonder if I already have.

14

BRADY

I stare at the string of unanswered texts on my phone, debating whether I should send another.

Because seven is the magic number and Piper will finally answer.

Fuck. Why isn't she responding? Did I do something wrong? Come on too strong?

Maybe the flowers were too much. Or worse, maybe she hated them.

"Last time I saw someone stare that intently at their phone, they were battling a porn addiction." Parker stretches his legs, luxuriating in the extra space our front row seats provide. "Just saying."

It's Friday afternoon, and even though we've got a bye this week, Coach is holding a team meeting. The entire team is gathered in the media room, waiting for the old man to show.

"I don't have a porn addiction, asshole."

He smirks. "The first step to overcoming addiction is admitting you have a problem."

"Did someone say porn?" Coop leans forward, craning to see around Parker. "Because I've got recs."

"Jesus Christ, DeLaurentis. Nobody wants your porn recs."

"Speak for yourself." Coop scoffs. "My shit is gold. Just ask the freshman."

Reid groans. "Please tell me you aren't actually sending porn links to the underclassman."

"Only the ones who ask." He smirks. "Can't have them embarrassing themselves when they hit Greek Row to blow off steam."

Parker snickers, but Reid is unimpressed. "I'm going to pretend I didn't hear that," he says, eyeing the clock. "If you end up in trouble with Coach, leave my name out of it."

"Aye aye, Captain, but mark my words, you're going to thank me when our guys roll into bowl season loose and totally stress free."

"Let's just get through the regular season and then we'll talk," Reid shoots back.

I glance around, making sure our teammates aren't listening, and wipe my palms on my thighs.

Quit stalling and just get it over with.

"What do you do when someone's ignoring your texts?"

My roommates stare at me, all three of them slack jawed.

So much for the band aid approach.

I don't know if it's the change in subject throwing them off or the fact that I'm looking for dating advice, but who else am I going to ask? I'm sure as hell not asking Gran.

It's bad enough she sent me a value pack of Magnum Gold condoms.

And yet that still wasn't as bad as the handwritten note she'd included: *Big hands aren't the only thing that runs in the family.*

I shudder at the memory.

"Oh, shit." Parker straightens in his seat. "Our boy has been ghosted."

Heat burns my cheeks, but it's a small price to pay. Every single one of these guys has more experience with women than I could ever hope to have. Sure, I was raised by two women and I've watched every rom-com under the sun, but none of what I know seems to work on Piper.

Maybe she's just not that into you.

Bullshit. Our date went well. Her body language was open. She didn't shy away from my touch, and she told me she had a great time when we said goodbye.

"I'm going to need more information." Coop leans forward, resting his elbows on his knees. "Is this someone male or female?"

"Does it matter?"

"Hell, yes, it matters." He gives me a disbelieving look. "Men and women are wired totally different."

I scrub a hand over my face, certain I'm going to regret my next words. "Her name is Piper."

"Has she blocked you? Taken out a restraining order?"

He can't be serious.

"This sounds like the voice of experience," Parker says, cutting in. "Please tell me you don't have a restraining order against you, DeLaurentis, because I feel like that's something Coach would want to know."

"No, I don't have a fucking restraining order. What kind of creep do you think I am?" Coop shoots him an indignant look and points to his chest. "I'm the protected party."

It's too late to turn back now.

"Look." Coop returns his attention to me. "I'm just saying that if I saw you coming at me on a dark street with that big ass beard..."

I give him the finger.

"Don't shoot the messenger." He throws up his hands in

self-defense. "There's a fine line between sweet and scary, and you're walking it."

"Screw you. I trimmed my beard last week." I stroke it for emphasis. "I'm surprised you didn't notice sooner since you're so obsessed with me."

"Can we get back on topic?" Reid asks, taking charge. "First things first. Is this woman playing hard to get or is she legit not interested? Because you don't want to be the entitled douche who can't accept the word no."

"Facts." Parker nods. "It's not a good look."

I scan my roommates' faces. "How do you know the difference?"

"Hell if I know." Coop flashes his trademark grin. "I've never had a woman turn me down before."

"Ignore baby biceps over there," Reid says. "He's just messing with you. Look, sometimes you just have to take control of your destiny and hope for the best."

Hope for the best? That's his sage advice?

Christ. This is what I get for seeking dating tips from serial bachelors.

The door bangs open and Coach Collins stalks in. Coach Walker and the rest of the coaching staff trail behind like ducklings.

"Listen up." He takes his place behind the podium at the front of the room. "I know all of you knuckleheads are looking forward to a few days off, but a bye is not an excuse to get wasted and make poor decisions."

"He's looking at you, DeLaurentis!" someone calls out.

Laughter erupts behind us, and Coop uses his middle finger to scratch the back of his head.

"Settle down!" Coach grumbles. "I'm serious. We've got recruits on campus this weekend and I swear to Christ, if I get a single call from campus police, you'll all be running laps until you puke."

"You know, the more he makes that threat, the less terrifying it sounds," Parker whispers from behind his hand.

Yeah, right. It's all fun and games until an underclassman pulls the group punishment card.

"You're the best and brightest Waverly has to offer, so act like it. Enjoy your time off and don't embarrass yourselves, this program, or the university."

Words to live by.

Thirty minutes later, Coach deems us sufficiently chastised and dismisses us. The guys make noise about getting food at The Diner, but I've got other plans.

After all, Piper can't ignore me if we're face-to-face.

THERE'S no answer when I knock on Piper's door.

Shit. This was stupid. It's Friday night. She's probably out doing whatever it is people with lives do on the weekend while I'm standing here like a sad sack, 'taking control of my destiny.'

I scrub a hand over my face and make a mental note to ignore all future dating advice from Reid. The guy may be a genius on the field, but this hope for the best philosophy isn't working for me.

That's because it's a terrible strategy.

I'm just about to give up when there's a muffled sound on the other side of the door.

My muscles tense and I strain my ears, waiting to see if it repeats.

The silence stretches on for nearly a minute, and I knock again, louder this time.

"Go *awaaaay!*"

A soft moan follows the request.

What the hell?

"Piper, are you okay?"

She doesn't reply, and my mind slips into overdrive.

What if she's hurt? She could've fallen and hit her head. Or slipped in the shower and broken a bone. She lives alone and it could be days before anyone finds her. The news runs horror stories like that all the time.

My gut twists.

Piper is all alone in there, and she might need help.

Or maybe she has a guy over and she doesn't need you busting up a good time.

Fuck. I really should've thought this through, because the mere possibility of another man touching her makes me want to rip his arms off and shove them down his hypothetical throat.

Which would definitely violate Coach's *'Don't do dumb shit'* policy.

Piper moans again and this time I'm certain there's no guy in the picture.

I may not be an expert on women, but I know the difference between pleasure and pain.

"Piper." I rap gently on the door and place my mouth close to the frame. "I know you're in there and I'm not leaving until I see for myself that you're alright."

And if she doesn't open the door?

I'll cross that bridge when I come to it.

She doesn't answer, but I'm prepared to wait her out.

I study the door, trying to figure out exactly how much damage it would do if I put my shoulder into it.

More than your broke ass can afford.

True, but it would be worth it.

A loud *thwack* shatters the silence and I step back from the door as Piper yanks it open.

Her hair is tied up in a messy bun and she's wearing red Hello Kitty pajamas.

It's the first time I've seen her without makeup and somehow, she's even more beautiful without it.

"How did you get my apartment number?"

I shove my hands in the pockets of my jeans. "Jenna."

"Why am I not surprised?" She rolls her eyes and leans against the door. "I'll deal with her later."

"Don't be mad. Jenna was worried about you. She said you missed class."

"If Jenna was worried, she could've come over. Or texted."

"So it's just my texts you aren't answering?"

I'd suspected as much, but hearing it confirmed is a kick in the gut.

She sighs and folds an arm across her midsection. "What are you doing here, Brady?"

"Like I said, Jenna and I were worried." I rock back on my heels, nerves taking root. What is it about this woman that leaves me totally unmoored? "I also wanted to ask you out on another date and since you've been ignoring my texts, I figured maybe I should do it in person. The old-fashioned way."

Which, now that I've said it out loud, sounds like a terrible idea.

"I can't deal with this right now." She flinches and her eyes snap shut. "You have to go."

Her voice is strained, and it's obvious she's not feeling well, even if she won't admit it.

"What's wrong, Piper? And don't tell me nothing when I can see with my own eyes that something isn't right."

"I'm fine. You don't have to worry about me." She huffs in

exasperation. "I'm...indisposed, so if you could just..." She makes a shooing motion with her hand.

"Nice try. You can hardly stand upright. I'm not leaving until I'm sure you're okay."

"Then I guess you'd better clear your schedule for the next three to five days."

Three to five days? It must be serious.

"Is it the flu? I've already had my flu shot, so—"

"Oh, my God. It's not the flu." She groans again. "I'm on the first day of my period and I'm leaking like a faucet and the cramps are killing me. And in case it's not obvious, I feel awful and I don't want company because I'm a cranky hot mess and I'm all out of Reese's."

"Oh."

She rolls her eyes. "Yeah, oh."

My cheeks heat and I take a step back, trying to unpack everything she's just thrown at my feet. This isn't how I imagined my visit, and I don't want to take it from bad to worse by saying or doing the wrong thing. Fortunately, I think I know how to make it better.

"I... You're right. I shouldn't have just shown up at your door without calling first. Get some rest and we can talk later."

15

PIPER

IF MEN HAD PERIODS, the world would cease to function for seven days every month.

I flop down on the couch and snuggle into my blanket fort, curling up on my side just as my uterus launches another vicious assault, reminding me I'm out of Tylenol.

I close my eyes and breathe through the pain as an old K-Drama plays out on the tv. Dae professes his love for Soo-jin and disappointment courses through my veins.

I'll bet he wouldn't leave his crush to fend for herself if she was in pain.

You're the one who told him to go. You have no one to blame but yourself.

I know that, but I'm up in my feelings and *spoiler alert*: they aren't logical.

That's the whole freaking problem.

Yes, I told Brady to go, but deep down, I'd been hoping he'd stay. He's the most determined man I've ever met, and after weeks of pole classes, I was actually starting to believe nothing could deter him.

Hell, I'd even been considering his request for a second date...*against my better judgment.*

But like most dudes walking the earth, talk of periods sent him running for the hills.

Just like you knew it would.

Ugh. Guys are so weird. How is it they can watch gory slasher flicks and play blood-soaked video games, but at the first mention of menstruation, they're out?

It's insulting.

No, it's for the best.

I don't have room in my life for a man, and even if I did, it's too risky.

This is what happens when you think with your hormones instead of your head.

Whatever. It's not like I can't take care of myself. God knows I've been doing it for most of my life. Nora sure as shit didn't comfort me when I was sobbing in pain during my first period. No, she's always been the 'Suck it up, buttercup' type, which is ironic given she expects to be waited on hand and foot when she's hungover.

That's because she's selfish.

I've always known it, even when I was little and didn't know the right word to describe her behavior.

My phone vibrates on the coffee table and I pick it up to find a text from Jenna.

Jenna: I emailed you the notes from Barnes' class.

I'd have done the same for her if our positions were reversed, but something tells me she's testing the water. Probably checking into see if Brady made use of the information she gave him.

Don't be mad. Jenna was worried about you.

Brady's words echo in my head, but I can't just ignore the fact that she gave him my address.

Me: Thanks. I had a surprise visitor today…

There's a long pause and then three little dots appear on the screen.

Jenna: Anyone I know?

I roll my eyes and pull the blankets tighter around myself.

Me: Don't play coy. I know you're the one who gave him my address.

Jenna: In my defense, I was worried. Besides, it's not like he's some rando serial killer.

Me: That we know of.

Even I huff a laugh at that, because no self-respecting psycho would subject himself to the humiliation that was Brady attempting pole.

Jenna: So? What happened?

Jenna: Are you going on another date?

Jenna: If you don't jump on that man, someone else will.

The messages pop up in a flurry. Jenna does this when she's excited, pressing send before she finishes typing.

I should let her stew in her own curiosity—it would serve her right—but apparently, I'm in a sharing mood, so I type out a quick message, explaining the situation.

Jenna's reply is swift and contains about a zillion skull emojis.

Me: Your support is duly noted…

Jenna: Nope. You don't get to be salty when you're putting that poor guy through it.

Guilt rears its ugly head and I hesitate before tapping out a reply.

Me: It's possible I didn't put my best foot forward.

Jenna: You think?

I sit with that, trying to decide if I've crossed the line from politely disinterested to asshole territory, and come up empty.

Not a good sign.

Another K-Drama starts and I try to lose myself in the story, but between the tug of war currently happening in my pelvis and my guilt, it's impossible to focus.

Something's got to give. I can't go on like this, seducing Brady in my fantasies and keeping him at arm's length in real life.

It's exhausting.

And if I'm not careful, I'm going to end up with whiplash.

I'm midway through a new episode of the K-Drama when my phone vibrates with an incoming text.

I check the screen and my pulse spikes when I see it's from Brady.

Brady: I didn't want to bother you in case you're resting, but I left some supplies by the door so you don't have to go out.

He...left me supplies.

Curiosity gets the better of me and I pad over to the door.

I open it to find two overflowing shopping bags and when I crouch down to peer into them, I find everything I could possibly need to ride out my period in comfort. There's a heating pad, a bottle of Tylenol, a carton of chocolate ice cream, a giant bag of Reese's, plus a romance novel and a white paper bag that smells a lot like takeout. To my complete and utter shock, there's even a box of tampons.

Holy shit. Brady bought me tampons.

A variety pack, nonetheless.

I'm absolutely speechless as I gather the bags and bring them inside.

Dammit. How am I supposed to resist the man when he goes and does thoughtful stuff like this?

I drop the bags on the kitchen counter and Jenna's words come back to haunt me.

If you don't jump on that man, someone else will.

Jealousy coils low in my gut and I grip the counter for support.

He deserves to be happy.

Of course he does. Brady is an incredible man, and he deserves an incredible partner. Someone who's as invested in him as he is in them. Someone who will go the extra mile to make him happy and bring out the sexy, dimpled smile he keeps hidden from the world. Someone who's willing—and able—to commit.

The thought of that person being another woman is too painful to even consider.

For weeks, he's tried to break through my defenses. Tried to convince me he's worth the risk while I've done everything in my power to keep him at arm's length. I've thrown out one excuse after another to protect my secrets and he hasn't wavered.

Not once.

The man is determined—today's visit proves it—but it can't last. If I keep throwing out roadblocks, if I keep pushing him away, he's going to move on.

And even though I should want it, should want to keep my distance and my secrets, I don't want him to give up on me.

On us.

The very real possibility of Brady walking away is enough to make me do the one thing I swore I'd never do.

I just hope I don't regret it.

16

BRADY

I'm about to exit Piper's building when my phone rings, and even though I know it's futile, hope flares in my chest as I step back into the lobby.

What can I say? I'm an eternal optimist.

That or a hopeless romantic.

I check the screen and I'll be damned if it's not Piper's name I see.

A grin splits my face as I swipe accept. "Hey, darlin'."

The guys on the team would probably call me a simp, but it's all good. I'm not ashamed to let my girl know I'm into her. Hell, I want the entire world to know.

"Hey." She's quiet for a beat and I imagine her worrying her lower lip on the other end of the line. "Thank you. For everything. It was really sweet."

"You're welcome, but it was no big deal."

I've done the same thing for my mom countless times, though she prefers Snickers to Reese's.

"Do you want to come back up? We could...watch a movie or something."

Hell yes, I want to go back up and watch a movie. That's

not even a question, but... "Are you sure you're up for company?"

It's probably stupid to give her an out because with my luck, she'll take it. But I don't want our time together to be an obligation or repayment for a simple kindness. And I sure as shit don't want her to feel like she has to entertain me when she's not feeling well.

"Yes." Her delivery is clear and confident this time. "I took two Tylenol that are bound to kick in any minute. Besides, it looks like you ordered the entire Great Wall menu and I can't possibly eat all this food."

I shake my head, though she can't see it. "Would it really be so bad to just admit you enjoy my company?"

She laughs, full and throaty. "I plead the fifth."

It's the same defense I used after our first pole class, so I'm not surprised when she disconnects.

Leave it to Piper to get the last word.

I chuckle and head for the elevator, pulse thrumming.

The door is open when I get upstairs, so I call out as I enter. "Piper?"

"Come on in. I'm unpacking the buffet."

I'm greeted by the scent of pumpkin spice as I step inside and close the door behind me. The apartment is small, but neat, and the open concept keeps it from feeling claustrophobic, even for a guy my size. It's furnished with the same stock pieces found in every apartment on campus, but Piper's added little touches like throw blankets and wall art to make it her own, and an orange candle burns in the center of the coffee table.

"Honestly." She gestures to the takeout containers that line the peninsula dividing the kitchen and living room. "I can't decide if I should be flattered or offended that you thought I could eat all this."

"I didn't know what you liked."

The hint of a smile curves her lips. "So you ordered the whole damn menu?"

"It was that, or call Jenna." I shrug. "I didn't want to get her in any more trouble."

"Fair enough. Jenna gets in plenty of trouble on her own." She opens a cabinet and takes down two white plates. "Now please quit hovering in the doorway and come eat some of this food so it doesn't go to waste."

"Sure." I cross the small space in a few strides. The kitchen seemed like a decent size, but once we're both behind the counter, it's tight. "What can I do to help?"

"Can you just grab us a couple of drinks from the fridge?" She maneuvers around me to grab silverware. "I'm good with whatever you're having."

I grab two bottles of water and then load up a plate with General Tso's, lo mein, a couple of wontons, and a pork egg roll. The food smells great and I'm starving since I didn't have time to grab anything after the team meeting.

Piper carries her plate into the living room and I follow her lead.

She settles in on the couch, sitting cross-legged with her plate in her lap. I take the spot next to her. Her knee brushes my thigh, but if she notices, it doesn't seem to bother her.

"I still can't believe you did all this." She plucks a dumpling from her plate using chopsticks. "I honestly thought the P word scared you off."

I snort. "You forget I was raised by two women. It'll take a lot more than period talk to scare me." I glance up, meeting her eyes. "It's a natural part of life, after all."

"Not all men share that view, but thank you. Sometimes I forget that under all this," she says, waving a hand to encompass all six and a half feet of me, "you're softer than a twist top cone."

"Thanks, I think."

She laughs and damn do I love the sound of it. "Oh, it's definitely a compliment."

"Why don't we keep that one between us? If the guys on the team catch wind of it, I'd never live it down."

Hell, Coop would probably have t-shirts made.

"My lips are sealed." She grins. "It's the least I can do since I've never had anyone to take care of me before."

"Not even your mom?"

The words are out before I can think better of them, but come on, what kind of mother is too busy to care for a sick child?

It's a fucking travesty.

Piper told me on our first date that her upbringing wasn't the greatest, but she didn't elaborate. Still, I know better than to ask intrusive questions.

Blame it on the nerves.

And that I want to know everything about her when she's ready to share.

"The idea of my mother playing nursemaid is laughable." She scoops up a bit of rice and pops it in her mouth. "Nora was never the mothering type, even when I was little. She's a bartender at the local watering hole so she works late, sleeps late, and brings home sleazy guys, who, as I got older, either hit on me or followed her lead and made cheap jokes about my body."

Disgust curls low in my gut and I grip my fork so hard it's a wonder the damn thing doesn't snap in half.

The scene she just described is disgusting, and the fact that her mother participated instead of protecting, leaves a dark cloud of rage hovering at the edges of my vision. I'm not a violent man, but if I could go back in time and break the fingers of every sick pervert who made her uncomfortable in her own home, I'd do it in a heartbeat.

Fucked up? Maybe.

But so was her childhood. It was clearly nothing like my own. My mom was always there for me when I needed her, sick or not.

Piper plucks a piece of chicken from her plate, not meeting my eyes. "It's in the past."

The hell it is. She wouldn't have brought it up if the memories didn't weigh on her and I hate that there's nothing I can do to make it right.

"I'm sorry your mother wasn't there for you when you needed her." I set my plate on the coffee table and shift so I'm facing her full on. Her gaze remains downcast, as if she's the one who should be ashamed. *Unacceptable.* I cup her chin and tilt her face up, forcing her to look at me. Her eyes shimmer with unshed tears and my throat tightens at the sight of them. "You deserved better, Piper. You still do. But for now, I'll have to do, because I'm not going anywhere."

"I still can't believe you're real."

The words are a whisper and I don't have time to respond because she leans forward, gently brushing her soft lips against mine. The kiss is sweet and tentative, just as I imagined it would be, but after weeks of yearning for this woman, of fantasizing about her, it's not nearly enough.

I need so much more.

More Piper. More heat. *More everything.*

I discard her plate on the coffee table and slip my arms around her waist, cupping the sweet, round globes of her ass as she climbs onto my lap, wrapping her legs around me. She deepens the kiss, her tongue skating past the seam of my lips as she tangles her fingers in my hair and pulls me closer, her breasts pressed firmly to my chest.

Christ Jesus.

The woman is hotter than a lit fuse.

I knead the tender flesh of her backside and she moans in approval. "That feels so good."

"*You* feel good." I trail kisses across her chin and down the long column of her neck. She smells like a dream, like roses in full bloom. I can't get enough of it. I bury my face in her hair, inhaling deeply. "You smell good, too."

Fuck. She even tastes good.

I nip at her ear, taking the lobe between my teeth. Her breath hitches and I bite down gently, coaxing another quiet moan from her lips before I kiss my way back to her mouth, licking and sucking as I worship every uncovered inch of her skin.

This is what Piper deserves, a man who will bathe her in adoration and shower her in affection.

I want so badly to be that man for her.

To be the one who makes her feel like she's walking on air, like nothing could ever bring her down. Because that's the way she makes me feel.

I crush my mouth to hers, determined to show her exactly how I feel as I capture her full lower lip and suck hard. She melts into me, her soft curves molding to mine, and when she rocks her hips, my body responds instinctively, desire taking control as blood rushes to my cock.

My balls tighten and I'm instantly hard, my erection pressing painfully against my zipper as she grinds on me.

She feels so fucking good, but if we keep this up, I'm going to come in my pants.

Should've jerked off before you came over.

I would have if I'd known things were going to escalate so quickly.

Shitfuckdamn. What am I doing?

I didn't come over here to pressure her. Thirty minutes ago, she was lying on her couch in pain and here I am, wishing she'd ride my dick.

Get it the fuck together, Vaughn.

"Hang on." I pull back and surprise flickers in Piper's eyes as I gently slide her onto the couch. "I, uh, can I use your bathroom?"

"Sure." Worry lines her brow as she straightens her Hello Kitty top, but she nods to the short hall branching off the living room. "It's the door on the left."

Once I'm safely inside the bathroom, I lean against the door and close my eyes.

I need to clear my head, something that's becoming harder and harder to accomplish when Piper's around.

The woman makes me feel all the things. Crave all the things.

For so long, my life has revolved around school, football, and the farm.

And now it revolves around your dick.

No way. I'm not in this for sex. I'm in it for Piper.

Hell, I don't care if we ever hook up.

Your actions just now would suggest otherwise.

Fuck. I'm screwing this up.

I open my eyes and brace my hands on the sink, staring into the mirror. But it's not the face reflected back at me that holds my attention. It's the words written on the mirror in looping red script.

Hello, beautiful.

My chest tightens and I flash back to our conversation at the brewery.

The words are a self-affirmation. A reminder to love herself.

I straighten. There are some things you need to learn for yourself. Things that have to come from within to hold meaning, and though this is one of them, I'll be damned if she's not going to hear the words aloud.

Every day, if that's what it takes for her to see herself the way I do.

Piper is gorgeous, but she's so much more than her appearance. She's smart and funny. Kind and compassionate. Strong and resilient.

Piper is mine.

She just doesn't know it yet.

When I return to the living room, Piper's right where I left her. I drop down beside her and pull her into my arms. She smiles, the worry in her eyes dissipating.

"Want to tell me about the words on the mirror?"

"The world doesn't make it easy to love yourself." She gives a one-shoulder shrug. "My therapist thought it might help."

Her delivery is plaintive, so matter of fact, it nearly guts me.

"The world is wrong." I cup her chin and level my gaze at her. "You're the most incredible woman I've ever met."

I lower my mouth to hers, determined to show her just how firmly I believe those words as the rest of the world melts away.

17

PIPER

I'M on cloud nine as I make my way to the College of Education to meet with Dr. Barnes. The sun is shining and a kaleidoscope of brightly colored leaves litter the ground in the quad, confirming fall has officially arrived in College Park.

I've always been a big fan of winter—of snowstorms and hot chocolate, roaring fires and cozy blankets—but I'm starting to see the merits of this in-between season. It's hard not to when Brady's turned my world upside down in the best possible way.

It's been five days since he showed up at my apartment armed with his own personal version of a period comfort kit, and though he's been busy with football stuff, we've been texting. Things between us have been surprisingly easy and because he's so busy, I've been able to get my schoolwork done and maintain my camming schedule without having to make excuses.

For now.

Whatever. I'm not trying to borrow tomorrow's problems.

I'm being careful, and that's what matters.

My phone vibrates with an incoming text, and I fish it out

of my pocket. At the sight of Brady's name, my stomach flips with the now familiar rush of excitement I get every time he messages.

Brady: Hey, beautiful. How's your day going?

God, where has this silver-tongued man been all my life? Not only is he a sweet talker, he's a good kisser. He took me from zero to one hundred with a single kiss, which has been great for my cam sessions, but terrible for my concentration. If Brady was ruling my thoughts before, he's now become a full-blown obsession.

Me: Good. I'm heading into my advisory meeting with Dr. Barnes. I think I'm getting my student teaching assignment today. You?

The prospect is equal parts thrilling and vomit inducing, which is probably why I didn't sleep last night. Then, because I was dragging ass this morning, I chugged a massive iced coffee and now I've got the full body shakes.

Yay, me.

Brady: Just sitting in class thinking about you.

I type my reply as I climb the stone steps to the College of Education.

Me: Sounds productive.

Brady: You have no idea.

The words send a thrill up my spine and though I'm tempted to reply, I drop my phone in my bag. No way am I going to be the reason he falls behind in...agriculture or whatever class he's currently zoning out in.

The door to the building swings open and Dr. Jeffries, who teaches Classroom Management, steps out. The guy is a talker, so I greet him and slip inside before he can engage me in a lengthy conversation. I cannot afford to be late for my meeting with Barnes.

When I get to the education office, the department admin sends me straight back.

"Ms. Reynolds." Dr. Barnes gestures to the empty chairs stationed opposite her desk. "Please have a seat."

I do as instructed, choosing the one closest to the door, just in case I need to make a quick escape.

"I've reviewed your observation reports."

My eyes dart to her monitor, but the text is too small to read. I completed my second classroom observation yesterday, and I thought my writeup was solid, but with the way Barnes is studying me, now I'm not so sure.

"I'd like to hear about the experience from you directly. How are things going in the classroom?"

"Things are going well." I clear my throat, determined to focus on the positive. After all, no one likes a whiner. "Mrs. Hanford's been incredibly welcoming. She even stayed after class yesterday to answer some questions I had about the lesson plan."

Barnes smiles, but there's an edge to it. "I understand she has a challenging class."

Understatement.

I've only observed her twice and I've seen some shit, but it will not deter me.

"That's true, but it was nothing she couldn't handle with a little redirection and a behavior chart."

Plus one trip to the principal's office.

Barnes nods slowly. "I'm going to be honest with you. This is usually when students start second-guessing their career choice."

"I—"

She holds up a hand. "I'm certainly not trying to discourage you, Ms. Reynolds. I simply want to ensure you're being honest with yourself and with me moving forward. Do not sugarcoat your observation reports." She arches a brow and I steel my resolve, resisting the urge to shrink into my chair. "You're not doing anyone any favors when you do."

I get what she's saying. Education is a tough path, but I'm going in with my eyes wide open.

At least, I think I am.

"I understand, but I'm committed and I hope to use this experience observing to prepare for student teaching in the spring."

I know it's going to be hard. I attended an under-funded school where classrooms were constantly over capacity, too many children were performing below grade level, and teachers had to manage students' social and emotional needs with little to no support.

Hell, I was one of those kids, until I wasn't.

If it wasn't for the teachers in the trenches doing the hard work, I wouldn't be sitting in Barnes' office right now.

"I'm happy to hear that." The professor gives a curt nod. "If at any point you feel overwhelmed, I encourage you to come speak to me."

Yeah-*freaking*-right.

The woman is terrifying. If I need to vent, I'll do it anonymously on the internet like a normal person.

"Now, as you've probably guessed, the real reason I wanted to see you today is to share your student teaching placement for spring semester."

Nerves coil low in my belly and I silently pray I haven't been placed anywhere near my small hometown. My mother hasn't contacted me since my birthday, and I have no interest in breaking the silent streak. I have to succeed—to focus on the future—and I can't do that if I'm constantly battling the demons from my past.

"Congratulations, Ms. Reynolds." Barnes slides a large

manilla envelope across the desk. "You'll be student teaching in the College Park School District."

The grin that splits my face is pure relief as I process her words.

CPSD is one of the top districts in the state, but more importantly, there's zero risk of running into Nora.

See? All that worry was for nothing.

The tight band of anxiety that's been wrapped around my chest snaps. For the first time in days, I can breathe freely.

"Thank you. I'm really looking forward to it."

I'm probably beaming at Barnes, but why shouldn't I? She's just given me fantastic news. Student teaching locally is the best-case scenario. I don't have to worry about finding short-term housing or dealing with a long commute during the snowy winter months. All I need to do is extend my current lease through the spring semester, and I'm set.

"I'm glad to hear it." She walks me through the paperwork and next steps for connecting with my student teaching mentor and by the time she's finished, my head is spinning. "Do you have any questions?"

Tons, but only one is pressing.

If you don't shoot your shot, someone else is going to take it.

I square my shoulders and deliver the line I've been rehearsing all week. "As the head of the department, I realize you probably get a lot of requests, but would you be willing to write me a letter of recommendation?"

As my advisor, she knows me better than any of the other professors I've had. More importantly, a recommendation from Dr. Barnes could be the difference between an interview request and a form rejection.

She purses her lips and my stomach drops.

Dr. Barnes is actually going to say no. I knew it was a possibility, but I'd hoped—

"Keep up the good work, and if at the end of the semester I'm satisfied with your performance, I'll consider writing you a letter of recommendation."

It's not a no.

But it's not a yes either.

The woman obviously knows the power of her influence and she's out here wielding it like the golden ticket it is.

She must sense my frustration because she adds, "You're an exceptional student, Piper, and you're going to be an exceptional teacher. In the meantime, it's my job to prepare you for the reality of a real-world classroom. Student teaching can make or break the start of a career."

There's a thick lump in my throat and I swallow past it as I nod at yet another reminder of my precarious position.

"When we send our students into the field, they're representing Waverly University and all the students who came before, as well as those who will come after. Not everyone wants to talk about it, but responsibility is inherent to the profession."

"I understand." I can do this. I just have to stay the course and get out of my own head. "I appreciate your consideration."

The meeting wraps up and though I'm uneasy about Barnes' parting words, I'm choosing to focus on the positive. I'm spending the spring semester in College Park and I've landed a plum student teaching gig.

For now, it's enough.

My phone buzzes as I step into the hall. I dig it out of my bag to find another text from Brady. It's a picture of a baby cow. Or, I guess technically, it's a calf.

Who cares? It's freaking adorable.

The calf is lying on a bed of hay and it has a rich, chocolate coat and big dark eyes that scream *love me*.

My fingers fly over the keyboard as I type my reply.

Me: That is literally the cutest thing I've ever seen. I'm going to die of cuteness overload.

Three little dots appear on the screen and a message pops up.

Brady: Where are you? I'll swing by and do a little mouth-to-mouth.

I snort-laugh. Did Brady just drop a terrible pickup line ironically?

I didn't think he had it in him.

That's what you get for underestimating him—again.

Me: I'll have to take a raincheck. I've got class.

Not to mention, a new incentive to ensure my grades remain top of the cohort.

Brady: I'm going to hold you to that. How was the meeting?

Me: Got my student teaching assignment. College Park School District!

Brady: Congratulations! Let me take you out to celebrate on Sunday. I owe you a proper second date.

Me: Proper is overrated. There's not a thing I'd change about our impromptu second date.

Just the memory of Brady's mouth on my throat is enough to raise my blood pressure.

Brady: Okay, then let me take you on a third date.

I grin as I type my reply. Classes will switch any minute and I need to get moving, but I'm having too much fun.

Me: I don't know. A third date is kind of serious. What did you have in mind?

There's a long pause and I'm about to put my phone away when another message pops up.

Brady: It's a surprise.

Me: I hate surprises.

Brady: Are you serious? What kind of monster are you that you hate surprises? Do you also hate the Easter Bunny?

Surprises in my house were rarely a good thing, but I trust Brady. Whatever he has in mind, it'll be something we both enjoy.

Me: No, but I'm not a fan of Santa. The Grinch is more my style.

Brady: I think it's safe to say you have a type.

Me: And what type would that be?

Brady: Hairy dudes with dad bods. And before you ask, no, I will not dye my hair green.

Did he just? Yup, new kink unlocked.

The way I cackle at the thought of a green Brady isn't even right, but it feels good to laugh. To let my guard down and just be a regular student with regular concerns. To not have to watch my every word for fear of slipping up and revealing the source of my income.

Me: Spoilsport.

Brady: I'll make it up to you on Sunday.

Me: It's a date.

And this time, I'm actually looking forward to it.

18

BRADY

"YOU STILL COOL if I borrow the Jeep?"

Reid looks up from the couch where he and Coop are watching the Steelers-Browns matchup. "It's all yours. I'm not planning to move my ass from this couch for the rest of the day."

Yesterday's game against Wisconsin was brutal and while I came home and crashed afterward, my boys hit up a Halloween party at Sig Chi. Looks like they're paying the price for it now.

"Thanks. I'll fill it up before I bring it back."

He waves me off, like always. Reid's father is an NFL legend and future Hall of Famer, but despite being raised with the kind of money I could only dream of, he's one of the most chill guys I know. "Don't worry about it unless you're planning to empty the tank."

It's a generous offer, but we both know I'm going to ignore it. That he's letting me borrow the Jeep is favor enough. I'm not about to take advantage of his generosity.

"Is it me, or is your beard shrinking?" Coop cocks his head like he's trying to see it from a different angle and then his eyes go wide. "Oh, shit." He nudges Reid. "He's borrowing the car. He broke out the hedge trimmers." The prick makes a show of sniffing the air. "And he smells like one *of* those pine tree air fresheners."

Reid's brows go flat. "I have no idea where you're going with this."

That makes two of us.

"Our boy has a date!" Coop howls. "Who's the lucky lady?"

Like hell I'm answering that question. With my luck, they'd track Piper down and tell her all kinds of embarrassing stories about me.

Nothing they say can be worse than your pole skills.

True, but I'm not about to risk it.

"A gentleman doesn't kiss and tell."

Coop smirks. "So you're saying there was kissing?"

"I'm not saying shit."

My roommates are all secretly hooking up, so why shouldn't I get the same privacy?

The front door opens and Parker comes lumbering down the hall with his backpack slung over his shoulder and a small cardboard box in his hands.

"I grabbed the mail." He hands me the box. "You got another care package from home."

They come every week like clockwork. I used to tell my mom to save her money, but I've given up wasting my breath. No matter what I say, she's going to send them and I'm going to enjoy them.

It's our thing.

"What did Mama Vaughn send us this week?" Coop asks, rubbing his hands together.

"She didn't send *us* anything." I clutch the box to my chest. No way am I opening it now. For all I know, Gran slipped another box of condoms in there. "She sent *me* cookies."

Which I know from her text a few days ago. "Sorry, boys. I'm taking them with me."

My mom is a great baker and Piper will love them. Given the situation with her mother, I doubt homemade cookies are a staple in her life.

Parker narrows his eyes. "Seriously?"

"Seriously."

"This is bullshit." Coop's face falls. "I can't believe you're sharing your mom's cookies with a chick you've known for like three weeks instead of your boys, who've had your back for three years."

"Didn't Coach put you on a special diet?" I shoot back. "From where I'm standing, it seems like I'm doing you a favor by removing temptation."

"Fuck that." Coop crosses his arms like a giant man-baby. "I can't live without carbs and sugar. Besides, what Coach doesn't know won't hurt him."

"Keep telling yourself that, Princess."

Coop flips me off—it's his love language—and I back out of the room, protecting the box of cookies the same way I'd protect the ball during a game.

Ten minutes later, I pull up to Piper's building to find her waiting out front. Her hair is blowing in the breeze and she's wearing an alpine green sweater dress that falls to mid-thigh, revealing her shapely legs. I can't take my eyes off her and nearly clip the curb as a result.

Get it together, asshole.

It's nothing I haven't seen before, but in my defense, it's been a few weeks and my memory doesn't come close to doing her legs justice.

My balls tighten and I force a calming breath out through my nose before I throw the Jeep in park and climb out to greet her.

"Hey, beautiful."

"Hey yourself."

"You didn't have to wait outside," I say, loping around the vehicle. "I would've come up to get you."

She quirks a brow. "Like a proper gentleman?"

"Exactly." I reach her side and she looks so goddamn tempting I want to pull her into my arms and kiss her, picking up where we left off last week. My cock twitches at the prospect, but since she just labeled me a gentleman, I go in for a hug instead, soaking up her sweet floral scent as her soft body molds to mine. "You look amazing."

"Thanks." She pulls back and gives me a slow once-over. "I wasn't sure what to wear, so hopefully this is okay."

I glance at her ankle boots and give silent thanks they don't have heels.

"It's perfect."

I help her into the Jeep and then I adjust my swelling cock as I make my way around to the driver's side. What is it about this woman that turns me into a walking hard-on?

That would be everything.

She flashes me a grin as I climb in and shut the door. "Nice ride."

"It belongs to Reid," I admit, buckling up. "He lets me borrow it occasionally."

"That's generous of him."

"Reid's a good guy. He'd give a stranger the shirt off his back."

"And you wouldn't?" Piper shoots me a pointed look, but doesn't press. I don't have a large circle of friends, but the ones I have are all standup guys. I wouldn't have it any other way. "Next time, we can take my car. It's not pretty, but it runs."

My heart skips as I put the Jeep in gear. "Next time?"

As if realizing her slipup, she flushes. "Of course, it'll depend on how things go today."

"Of course."

"Speaking of which, are you going to tell me where we're going?"

Not a chance. "I told you, it's a surprise."

She groans and tosses her head back as we pull out of the complex. "At least give me a hint."

"What would be the fun in that?" I point the Jeep north and reach around to grab the small box off the floor in the back. "Do me a favor and open this up."

Her brows knit together, but she takes the package. "You... want me to open your mail?"

I chuckle. "Trust me. You'll be glad you did."

She removes the tape and when she opens the box to find a plastic tub of cookies, her eyes go wide. "Oh, my God. This is a care package, isn't it?"

My throat tightens. That she even has to ask is a fucking travesty, but I don't want to ruin the moment and something tells me she wouldn't take kindly to being pitied.

"My mom likes to bake." I gesture to the container sitting in her lap. "Try one. Rumor has it they're pumpkin chocolate chip."

It's one of my favorite cookies and my mom makes them by the tray load every fall.

She hesitates, worrying her lower lip between her teeth. "You really don't mind?"

"They're meant to be shared." I reach over and gently squeeze her thigh. It's as much to reassure her as it is to silence the part of me that's desperate to touch her. She opens the container and the scent of pumpkin spice fills the Jeep. My stomach growls like one of Pavlov's dogs, and she grins. "I should probably warn you; they're addicting."

Piper grabs two cookies and offers one to me.

"Ladies first." Sure, it's good manners, but the truth is, I enjoy watching my girl eat.

She bites into the cookie carefully, one hand cupped underneath to catch any crumbs, and when it hits her tongue, her eyes roll back in her head. Her throat bobs delicately as she chews, and when she swallows, she turns back to me.

"That might be the best thing I've ever eaten." She takes another bite, that blissful look still on her face. "I swear it's like an orgasm for your mouth. Like a mouthgasm."

Heat floods my cheeks and I sputter something about passing her compliments to the chef, which earns me one of those husky laughs I love so much.

"Maybe leave out the orgasm part," she suggests as I stuff my cookie into my mouth.

That definitely won't be an issue. My mom and I are close, but we're not *that* close.

"You played a great game yesterday." She cranes her head to look out the window, and I'm not sure if she's taking in the colorful foliage of the mountains surrounding College Park or if she's trying to figure out where we're headed. "The team is 7-1 now, right?"

I nod. "It's starting to feel like we might actually have a shot at the championship."

We're over halfway through the regular season and all our guys are healthy. We've got a few injuries here and there, but nothing major, which is a blessing in itself.

If we stay focused, we could go all the way.

"I don't know how you do it." Piper gives a self-deprecating laugh. "I barely survived midterms. I can't imagine juggling school and a high-profile sport."

"It's intense, but other guys on the team have it worse. Reid and Coop are under constant scrutiny. The scouts are watching them like hawks, analyzing every move they make." My grip tightens on the steering wheel. "I just don't want to let them down."

Piper's hand settles on my thigh, a comforting weight to anchor me in the moment. "Anyone who watched yesterday's game can see you're giving it your all."

I just hope it's enough.

We round the bend and a hand-painted sign appears on the right side of the road.

"Are we going to a pumpkin patch?" she asks, voice climbing several octaves. "Please tell me we're going to the pumpkin patch."

"Even better." I tap my blinker and pull off on the gravel drive, the Jeep throwing up a cloud of dust in our wake. "We're visiting a pumpkin patch on a working farm."

The squeal she releases is high enough to shatter glass, but I'm here for it.

After weeks of struggling to break through Piper's defenses, seeing her let go is everything.

"They've got hay rides," she announces, reading the first of many white signs staked along the drive. "And a corn maze!"

Her enthusiasm is infectious. "Have you ever gone punkin chunkin?"

"I don't even know what that is, but I'm game for anything." She laughs and shakes her head as we bump along the gravel road leading to the parking lot. "I've always wanted to visit one of these places."

"What's been holding you back?" I ask, maneuvering the vehicle into the grassy lot.

"No time." She shrugs. "I always figured I'd get around to it someday."

"I used to think that way too, but then my grandfather passed…" I pull into an empty spot and throw the Jeep in park.

"It's cliché, but losing him taught me to make the most of every day."

Because tomorrow isn't guaranteed.

Piper takes my hand, enveloping it within her own. "No child should ever have to learn that lesson."

She's right, but the powers that be clearly don't give a shit about our opinions.

"What do you say we go find ourselves some pumpkins?"

19

———

PIPER

"Welcome to the Ross Family Farm."

Brady grins and I know I must look like a kid in a candy store, but it can't be helped.

I spin, soaking up the cozy fall aesthetic. The property is bathed in the colors of the season and stretches as far as the eye can see, though that's probably because of the hilly landscape. There's a rustic red and white barn near the parking lot that's been converted into a general store. A covered porch runs the length of the building and wooden rockers are lined up from one end to the other while the side yard is overflowing with potted mums and wooden displays filled with pre-picked pumpkins in all shapes, sizes, and colors.

The whole place is giving fall influencer vibes, and I am obsessed.

"This place is amazing."

"If I'd known pumpkins were the key to winning you over," Brady says, raking a hand through his short hair. "I'd have suggested this weeks ago instead of humiliating myself on the pole."

"Yeah, but then you wouldn't have perfected your fireman spin."

He groans.

"And don't even get me started on your floor work."

"Let's never talk about that again." He cringes. "My lower back still hasn't forgiven me for attempting a speed bump."

"What?" I clasp a hand to my chest, feigning shock. "You nailed it. The way you rolled your hips was—"

"Please don't finish that sentence."

Brady grabs my hand and electricity crackles across my skin as he leads me up the path toward the barn. His palms are rough, but warm, and when he laces our fingers together, it feels natural.

A nagging voice in the back of my head reminds me that every moment I spend with this man is a risk and that if he knew the real me—the one who bares it all for cash—he'd walk.

It doesn't matter because he's not going to find out.

Besides, it's only our third date. Surely we haven't reached the point where we're obligated to spill all our secrets?

As we approach the barn, Brady points to a giant trailer that's attached to an idling tractor. "Your chariot awaits, my lady."

I stare at the neatly stacked bales of hay piled high on the trailer. "We're going to ride that?"

"It's part of the experience." He chuckles and tightens his grip on my hand. "Don't worry. I won't let you fall off."

My stomach drops. "You're kidding, right? People don't actually fall off these things?"

His lack of reply is far from comforting, but I follow his lead, assuring myself I won't become a meme.

Brady helps me climb into the trailer and I'm relieved to discover a safety rail as we take seats on a bale of hay. It's itchy against my exposed skin, but with Brady's hard thigh pressed against mine, I barely notice.

The trailer fills quickly and then we're off, the steady rumble of the tractor filling the air.

"I can't believe how busy this place is." I scan the faces packed into the trailer with us. It's a mix of couples, teens, and families, and everyone appears to be in good spirits.

"Agritourism has become big business." The trailer bounces and I lean into his broad chest for support. "People are more conscious than ever of their carbon footprint and they want to buy locally sourced produce. Combine environmentalism with a unique experience that can be posted for clout on Insta and Snap and it's a no-brainer, if you can afford the insurance premiums."

I poke him in the side. "That's a cynical take."

"Not at all. I'm behind agritourism one hundred percent. It's a great way for communities to learn more about local agriculture and it's a profitable venture when done right." He pauses and wipes his hands on his thighs. "I actually wrote a business plan over the summer suggesting we open Willow Bend to the public during key seasons."

I'm no expert, but I know farming is a tough business and anything that brings in extra income is probably worth exploring.

"And?"

"It's been months and my mom has yet to read the proposal. She keeps finding excuses to put it off." He grimaces. "We're barely making ends meet, but she and Gran are so stuck in their ways, it'll take a miracle to convince them."

"I'm sorry. That must be really frustrating."

The words are meaningless in the grand scheme of things. They'll do nothing to improve his situation, but I don't have it in me to stay quiet.

Not when heartbreak is etched in the very lines of his face.

"You have no idea." His gaze travels the horizon. "We could do all the things they do here. A pumpkin patch, apple picking, hayrides. And the margins are far better than what we get selling our produce at wholesale."

"Change is never easy." I'd know. My entire childhood was wrought with upheaval. "Maybe they just need more time to warm up to the idea."

"Maybe. I just wish there was something more I could do." He huffs out a breath. "Willow Bend is breathtaking and opening the property to our community would be good business. I know it in my bones."

"If that's true, then why do you sound like you're giving up?" I nudge him with my shoulder. "You've got to be the most stubborn man I've ever met. If your mom is stonewalling you, find another way."

"You're right. A defeatist attitude won't solve my problems. It's just that..." He scrubs a hand over his face and there's actual fear in his eyes. "If things don't improve soon, Gran will be forced to sell off some of the land."

Land that's been in his family for five generations. Land that should be his legacy.

I can't imagine what that must feel like because I wasn't raised to put down roots. Nora and I moved from one shithole apartment to another. We didn't have a home and forget about fond memories.

They were few and far between.

It's one of the many differences between Brady and me, and I'd hate to see him lose even a tiny bit of the life that shaped him into the incredible person he is today.

Yeah, well, life isn't fair.

No kidding.

"Willow Bend is a problem for another day," he declares,

snapping me back to the present. The tractor rolls to a stop alongside a lush green field where orange, white, and yellow gourds still grow on the vine. "Today is all about spending the day with my girl and finding her the perfect pumpkin."

"No way." I laugh as he pulls me to my feet. "Everyone out here is looking for the perfect pumpkin. Those gorgeous, Gram-worthy gourds will all find a home. I'm looking for the saddest, most awkward little pumpkin I can find."

He laughs quietly. "Does this mean you're one of those people who always roots for the underdog?"

"Abso-freaking-lutely."

"I'll keep that in mind." He climbs down from the trailer and turns to help me, slipping his hands around my waist as he all but lowers me to the ground. I'm a big girl, and yet, in Brady's arms, I feel almost dainty. I knew he was strong, but having those massive hands clamped around my waist and seeing how easily he supports my weight is the ultimate turn-on. "So, how was your first hayride?"

I take my time, considering. "Eight out of ten."

"Just eight?"

"Full marks for fresh air and good company, but I'm deducting two points for hay because it's itchy as hell and I'm not a fan of bouncing."

Not in this context, anyway.

My sweater dress might be giving fall, but it's collected every loose piece of hay on the trailer. I pluck the stray flakes from my clothes and toss them into the grass. "Did I miss any?"

Brady makes a twirling motion with his finger and I spin for him, channeling the flirty side I unleash when camming. And why not? I'm feeling myself in this dress and I'm on a date with a sweet, sexy man who's looking at me like I'm the hottest thing on the farm.

Now there's a phrase I never thought I'd say.

"You have some hay on your, uh..." Brady gestures to my ass, cheeks turning scarlet.

"Give me a hand?" I bat my lashes and flash him a smile that's anything but innocent as I turn, giving him my back. I watch over my shoulder as he carefully picks every piece of straw off my backside, and though he's a perfect gentleman, I nearly swoon when his fingers brush my lower back. "Thanks."

"Any time." His eyes narrow and he nods like a man on a mission. One determined not to fail. Is this his game face? The one his opponents see when he stares them down on the field? If so, consider me jealous because *damn*. "We'll have to do better with the pumpkins. I'm shooting for a perfect ten this time."

Naturally. Brady doesn't have it in him to give anything less than his best. "Lead the way."

We walk up and down the rows, Brady searching for the prettiest pumpkin he can find while I trail behind, my gaze fixed on his perfect butt.

"What do you think of this one?" He squats to examine a large white pumpkin and his jeans pull taut across his thighs and ass. *Thank you, Jesus.* "It's nice and round."

"It really is."

He turns to me, his dimple on full display. "I'm talking about the pumpkin."

"Same." We both know I'm full of it, but there's zero chance I'm going to cop to ogling him, so I turn to my right and scan the ground, spotting a little orange gourd that's shaped more like a pomegranate than a pumpkin. "Oh! I found mine."

It's a sad little guy and I doubt anyone else will take it home, but it'll look great in my kitchen.

I reach down to grab it and the instant I wrap my fingers around the vine, I'm struck by a sharp pricking sensation.

"Ouch!" I leap back, cradling my injured hand.

Brady's on his feet in an instant.

"Let me have a look." He takes my hand in his and examines my palm. "I should've warned you. The peduncle is prickly."

I snort-laugh. "I'm sorry, did you just say peduncle?"

"It's the proper name for the stem." Brady chuckles, but his gaze stays fixed on my stinging hand. "Hold still, okay? You've got a few spines stuck in your palm and I need to remove them so the skin doesn't get irritated."

His touch is gentle as he removes the tiny prickles and when he's done, he brushes his fingers over my palm to ensure he hasn't missed any.

Awareness floods my body, raising a trail of goosebumps on my forearm. The man may look rough and tumble, but damn if he doesn't know how to handle a woman. One touch —hell, one look—is all it takes to send my hormones into a tailspin.

"How does that feel?" he asks, voice low and husky.

Like I want to wrap my legs around you and climb you like a pole.

"Good."

Maybe Brady hears the longing in my voice because he lifts my hand to his mouth and brushes his lips against my palm.

My knees turn to jelly and it's a wonder I don't melt on the spot.

"That's nice, too." *Really nice.*

I stretch up on my toes, desperate to feel his lips on mine, but the tractor chooses this exact moment to return, shattering the spell.

Brady drops my hand and pulls a folding knife from his back pocket. "I'll cut the pumpkins loose and we can catch a ride back to the barn."

I flick my gaze to the small blade. "Let me guess, you were a Boy Scout?"

"Would you believe me if I said I just like to be prepared?"

"Not even a little." I jab him playfully in the chest. "I've finally got your number Brady Vaughn, and there's nothing you can say or do that will surprise me."

20

BRADY

I MAKE quick work of the pumpkins and after we pay, we stash them in the Jeep and check out punkin chunkin. It's a first for Piper, but she takes surprisingly well to the giant slingshot, sending her gourds sailing across the farm's tiny pond with ease. She hits the target every time, the tiny pumpkins exploding on the wooden board while mine go splashing into the lake.

When she's done gloating, we decide to check out the corn maze.

We grab two cider donuts and munch on them as we make our way across the property. They aren't as good as my mom's cookies, but that doesn't stop me from demolishing the apple cinnamon ring.

A guy's got to eat, after all.

"What's our strategy?" Piper asks, the tip of her tongue darting out to lick cinnamon from her fingertip.

The only strategy I've got right now is don't get hard, and that's probably more of a plan.

But seriously, how can I not get turned-on when she's using her tongue like that? With a single move, she's transported me back to her apartment, to the night her tongue was gliding along my own in sweet seduction.

Piper must take my silence for confusion because she elaborates.

"You know, how are we going to find the exit?" Her brow furrows. "Like, some people only make left turns or whatever."

"Hope for the best." I pop the last bit of my donut into my mouth and dust off my hands. "Fair warning, my sense of direction is...*lacking*."

Piper smirks. "You realize you're probably the first man in recorded history to admit that, right?"

"I'd rather be directionally challenged than be a toxic creep who can't admit his own shortcomings."

"Fair enough."

It probably sounds like pandering, but it's the truth.

I'm not such a prick that my self-worth is defined by an innate ability to sense true north.

We approach the maze, and I study the outer wall, though I'm not sure how much good it will do. The corn stretches a couple hundred feet in either direction from the narrow entrance and the stalks are eight feet tall, preventing even the tallest of explorers from peeking over the top.

Piper turns to me, uncertainty flashing in her eyes. "How big did you say this thing is?"

"Five acres." I hand our tickets to the attendant and turn to my date, gesturing toward the entrance. "Ladies first."

The sun is slipping lower in the sky, but we probably have another solid hour of daylight.

It should be plenty of time.

Piper hesitates, and I place a hand on her lower back. "We've got this."

"I don't know why I'm nervous. I—"

A boy with white-blond hair rushes past, bolting into the maze without a backward glance.

She squares her shoulders and straightens her spine, as if waging an internal battle with herself. "If that kid can do it, so can we."

"That's the spirit."

Determination restored, she steps into the maze, with me close on her heels.

We follow the dirt path and though I've never been claustrophobic, I can't help but feel like the walls are closing in as we reach our first decision point.

"Left or right?" Piper turns to me. "And don't you dare say lady's choice. Chivalry will only get you so far."

"There's that stubborn streak I love so much." I sling an arm around her waist and pull her close, savoring the warmth of her body against mine. She fits perfectly under my arm, as if the spot were carved for her alone. "Let's go right."

We take turns choosing directions and on our fourth turn, we nearly bump into a couple doubling back.

"It's a dead end," the guy on the right warns as his boyfriend tugs on his hand, urging him to hurry.

"Thanks."

We make a U-turn and follow them down the path.

At the next fork, they go right, and Piper gestures to the left. I nod and we split off from the other couple, proceeding independently.

We plod along for another ten minutes before she turns to me. "How do you think we're doing?"

Honestly? Not great.

"We've been here before." I stop and she pulls up short next to me. I survey the clearing and my gaze settles on a gap in the corn where it looks like several stalks have been trampled. "We passed this way two turns ago."

Piper studies the area. "No, we didn't."

Everything looks the same—that's why it's easy to get turned around—so I can't exactly fault her for disagreeing.

"You sound awfully confident for a woman wading through five acres of corn."

"You're the one who said you're directionally challenged." She shrugs. "You don't get to be surprised when I believe you."

The corner of my mouth twitches. I fucking love this side of her. The one that doesn't take shit and gives as good as she gets. "If you're so sure, why don't we bet on it?"

She cocks a hip. "What's the bet?"

"We each go our separate ways, and the first one to the exit wins."

"What do I get when I win?"

Not if, *when*. The confidence she wears like a second skin is sexy as hell.

"What do you want?"

She taps her chin, considering. "I tweaked my shoulder in class this morning and I'd kill for a massage."

"Done." I'll happily massage her shoulder, whatever the outcome. "If I win, I want a fourth date."

"Deal." She turns to go and then seems to think better of it, throwing a challenging glance over her shoulder. "See you at the exit."

Win or lose, I'm making out in this bet, but you don't play DI football without developing a taste for victory and I'm not about to hand Piper the W.

I take off in the opposite direction, choosing my path instinctively. I don't have a clue where I'm going and I'm not about to waste time overthinking. As long as I keep moving, I'll find the exit...eventually.

I race through a series of turns at a breakneck pace and

yeah, I'm probably moving faster than I should, but I haven't seen another person in at least ten minutes.

Hell, the maze is all but silent, the sounds of the farm and its guests a distant melody.

I hit a dead end and retrace my steps, but I must take a wrong turn, because I end up in the same clearing where I started.

Fuck.

It's not supposed to be this hard. It's just a corn maze for chrissake.

It's supposed to be fun. For families. With small children.

Yet your dumb ass can't find the way out.

The sound of pounding feet arises on my left and I turn just in time to see Piper burst into the clearing.

She looks around and curses under her breath. "How is this even possible?"

It's a valid question. Even so, I have to stifle a laugh. "I'm starting to think we're both directionally challenged."

She plants her hands on her hips and when she levels her gaze at me, there's a spark of mischief in her blue eyes. "Why Brady Vaughn, are you saying we're lost?"

A big ass smile splits my face. "Hopelessly."

We're deep in the maze, our labored breathing the only sound to be heard. The air is charged and when she takes a step toward me, I know exactly what she's thinking.

"Since we're stuck out here, we might as well make the most of it."

Hell yeah.

Anticipation surges through my limbs and I cross the clearing in two quick strides, the urge to claim the woman before me a throwback to some latent Stone Age instinct. I'd like nothing more than to take her in my arms and crush my lips to hers, but I force myself to take it slow.

I've been aching to touch this woman—*really touch her*—all day. Aching to feel her soft lips pressed to mine. To run my hands over her generous curves.

I won't ruin the moment by rushing the play.

I cup her cheek, tipping her face to mine even as I tangle my other hand in her golden locks. Her hair is smooth and silky and it smells like strawberries. "Have I told you how much I love your hair?"

She grins. "I think you just did."

"I love everything about you." Her breath hitches, her full breasts pressing against my chest. "The way your eyes sparkle in the sunlight." I brush her cheek with my thumb and drop a gentle kiss on her forehead. "The smell of your skin." I duck my head and place a kiss just below her ear. "The way you taste." I brush a final kiss against her collarbone and when she shivers, a bolt of lust goes straight to my cock.

"If this is your idea of foreplay," she says, hooking her fingers in my belt loops and pulling me closer. "It's working."

"Darlin', I'm just getting started."

I lower my mouth to hers and our lips crash together, a desperate joining fueled by mutual attraction and pent-up frustration. Not a day has passed since our first kiss that I haven't fantasized about this moment, about holding Piper in my arms and feeling her lips on mine.

Hell, not a day has passed where I haven't jerked off to the memory.

Her tongue glides along the seam of my mouth, seeking entry, and I don't have it in me to deny her.

Our tongues mate in a complex dance and my balls tighten, desperate to get in on the action.

It's not going to happen. Not here, anyway.

But that doesn't mean I can't touch my girl.

My hands skate along her back and over her voluptuous

hips and then I'm cupping her breast, the tender flesh filling my palm. Her nipple strains against the soft fabric of her dress and I flick my thumb across the hardened peak.

Piper moans, the guttural sound going straight to my cock.

"Again," she pleads, a frantic edge to her voice.

I repeat the motion and she melts into me, positioning my erection so it's flush with her belly.

"Christ, you feel good."

She captures my lower lip between her teeth and I damn near come when the little tease sucks on it, delivering her own brand of foreplay.

"Get a room!"

I freeze and Piper releases her grip on me. Heat floods my cheeks as we turn in unison to find a child staring up at us with the kind of disgust only a pre-teen boy can muster. It's the same boy who entered the maze ahead of us, and he's way too young to know what 'Get a room' means.

"That wasn't very nice." I give him a pointed stare.

"Yeah, well, neither is making out with your girlfriend in public."

Piper covers her mouth with her hand and I have no doubt she's laughing at the little menace. I'm about to ask where his parents are when he takes off, disappearing into the maze.

"What do you say we go back to my place?" Piper drapes her arms around my neck. "We can finish what we started...in private."

21

BRADY

EVERY MUSCLE in my body is stretched taut as I close the door to Piper's apartment. The drive back to campus was the longest ride of my life and I spent every second steeped in arousal, fantasizing about all the ways I'd like to pleasure the woman at my side.

With my mouth. My fingers. My cock.

My dick is so hard it's a wonder I haven't split my zipper.

Piper must share my frustration because she pushes me up against the wall, and before I can even get my bearings, her lips are on mine. Her kisses are ravenous and there's no doubt she's as desperate for me as I am for her. I cup her ass and pull her close, letting her feel the hard ridge of my erection as she runs her hands over my chest and up through my hair. Her nails scrape my scalp, sending a fresh wave of desire coursing through my veins.

"Christ," I pant, coming up for air. "I want you so bad it hurts."

She throws her head back, exposing her throat and I pounce, peppering her skin with openmouthed kisses as I nip and suck the tender flesh.

"I need more." She rolls her hips, but it's not enough. For either of us, judging by the soft whimper that escapes her lips.

I spin us around, pressing her back to the wall with more force than intended, and when I open my mouth to apologize, her lips slam into mine, our teeth knocking together from the force of it.

"Don't you dare apologize," she murmurs, punctuating each word with a kiss.

I'm not about to argue. Piper is a strong woman. She knows her own mind, so who the hell am I to tell her what to think or feel?

I slide my hands down her outer thighs and hook my fingers in the hem of her dress. "Is this okay?"

She nods, eyelids at half-mast.

I hitch the dress up to her waist, pausing just long enough to admire the lacy red scrap of fabric covering her pussy before I cup her ass and lift her into the air. She wraps her legs around my waist and then she's grinding against my cock as I support her weight.

It's the sexiest damn thing I've ever seen, and her soft moans are nearly my undoing.

Tension coils at the base of my spine, each glide of her sweet pussy sending a bolt of pleasure straight to my brain.

"That's right, darlin'. Take what you need from me."

Her eyes snap open and fix on mine as she tightens her grip on my hair, tugging gently.

A flush creeps up her neck, but she doesn't stop.

Piper holds my gaze as she rides me, hips rocking faster as she chases release.

"I want to see the look on your gorgeous face when you shatter."

No, I want to see the look on her gorgeous face when she shatters *for me.*

I've fantasized about this moment for weeks and though it hasn't played out as I'd imagined, this is even better because it's real. Raw. *Frenzied.*

"I'm. Going. To. Come."

The words are little more than a breathy whisper, but I'm ready when the orgasm takes her. She stiffens in my arms before going limp, her head falling back against the wall as she rides out the aftershocks.

She's so damn beautiful, cheeks flushed, hair mussed, walls down.

I close my eyes and commit the image to memory before I lower my mouth to hers, kissing her slow and deep.

"That was...amazing," she says, voice husky as I pull her close and carry her boneless body to the couch. "We definitely have to do that again sometime."

Screw sometime.

My appetite is far from sated.

"Why wait?" I drop to my knees before her and spread her thighs wide, peppering kisses along her inner knee. "I'm nowhere near finished with you."

A smile tugs at the corner of her mouth. "And what if I'm finished?"

"That would be a real shame." I dig my fingers into the powerful muscles of her thigh, massaging as I work my way north. "I was hoping to give you another orgasm. With my tongue."

Her breath hitches and I don't miss the slow rise and fall of her chest.

"I've never had back-to-back orgasms before."

"Then let me be the first, darlin'. I've been dying to get my mouth on you."

To emphasize my point, I spread her thighs wider, giving myself an unparalleled view of her pussy. Her panties are damp, the red lace dark where arousal has soaked through, the musky scent causing my cock to grow impossibly hard.

Fuck, that's hot.

My balls go tight as I lower my mouth to her pussy and lick straight up the center.

Her hips wiggle and when I press my tongue against her clit, she moans, low and long.

"Take off your panties and let me do it right."

I need this as badly as she does. Need to taste her, to bury my face in her pussy and give her an orgasm the likes of which she's never experienced before. I want her arousal to soak my beard so I can savor her sweet flavor long after we're finished.

Without a word, Piper slams her knees together and yanks the panties off.

She moves to toss them on the floor, but I catch them and stuff the red lace in my pocket.

Her eyes widen, and I don't know if it's surprise or lust, but her knees fall open again, revealing her slick pink folds.

Fuck me.

I haven't gone this far with a woman since I was in high school, and it hits me I've been talking a big game for a guy who doesn't actually know much about pleasing a woman.

Doesn't matter. I'll figure it out.

There's no way in hell I'm going to walk away before I deliver the promised orgasm.

My brain tells me to start slow, to lick and suck and give her gorgeous thighs the attention they deserve, but instinct takes over and I descend on her like a starving man at a feast.

I devour her pussy, lapping up every drop of her arousal with the flat of my tongue. She tastes so fucking good I can't control myself, but I must be doing something right because Piper moans and threads her fingers through my hair, pulling me closer and rolling her hips every time I circle her clit.

"Jesus, Brady. You're going to make me come again."

I huff a laugh. "That's the idea."

Fuckin' right it is.

I want Piper to think about this moment every night while she's lying in bed.

Hell, I want her to think about it when she wakes up in the morning. When she's in the shower. Even when she's in class.

I want to rule her thoughts the way she's ruled mine since the day we met. If orgasms are the key to achieving my goal, I'm down. There's nothing I wouldn't do for this woman.

I swirl my tongue around her clit and suck, earning another moan of approval as she clamps her thighs together, caging my head between them.

"I don't think…" She whimpers, and there's something like panic in her voice. "I can't take anymore."

The hell she can't. This isn't about overstimulation. It's about giving up control. About letting herself be vulnerable on terms other than her own.

It was easy for her to ride my cock because she was in charge, setting the pace, taking what she needed. But now that she's spread out before me like an offering, completely vulnerable, she wants to slam those walls back into place.

I can't let that happen.

"Just let go, darlin'. I've got you."

Piper looks down at me kneeling between her thighs, and a silent understanding passes between us. She throws her head back, giving herself over to pleasure, and I slip a finger inside her tight channel, moving it in concert with my tongue.

It only takes a few thrusts to send her flying over the precipice. Her inner walls clamp down on my finger and she cries out, the orgasm taking her body by storm.

I work her until the last shudder has passed, drinking in

her pleasure, and when I'm finished, I suck the remnants of her arousal from my finger.

"Holy shit." Piper tugs her dress down as I climb to my feet. "That's literally the hottest thing I've ever seen."

I smirk. "Couldn't let it go to waste. Not when you're so damn delectable."

Her cheeks flush and she lowers her gaze to my cock, which is still hard as fuck.

"What do you say we go for lucky number three?" She licks her lips slowly. "If you have a condom, we could…"

If I have a condom?

I've got about three thousand in my nightstand at home, thanks to Gran.

I've also got one in my wallet.

It's just a precaution, but…

Shit. I didn't actually think things would go this far. Not yet, anyway.

Piper stands, and without another word, unbuckles my belt.

Her touch short-circuits my brain.

Are we really doing this? Here? Now?

I haven't even told her I'm a virgin. What if the sex is terrible? It could ruin everything. I've heard plenty of horror stories from guys who were ghosted after a sub-par performance.

Most of which involved alcohol.

Still, it's a risk. One I'm not sure I'm ready to take.

I capture her hands in mine before she can unzip my fly. "Can I use your bathroom?"

I need a minute to think. To sort myself out before we go any further.

"Sure." Piper grins. "You remember where it's at?"

I nod and dart down the hall like the coward I am. I barrel

through the door on the right and it's only when I flip the light switch that I realize my mistake. The bathroom was on the left side of the hall.

I've entered Piper's bedroom. Like the living room, it's somewhat sterile. There are no pictures or personal items, no Waverly fan gear, and her desk is uncluttered with only her laptop on the surface.

A tripod and camera have been set up in the corner, along with a photography light, all of which are pointed at the neatly made bed. The bed that has a red and black flogger lying beside a paddle with the word *Daddy* imprinted on it.

What the hell?

I blink, not trusting my eyes, but the paddle remains.

This can't be what it looks like. There has to be a rational explanation.

Behind me, Piper clears her throat.

I turn to find her standing in the doorway with her arms crossed, all traces of post-orgasm bliss erased.

What did you expect? You just invaded her privacy.

It was an accident, but that doesn't change the facts.

Her eyes cut to the items on the bed and her frown deepens. "What are you doing?"

"Sorry. I was flustered and I opened the wrong door. I didn't mean to pry, but..." I gesture at the camera and the toys. "What is all this?"

"This," she says, lips tight, "is how I pay for school."

22

———————

PIPER

Damn it all to hell. How could I be so freaking careless?

It would've taken five minutes to pack up my camera before our date. But no, I had to go outside and get fresh air because I was nervous and there was no way Brady was going to see the inside of my bedroom.

Stupid. Stupid. Stupid.

I can only imagine what's running through his head right now. Despite what we just did on my couch, Brady is sweet and wholesome. He probably doesn't even watch porn.

The way he just went down on you would suggest otherwise.

Fair. The man ate my pussy like it was his last meal.

The last time I came that hard was the night we met, and he wasn't even here for it. Not in the flesh, anyway.

So not the time, Piper.

I close my eyes, banishing the memory of his tongue on my clit.

The only thing I should be thinking about right now is protecting my secret. That's what matters. If Brady doesn't want to see me again, if he wants to break things off, I'll deal with it.

"I don't understand." He stares blankly at the paddle on my bed.

Of course he doesn't understand because his life is so completely different from mine.

We might as well have been raised on different planets.

My pulse thrums at my temple and I exhale slowly, willing it to settle.

I need to stay calm. In control.

"I'm a camgirl, Brady." I square my shoulders and lift my chin because no way am I going to be ashamed of the work I do. "I film myself and stream it online for cash."

His eyes narrow and something tells me he doesn't like the idea of other men watching me. Brady's usually even-tempered, but right now he looks like he wants to throttle something.

Or someone.

His nostrils flare. "Are we talking about...sex stuff?"

Tread carefully.

I won't lie to him, but this is a lot to take in and I don't want to give him the wrong impression. Yes, I share adult content, but plenty of it is PG-13. Some of these guys just want someone to talk to and others are perfectly happy to watch me study or clean my apartment in my underwear.

"Yes, there is adult content on my channel."

The color drains from his face and I curse my pre-date jitters.

If only I'd packed up. Or reminded him the bathroom was on the left. Then I wouldn't be in this mess.

He scrubs a hand over his face. "I really didn't see this coming."

That makes two of us.

What started off as the perfect date is starting to feel like a runaway train. Worse, I have no idea how to get it back on track, or if it's even possible.

"I'm sorry. Maybe I'm being thick here, but this is all new to me." Brady scans the room as if he's searching for the right words. "I don't understand why you would do this? Sex should be meaningful. An intimate act shared between two people who care about each other deeply."

I've never viewed sex through such rose-colored lenses, but I'm not about to knock his beliefs because they're different from my own. Our experiences have shaped our world views, so it's hardly a surprise that he places high value on intimacy while I've been trading it like a commodity.

"Not everyone feels the way you do," I say quietly.

"I know." He throws up his hands. "There are plenty of people who use sex as an outlet for stress relief or self-care or hell, even self-discovery. I'm just not one of them. I'm not built that way."

It's not the revelation he thinks it is.

I knew from the moment we met that Brady's values were old school.

It's one of the things that first attracted me to him, but it's also one of the most frustrating.

Because even though he's not trying to throw shade, his words sting.

"When I applied to Waverly, I was granted an academic scholarship." I lean against the doorjamb and fold my arms tightly across my chest. "It was only a partial, so I had to work part-time to cover room and board. Still, I was thrilled. I'd worked throughout high school and it was never an issue, but it turns out college is harder than high school. The long hours I put in tutoring at the academic center caused me to fall behind in my classes, and my grades slipped. I knew my scholarship would be at risk if my GPA fell below a three-point-five, but I couldn't quit tutoring. I needed the money for food and incidentals." Add in the fact that studying in the dorm was nearly impossible because my neighbors were always partying and yeah, it wasn't a great situation. "By the time I went home for summer break, my scholarship had been rescinded for failing to maintain academic excellence." I throw up air quotes for that last bit.

"Jesus." Brady shakes his head in disgust. "They expected you to work and maintain a three-point-five GPA? That's brutal."

"Tell me about it."

"Most guys I know are lucky to stay above a three-point-oh."

"That wasn't even the worst part. When my mother found out I'd lost my financial aid, she was thrilled." I laugh bitterly. "I've never heard such a gleeful *I told you so* in my life."

My stomach churns at the ugly memory and I want to stop talking, but I can't. Brady needs to hear it, if only to understand why I've made the choices I have.

"Most parents want to see their kids succeed, to have a better life, but not Nora. She reveled in my failure, secure in the knowledge that I was no better than her."

Talk about a one-two punch.

That it came from the one person who was supposed to love me unconditionally was the least surprising, but most damaging of all.

"Nora wanted to see me brought low, but the joke was on her because every snide comment she made fueled my determination to get back to Waverly and prove her wrong." I sigh. "I couldn't get student loans because I didn't have a cosigner and working for nine dollars an hour at the local grocery store wasn't cutting it. I'd blown through my savings by that point, and I was desperate. That's when I turned to camming."

The first time I stripped on camera, I was terrified, but over time, I came to love it. Camming's helped boost my confidence, strengthen my body, and broaden my horizons. I never would've started taking pole classes if it hadn't been a tax write-off for my business.

"I know what it's like to feel desperate. To feel like your back is against the wall." Brady takes a step forward, but then seems to think better of it. "You shouldn't have to do this to get an education."

Irritation flares deep in my belly at the insinuation that there's something wrong or inherently dirty about camming, but I tamp it down.

Lashing out won't get us anywhere.

"No one is forcing me to do it. It's my choice." Everything that happens on my channel is my choice. That's what makes it so empowering. "Camming allows me the flexibility to set my own hours and the money is good."

Sure, it's hard work and keeping things fresh can be a challenge, but I enjoy it.

Brady frowns. "Some things are more important than money."

After all that I've shared with him, does he really think I don't know that?

"Trust me, I know what matters. Camming has changed my life. I'm more confident in my body and in my ability to support myself."

"Is it even safe?" he asks, though his tone suggests he's already decided. "You have no clue who's out there watching you or what they're thinking."

I have a pretty good idea what they're thinking, but I don't say that because it will not improve his perception of my work.

"I'm extremely careful. I don't use my real name or share personal details from my life." I pause, hoping he can understand where I'm coming from. "It's why I live alone and don't have many close friends. Not even Jenna knows I'm camming because if it were to get out, it would ruin my future. No one is going to hire a teacher who bares it all on the internet."

"And yet you're still doing it," he deadpans.

"Only until graduation." I shoot him a pointed look. "Camming is just a means to an end. Sort of like football."

He huffs. "It's not the same."

"It's exactly the same." My voice rises, but this time, I don't bother tamping it down. "For the record, this is why I don't date. When you let people in, it gives them the ammunition to hurt you."

He flinches, but I refuse to apologize for speaking my truth. I took a chance on Brady and I really care about him—far more than I ever expected to—but if he can't accept my work, if he can't accept me, then this thing between us is over.

"I— This is a lot to take in." He shoves his hands into his pockets, but he doesn't quite meet my eye. "I had a great time at the farm, but maybe we should call it a day. I need some time to process."

I nod, because what else can I do? Brady's request is perfectly reasonable.

So why does it feel like my chest is collapsing?

23

BRADY

HOW IS THIS MY LIFE?

Three days ago, I was going down on the most beautiful woman on campus and today I'm watching B-grade porn alone in my bedroom. Probably not a wise decision given I have to leave for mandatory team study hall in half an hour, but they say love makes people do foolish things.

It doesn't matter that Piper and I have only known each other for two months.

Gran's right. When you know, you know.

I love Piper.

Maybe it started the night we met, or maybe it's been building little by little each week, but when I saw her standing in the field holding that hideous little pumpkin, I knew.

I'm completely and totally head over heels for her.

Which makes my current situation doubly frustrating.

I handled the discovery of her income source poorly.

I've been stewing on it for days. Despite what she probably thinks, I'm not a judgmental asshole. Camming isn't something I'd do, but I'm surrounded by dudes who regularly watch porn, so it would be pretty damn hypocritical to judge Piper for profiting off the adult entertainment industry.

I just don't like the idea of sharing my girl with the world.

She's her own person.

Fuck. I know I don't actually have the right to dictate who gets to see her naked, but damn if I want anyone seeing her O face but me.

Just the thought of it has my gut twisting in knots.

The woman on-screen moans—loudly. She's on her hands and knees, doggy-style, and there's a giant dildo suction cupped to her headboard. Her tits bounce with every thrust and she's giving an enthusiastic performance, but it's not doing shit for me.

The only woman I want to see in the throes of passion is Piper.

Yeah, but are you man enough to please her?

The insidious question is the real reason I bolted Sunday. Sure, she seemed to enjoy oral sex, but for all I know she was faking.

Christ. I hadn't considered the possibility until this moment.

I'd just been wondering how I could deliver in bed when she's got so much experience and I'm a goddamn virgin. Sure, I know the mechanics of sex, but that doesn't mean I'll be good at it. I have no idea how to please a woman in that regard.

Or how to tell if she's faking.

The prospect of disappointing Piper, of not being enough for her, sits like a stone in my gut.

The woman on-screen climaxes and I'm comparing her performance to the sounds Piper made when my bedroom door swings open and Parker barges in.

"What the hell are you doing in here?" His eyes go straight

to my computer and I attempt to close the laptop, but he's too quick.

He grabs it off the desk and holds it up for closer inspection.

"Ever hear of knocking?"

He snorts. "Bruh. Rule number one of watching porn is to lock the door."

"I'm not watching porn."

I'm studying it.

"Whoswatchinpor?" Coop appears at the door. There's a blob of white foam at the corner of his mouth, and his toothbrush dangles from between his lips.

Jesus Christ. Does he have some kind of internal radar that helps him home in on sex talk?

"If that shit drips on my carpet, you're cleaning it up."

"Uh, uh." He shakes his head. "Don't try to change the subject."

"Vaughn was getting a little triple X action before study hall," Parker offers.

Coop snorts. "Looks pretty vanilla to me."

Great. I don't even know how to watch porn correctly.

If you want advice, go to the experts.

I study my roommates, debating.

Am I really going to take advice from a guy who's got toothpaste dripping from his mouth?

Yes, I am. My boys might be commitment phobes, but they've got more experience than me.

Talk about irony.

The one guy in the house who actually wants a relationship is also the most clueless.

"Can I ask you a serious question?"

"Whassup?" Coop asks, sending toothpaste flying.

"Dude." Parker leaps back, barely clearing the line of fire.

"Go spit that shit out before you get it all over me. I'm not rolling up to study hall drenched in your saliva."

"Your loss." Coop blows him a kiss and backs down the hall. "Eau de DeLaurentis is a hot commodity."

Parker shakes his head. "It's a good thing he's pretty."

"I heard that!"

I scrub a hand over my face, second guessing all my life choices.

"So what's the question?" Parker returns my laptop, which is now streaming a dude railing his partner, to the desktop.

I slam the lid closed, silencing the endless *slap-slap-slap* of flesh.

"Have you ever dated a woman who had more experience than you?"

"You'll have to be more specific." He grins. "What kind of experience are we talking about? Agriculture? Video games? Football?"

He's messing with me. He knows exactly what I'm asking.

"Forget it." I point to the door. "I'll figure it out on my own."

Coop strides in like he owns the place and flops down on the bed. "What did I miss?"

"Nothing. In fact, we should probably get going." I stand and grab my bag. "We don't want to be late for study hall."

"Our little boy is growing up." Parker jerks his chin toward me.

"Screw you."

"Woah." Reid appears at the door and does a quick scan of the room. "Family meeting?"

"Yes," Coop and Parker say in unison, drowning out my emphatic, "No."

"Two to one." Reid rests his forearm against the doorjamb. "You've been outvoted."

"Come on." Parker makes an *out with it* gesture. "Just tell them."

I drop my bag on the desk and cross my arms, not caring if it makes me look like a defensive asshole. "I was just wondering if any of you have ever been with a more experienced woman and how you handled it."

"Are you serious?" Coop smirks. "That's the dream. A sexually adventurous woman is a golden ticket."

I glare at him and he throws up his hands in self-defense. "You know what I mean."

I really don't, but I keep that to myself.

Parker rubs the back of his neck. "I have some experience in this area and the best advice I can offer is this: forget about the golden ticket and follow the golden rule."

"Which is?"

"Whatever the fuck you do, make sure she comes first. Every. Single. Time. That's the most important thing."

Okay. That feels like solid advice. Then again, I'm so tangled up in my head, I probably couldn't get it up right now, even if I wanted to.

"What he said," Coop chimes in. "When it comes to sex, women are no more complicated than men. They want to have a good time and get off."

"This from the guy who has the emotional maturity of a spork." Reid snickers. "Open communication is key. We don't need another stalker situation in this house."

Coop frowns. "We don't talk about Brenda. Besides, I was talking about the deed itself, not what comes after."

Reid rolls his eyes and turns his attention back to me. "Look, I'm no expert, but you're coming at this all wrong. It doesn't matter who has more experience and who has less. If you've got good communication and you're on the same page, you're—"

"Golden?"

"Exactly." He grins, like he's letting me in on a little secret.

Hell, maybe he is.

For as long as I've known Reid, he's been single-minded, focused only on the game. But lately he's been spending a lot of time with our new kicker. Maybe it's changing his priorities.

"If this woman is someone you plan to see more than once, you'll have ample opportunity to discover what she likes," Parker adds. "That's half the fun."

I sit with their advice, mulling it over.

Could it really be that simple? Tell Piper the truth and then dedicate myself to learning what turns her on. If so, I can do that.

There's nothing I want more than to master every dip and swell of her gorgeous body.

Yes, she's more experienced, but it's like Reid said. That means she knows what she likes, and if she's willing to teach me, I'll for damn sure learn.

Hell, I'll be a straight-A student.

"So," Coop says, drawing the word out. "Who's the special lady?"

I shove my laptop into my backpack. "None of your business."

"What?" He springs off the bed and plants his hands on his hips. "You can't ask us for advice and then leave us hanging."

"Watch me." I sling my bag over my shoulder and saunter out the door, a plan taking shape in my head.

24

PIPER

So much for needing time to process.

The wind whips at my hair as I trudge up the steps to the education building, my coat pulled tight around me. It's been three days since Brady bailed on me, and I haven't heard a peep from him.

No texts. No calls. Nada.

He's completely ghosted me.

You haven't reached out to him either.

Yeah, because he asked for time and I'm giving it to him.

It hasn't been easy. I've picked up the phone several times to send him a meme or tell him something funny that happened in class, but then I remember the look on his face when I told him I'm a camgirl and I'm right back in that moment, my chest collapsing all over.

That wasn't your chest, darlin'.

Nope. I'm definitely not going there.

I already feel like I've been turned inside out and flayed. I'm not going to subject myself to another round of emotional flagellation.

If Brady can't handle a camgirl, that's on him.

Then again, maybe if I'd been upfront with him or if he'd discovered my secret in a way that didn't involve an imprint paddle, the conversation might have gone differently.

But I can't sit around playing the *what if* game.

If it wasn't going to work out, it's better to know now than to find out six months down the road. Unfortunately, the knowledge doesn't make it any easier to accept.

The only upside—if such a thing exists—is that Brady will keep my secret. He may not approve of my side hustle, but he knows how important my education is, and he's not the kind of person to spread rumors or stir the pot out of spite.

It's a small comfort.

Especially when I can't even talk to Jenna about the situation. Telling her about Brady would mean telling her about Fangirl, and I'm not about to spill my secret now. Not when Brady reacted so poorly.

Jenna would understand.

Maybe. But I'm not about to put her in a compromising position. She's an education major too, and the less she knows about Fangirl, the better.

The building is quiet when I enter. No surprise there. It's nearly six and most classes are finished for the day. I'm meeting with Dr. Barnes' teaching assistant, Mike McConnell, though he wasn't exactly forthcoming about the agenda for the meeting.

Nerves coil tight in my belly, my mind going to the worst-case scenario.

Which, given the week I'm having, would be par for the course.

Shit. What if Dr. Barnes is unhappy with the classroom observations I turned in yesterday?

Our last meeting flashes through my mind and I can't help but remember her promise: *Keep up the good work, and if at the end of the semester I'm satisfied with your performance, I'll consider writing you a letter of recommendation.*

It's only the end of October. It's too soon for a decision.

Stop worrying. You'll have your answers soon enough.

It's sound advice, but easier said than done.

The department office is quiet when I enter. The admin has left for the day, and from the looks of it, so have the teaching staff.

Can you blame them?

Not even a little. If I was a tenured professor, I wouldn't be holding office hours in the evening either.

I make my way back to the cramped communal office shared by the TAs and find Mike McConnell waiting, his laptop open on the desk.

"Hi." I force a note of cheer into my voice, though I'm nervous as hell. "Are you ready for me?"

"Yes. Come in." His dark hair curls over his forehead and his midnight eyes are unreadable as I take a seat across from him, the narrow desk separating us. "Would you mind closing the door?"

My stomach bottoms out.

That can't be a good sign.

At least he's respecting your right to privacy.

I've never liked it when teachers post grades publicly or point out a student's shortcomings in front of their peers. It's demeaning and promotes an unnecessarily competitive environment.

I do as he asks, reaching behind me to close the door to the office.

When I turn back to the TA, my pulse is thrumming, and not in a good way.

"I don't believe in wasting time." He folds his hands on the desk. "I'll get right to the point."

"Okay." I nod slowly, impressed I squeaked out two whole syllables.

"It's come to my attention that you have a Fangirl account where you engage in and provide adult entertainment."

A cold sweat beads long my brow and bile rises in the back of my throat.

My hands begin to shake and oh, God. I'm going to throw up.

This can't be happening.

How does he know? Was it Brady?

No. Brady would never do that. He might not approve of my choices, but he'd never intentionally hurt me. He's not that kind of person.

"I— I can explain," I stammer, clasping my hands in my lap.

"That won't be necessary." The TA looks down his thin nose, judgment radiating off him like smoke from a fire. "I believe I understand the situation quite clearly."

Christ. He actually sounds smug.

Like he's just been waiting for the opportunity to ruin someone's life.

"Dr. Barnes doesn't know about your exploits." Hope flares in my chest as a slow smile curves his lips. "Yet."

The word echoes through my brain, snuffing out my naïve optimism.

Dr. Barnes doesn't know about my exploits *yet.*

"If Dr. Barnes knew what you've been up to, she'd be so disappointed," he says, voice dripping with condescension. "You know how she feels about personal conduct."

Me and everyone else in the College of Education.

It's not exactly a secret.

My mouth goes dry and though I want to rage against the

unfairness of it all, I force myself to remain calm. Melting down won't change the facts.

Facts? What facts? This whole thing is bullshit.

What I do online has no bearing on my ability to be a successful educator, and if higher education wasn't so damn expensive, I wouldn't even be in this position.

"Dr. Barnes would probably cancel your student teaching assignment, and she definitely wouldn't provide you with a letter of recommendation."

The TA flashes another oily smile and understanding clicks into place.

He hasn't told Barnes...*yet.*

Why not? He should've reported it immediately. She's his direct supervisor.

He didn't report it because he wants something.

That's why he's been watching me all semester. He's been biding his time, just waiting to make his move when it would have the greatest impact.

Now that I've received my student teaching assignment, I've got the most to lose and he knows it.

Bastard.

"What do you want?"

The prick doesn't even hesitate. "Money."

He's got balls, I'll give him that.

"You know this school isn't cheap." I have to force the words past my lips. "What makes you think I have cash to spare?"

"Come on, CurvyGirl. Let's not play games." He flips the laptop around to reveal my Fangirl profile. "I've been following your channel for a while now. You've got quite the following."

He's been watching me online.

My skin crawls at the revelation.

I've got thousands of fans online, but they're strangers, not people I know in real life. People I have to face every day in class. People who grade my freaking papers and have influence over my future.

Talk about *ick*.

I've never felt uncomfortable camming, until now. In one fell swoop, he's stripped my control. I'm not sure I'll ever look at Fangirl the same way again.

"Why are you doing this?"

He shrugs, like he's not trying to fucking blackmail me right now. "Higher education is expensive." *No shit*. "Do you have any idea how many student loans I have?" Irritation creeps into his voice. "I'll never pay them off working in education, but as they say, every little bit helps."

That he'd rather blackmail another student than find a productive—and legal—way to pay his debts is nauseating.

You're not the only one out here disappointing Dr. Barnes tonight.

"How. Much?" I ask through clenched teeth. I don't bother trying to feign cheerfulness. He'll know it's a farce and frankly, he's not worth the effort.

"Five grand."

"Five thousand dollars?" I shout, voice reaching a pitch only dogs can hear. "You're unhinged."

It would take me at least a month to raise that kind of cash.

He narrows his eyes and leans forward, resting his forearms on the table. "You have three days."

Three days? He can't be serious.

"That isn't nearly enough time. I don't have that kind of money lying around."

"Then I suppose you'll have to find it." He picks a piece of lint off his button down. "Because if you don't, I'll expose you, and I really don't think Dr. Barnes will react well to learning one of her students is a sex worker."

I'm going to have to tap into my savings. There's no other choice.

I can't afford to call his bluff, and I can't go to Barnes.

Not if I want to finish my degree and get my teaching certificate.

My chest tightens and I rub it absently, trying to figure out how things have gotten so screwed up in such a short amount of time.

"Here." Mike slides a business card across the desk. His Venmo handle is scrawled on the back. "If the money isn't in my account in three days, Dr. Barnes will receive an email with a link to your Fangirl account."

25

BRADY

It's now or never.

I draw a steadying breath and knock. I have no idea if Piper's home, and I probably should have called first, but I was afraid she might blow me off and what I have to say needs to be said in person.

My palms begin to sweat and I force myself to relax my grip on the flowers I'm holding before I crush the stems.

Whatever happens tonight, I'll have to be okay with it.

After all, I brought it on myself with my stupid insecurities.

There's movement on the other side of the door, and I hear the *thwack* of the deadbolt being thrown before the door swings open.

Piper's eyes go round when she sees me, but she recovers quickly, wariness settling over her features. "This is a surprise."

I hold out the flowers, lilies wrapped in brown paper. "Can we talk?"

She takes them without comment and steps aside to let me enter.

The pumpkin spice candle is burning, just like on my first visit, and textbooks are spread out on the coffee table, making it clear she was studying.

"This won't take long," I promise, turning as she closes the door.

"It's fine." She crosses to the kitchen and places the flowers on the peninsula, careful to keep her distance. It's a gut punch, but no less than I deserve. "I take it you're done processing."

Her face remains guarded and I hate that I've made her feel like she needs to protect herself from me. It took weeks to break down her walls, but only seconds to erect them again.

"I came here to apologize."

She worries her bottom lip, but says nothing.

"I reacted poorly to the news that you're a camgirl and I'm sorry. The last thing I wanted to do was hurt you. If I could take it back, I would."

"What's done is done."

"I know." Just like I know she might never forgive me, but still, I have to try. I couldn't live with myself if I walked away now. "I didn't leave for the reasons you're probably thinking."

She cocks a hip and leans against the counter. "You have no idea what I'm thinking."

"No, not exactly, but I know how it looked when I bailed on you."

"So you didn't leave because you were disgusted by my work?" She snorts. "Could've fooled me."

"I could never be disgusted by you." Christ. I want to go to her, to take her in my arms and forget the other night ever happened, but that's not an option. For either of us. "I admit I don't understand why you would choose to cam, but—"

"It's a job, just like any other job." She straightens, pulling herself up to her full height. "Yes, I perform on camera, but it's not personal. I don't meet up with these guys or let them touch me, and I set the boundaries. I don't do anything I'm not comfortable with and if you can't handle that, that's on you." She sucks in a breath, chest heaving as she levels a dark look in my direction. "Sex work isn't something to be ashamed of and not all sex workers have daddy issues or whatever it is you're thinking. It's actually pretty empowering."

Shit. I'm totally screwing this up. I've put her on the defensive when I'm supposed to be apologizing.

"And for the record, a lot of the guys who subscribe to my content are just lonely. They want a human connection in a digital world and they're willing to pay for it."

This, at least, I understand, so I jump on it.

"I get it. Waverly is expensive." I shrug, remembering how she compared my sport to her job. *It's just a means to an end.* "Hell, I wouldn't even be here if Coach hadn't offered me a football scholarship."

I'd be at home, helping on the farm.

And you never would've met Piper.

The time away from home is a more than fair trade. I couldn't see it before, but now...

Now I realize just how lucky I am.

Not only am I getting a world class education, I had the opportunity to fall in love with the incredible woman before me.

The woman I'm going to lose if I don't pull my shit together.

I'm still not wild about the idea of other guys fantasizing about my girl, but it's not my place to tell her what she can and can't do. It's her body and her decision.

If she finds camming empowering, then I need to support her. That's what it means to be a good partner.

"I don't need your approval," she says, as if sensing my inner turmoil.

"I know." I shove my hands into my pockets, praying she won't throw my next words back in my face. "As much as I hate the idea of sharing you, I'm not going anywhere. I plan to be at your side as long as you'll have me."

She arches a brow. "That's not the tune you were singing on Sunday."

"I made a mistake. I'm not proud of it, but I can admit when I'm wrong." She opens her mouth to speak, and I press on before I can lose my nerve. "I freaked out because I'm a virgin and I felt inadequate."

The words come out in a rush, but it's a relief to get them off my chest.

Piper's mouth drops open and then snaps shut. "You're...a virgin?"

Heat crawls up the back of my neck, but I nod. "When I saw the toys on your bed, I realized you were more experienced and I was afraid I wouldn't to live up to your expectations."

She laughs and my mortification multiplies, the heat on my neck fanning out to blaze across my cheeks.

"I'm sorry. I shouldn't laugh." No kidding. Here I am baring my soul and she's cackling like it's the funniest thing she's ever heard. "It's just that I'm only experienced in the same way you're probably experienced."

What the hell does that mean?

"I...don't understand."

"I'm a pro at self-gratification." She grins. "But I've never had a partner."

Is she saying what I think she's saying?

"You're a virgin, too."

She nods and a disorienting mix of shock and relief wash over me, immediately followed by guilt. I jumped to the wrong conclusion because of her job and instead of talking to her about it, I ran home with my tail between my legs.

Like an asshole.

"It doesn't matter to me, Piper." It was never some antiquated concept of purity that sent me spiraling. It was my lack of experience. "My insecurities are my own, and I know they're not your responsibility, but if you're willing to teach me, to show me what you like, I want to learn."

Hell, I want to learn everything there is to know about her.

She takes a tentative step forward and my pulse quickens.

"I like you, Brady. A lot. I've been fighting it since the night we met, but I'm tired of pretending my heart doesn't flutter when you walk in the room. Of pretending you don't rule my thoughts when you're not around. I want to be with you. And not because we have great chemistry or because you gave me a toe-curling orgasm. I want to be with you because you're a great guy and I think we could be really good together."

I beam at her, feeling like a kid on Christmas.

Hearing that I gave her a toe-curling orgasm feels damn good, but knowing that she wants to be with me? It's more than I could've hoped for and I will not blow it.

"So." I grab one of her belt loops and pull her in close, cupping her cheek with my free hand. "Just to be clear, you're not expecting a sexual savant?"

She laughs, low and husky. "I mean, I wouldn't complain, but if we're even half as good in real life as we are in my fantasies, I'll be a very satisfied woman."

Hell, yes. "Did you just admit to fantasizing about me?"

"The night we met, I came home and filmed selfie-time with my favorite vibrator." She looks up at me from under her lashes. "It was your cock I imagined filling me, sliding in and out of my pussy until I came so hard my back bowed off the bed."

Jesus Christ, that's hot.

My dick hardens and when I try to speak, the words come out deep and gravelly. "I'd like to see that video some time."

"I'll bet you would." She trails a finger down the center of my chest. "Play your cards right and you just might. It's part of my personal collection. No one has seen it but me and I've watched it many, many times."

I lower my hands to her ass and pull her flush to my body, letting her feel the effect her words have on me. "You keep talking like that and I'm going to embarrass myself, darlin'."

She stretches up on her toes and brushes a soft kiss across my lips. "You never have to be embarrassed with me. We'll figure things out together."

Fuckin' right we will. And we're going to enjoy every damn second.

"I like the sound of that. Can I take you out this weekend? We could have dinner at The Inn and try again."

The Inn is one of the most romantic—and expensive—restaurants in town. It would normally be out of my budget, but I can dip into my savings just this once.

Piper deserves the best and I'm going to give it to her.

"I don't need a fancy date or an overpriced meal." She holds my gaze and when she speaks, her voice is thick with emotion. "I just need you, Brady."

It's all the encouragement I need. I lower my mouth to hers and claim her full lips, pouring the love and desire that threatens to overwhelm me into the kiss. I want to tell her how I feel, but I'll have to settle for showing her. She's not there yet, or if she is, she's not ready to voice it, and I'm not going to pressure her.

Piper will get there in her own time. There's no need to rush.

Not when we've got all the time in the world.

When we finally break apart, her lips are red and swollen, her chin pink from the brush of my beard. She's never looked more beautiful than she does in this moment as she cups the back of my neck and whispers, "What do you say we try again right now?"

26

PIPER

"Right now?" Brady's eyes darken, his pupils blowing so wide the whiskey irises deepen to a rich cinnamon.

"Yes."

I want him, and I want him now.

My core clenches and the hollow ache between my legs intensifies.

This is it. I'm finally going to have sex. With Brady.

The thought of his cock filling me sends a fresh wave of arousal to my pussy and my panties grow damp. I've never wanted a man the way I want him and though this is a big step for both of us, there's no one I'd rather share it with.

I trust Brady.

With my body and my heart.

I was hurt by his reaction to my Fangirl site, but I understand it now. Perhaps better than he realizes, because it's taken two years of therapy to fully face my own insecurities and gain the confidence to love myself exactly as I am.

"If we're doing this, we're doing it right."

He cups his hands under my ass and lifts me into the air. I instinctively wrap my legs around him as he carries me to the bedroom with ease. His eyes never leave mine and there's such tenderness in his face that I feel my chest expand with a rush of emotion.

"I can't believe this is finally happening. I've thought about it so many times..."

My words trail off as Brady deposits me at the foot of the bed, my body sliding down the length of him. He's only got about eight inches on me, but it's enough. My pussy slides over his cock, a delicious tease that delivers a zing of pleasure straight to my brain.

"You and me both, darlin'."

His slow drawl is more pronounced than usual and I don't hate it. In fact, I love that he's as enamored with me as I am with him.

He lowers his mouth to mine, claiming me with a languid kiss as I slip my fingers under the hem of his black t-shirt and tug. We break apart just long enough for me to pull the shirt up over his head and then his lips are on mine again as I explore his body, running my fingers over the taut muscles of his chest and biceps.

I've never felt small in my life, but next to this man?

I'm positively dainty.

His wide chest is covered in dark, wiry hair and as I skim my nails over his pecs, I'm taken by the urge to feel him skin-to-skin.

I open the top button on my shirt. "We need to get rid of all these clothes."

"I couldn't agree more." He brushes his knuckles across my cheek and tucks a loose strand of hair behind my ear. "I want to admire every gorgeous inch of you."

"Ditt—" I freeze, my gaze locked on his tattoo. The familiar roses creep up his forearm, a compass nestled among the blossoms as they continue up his biceps, winding around an intricate clock with roman numerals. I've seen the sleeve before and it's just as gorgeous as I remember, but there's an addition branching out from his shoulder that looks new. The ink is darker, the skin surrounding it red and raw.

Brady notices my stare and glances down at his left shoulder.

"I got it to remind me of you."

Lilies. He got lilies. *To remind him of me.*

Tears sting my eyes as I study the addition, but I can't seem to find my words.

"I've known from the moment we met that you're the one for me, Piper. I'm crazy about you and there's nothing I won't do to make you happy."

"I..." My throat tightens. What can I even say? I'm blown away by the implication. He's so confident we're end game he tattooed it on his body. No one's ever done anything like this for me before and I certainly wasn't expecting it, but damn if it's not completely Brady.

Once he sets his mind to something, it's a done deal.

I open my mouth to say as much, but he presses a finger to my lips. "You don't have to say anything. I'm a patient man, Piper. I won't rush you, and I'm not going anywhere. Just being with you is enough for me."

It's far more than I deserve, but I grab onto the sentiment with both hands and hold on tight as I crush my lips to his.

We make quick work of our remaining clothes and when I stand before him, completely naked, Brady looks his fill.

I do the same, mouth watering at the sight of his cock.

It's long and thick, standing proudly at attention. A bead of moisture glistens on the tip and I want so badly to touch him, to join my body with his, but he's right, there's no need to rush.

We have all night.

"Damn." He skims his fingertips over my hip and anticipation sizzles up my spine. "Every time I think you can't get any prettier, you prove me wrong. Your body is perfect."

I'm not shy and I love my curves, but hearing the words from him?

It's a whole other level.

"Thanks. You're not so bad yourself."

Despite his muscular frame, Brady's soft in the middle and I freaking love it.

He chuckles and pulls me close, the soft curves of our bodies melding as he captures my mouth, his beard scraping my chin as he deepens the kiss. The gentle burn is a welcome sensation, one that will leave its mark on me, irrefutable proof that I'm his and he's mine.

My pussy clenches at the realization and I break off the kiss, gasping for breath as Brady trails kisses down my throat and across my collarbone.

The man is relentless in the pursuit of pleasure.

My pleasure.

It's a heady feeling. I thread my fingers through his hair and guide him to my breast, desperate to feel his mouth on me.

True to his word, Brady's an eager student.

He cups my left breast, massaging gently as he flicks his tongue across my hardened nipple.

Pleasure radiates from the point of contact and I arch my back, encouraging him to do it again. He repeats the motion, but this time he sucks the puckered flesh into his mouth and it feels so damn good I can't help but moan.

His mouth is hot and wet and I need to feel it on every inch of my body.

"Your mouth feels so good."

"Yeah?" He looks up at me with a question in his eyes. "What about this?"

He takes my nipple between his teeth and bites down. The sharp sting is immediately followed by a dark wave of arousal, and I squeeze my thighs together, attempting to satisfy the growing ache between my legs.

"I need more." The words are part plea, part instruction. "I need your mouth. Your fingers. Your cock."

With Brady, I want it all.

He continues the trail of kisses, nipping and biting as he cuts a path down the center of my abdomen. The man is clearly on a mission and when he licks my pussy and sucks my clit between his lips, I nearly come.

The tension in my core skyrockets and I dig my nails into his scalp, attempting to ground myself in the moment.

"*Ohmygod.*" My hips roll forward, my body determined to find release. "That feels so fucking good."

He repeats the combination, this time sucking longer and harder. The sensation is like nothing I've ever felt before and I moan shamelessly, reveling in the feel of his mouth on me. When he finally lets up, my knees buckle from the loss of contact.

Brady's hands clamp onto my hips and when he looks up at me, there's a smug grin on his face.

"You're sweeter than a bowl of cherries. I could do this all day."

As if to prove his point, he dives back in, licking and sucking with renewed vigor.

Pleasure sings through my body, each note higher and brighter than the last as I soar toward the inevitable crescendo.

"More," I pant. "I need more, Brady. I need to feel you inside of me."

In answer, he drags a finger along my slit, spreading my arousal before he plunges the thick digit into my pussy.

"Like this?" he rasps, eyelids at half-mast.

"Mmmhmm." I rock my hips, angling for the spot that will give me the most intense orgasm.

"Or maybe you want it like this." He eases another finger inside of me and *damn*. I knew his hands were big, but I never imagined just two fingers could fill me up so good.

He circles my clit with his tongue and the moan that escapes my lips is loud enough to be heard throughout the building.

I should probably turn on some music, or at least feel some level of shame, but I've got nothing. Brady is out here doing God's work, and I am here for it.

"I'm so close," I whisper, rocking my hips.

"Tell me how to get you there." He punctuates each word with a thrust of his fingers. "I want to make you feel so good, Piper."

Despite his obvious arousal, it's clear he means every word. That he wants to get me off before we go any further speaks volumes, and I'm not about to hold out on him. Not when clear communication will lead to a more gratifying experience for both of us.

"Curl your fingers just a bit."

He does as instructed and my body hums in response. "Like this?"

"Yes." The tension in my core ratchets higher with each brush of his fingertips against my G-spot. "I'm so close, Brady, but I need your mouth, too."

He doesn't hesitate. The next thrust is paired with a flick of his tongue. The added pressure on my clit is divine and with only a few more thrusts, I'm shattering, my orgasm exploding with an intensity I've never felt before. Pleasure radiates through my body and Brady gives no quarter, working me until the very last aftershock subsides.

By the time he climbs to his feet and drops a soft kiss on my lips, my knees are weak and I'm hyperstimulated.

"You're a quick study."

He grins, revealing the dimple I love so much. "What can I say? I have an excellent teacher."

It's silly banter, but his words are laced with lo— *affection*, and a familiar warmth fills my chest. "Does that mean you're ready for your next lesson?"

27

BRADY

"Darlin', I will always be ready for another lesson."

Piper smiles up at me, almost shyly. "You're not the only one who's eager to learn. I want to know what you like and how you taste."

My cock twitches at the prospect. I'm so damn hard right now, it's a wonder my balls haven't exploded.

Piper huffs a laugh and glances down at my erection, which just poked her in the belly. "I'm going to assume that means you have no objections."

I couldn't tell this woman no, even if I wanted to.

She may not realize it yet, but she's got me wrapped around her finger.

"I'd be a fool to deny you, and we both know it."

I want to be with her in every way that counts. Sex and intimacy are part of that equation and I'm not about to shy away from her when all I want to do is get closer.

Piper drops to her knees and fuck me. It's the hottest thing I've ever seen. She looks up at me, and maybe it's wishful thinking, but there's adoration in her eyes. Anticipation prickles along my skin and I hope she sees the same emotion reflected in mine.

I scrape her hair back from her face, fisting it in my hands as she wraps her fingers around the base of my cock.

"I want to watch." I tighten my grip on her hair so it doesn't slip free.

"Then I guess it's a good thing I enjoy putting on a show." She flashes me a wicked grin and licks her lips seductively. Then she lowers her mouth to my cock and licks the pre-cum from the tip.

"*Mmm.* You taste so good, Brady." She swirls her tongue around the head like she's licking a goddamn lollipop and tension coils at the base of my spine. "Do you have any idea how many times I've fantasized about taking you in my mouth?"

"No." But it can't possibly rival my own count.

"I've thought about it so many times. Wondered if I'd be able to take your entire cock. Whether it would reach the back of my throat. If you'd be sweet or salty."

Christ. The things she says... The way she says them so confidently...

It's a huge fucking turn-on.

"My girl has a dirty mouth." She smirks and there's a silent challenge in her eyes. One I have to meet, because while I might be vanilla, she's salted caramel. Sweet, sophisticated, and perfectly decadent. "So what's the verdict? Do you think you can handle my cock?"

I've always tried to be respectful of women. I don't swear in front of them, and I've sure as shit never used the word cock when speaking to one, but Piper said herself that sexuality is empowering, so maybe I've got it all wrong. Or maybe there's a time and place for everything.

And in this bedroom, in this moment, it's exactly what she needs.

What we need.

"I have to admit." She trails a finger up my shaft. "It's bigger than I'd imagined." *Fuckin' right it is.* "But I'd like to try."

Her tongue darts out, and she swirls it around the head before she takes it in her mouth, sucking gently.

I've died and gone to heaven.

Piper's mouth is hot and wet and her lips slide over my sensitive flesh with ease as she takes me deeper. She works me with her tongue and it's all I can do not to thrust into her mouth as tension coils at the base of my spine, urging me toward release.

Her head bobs and my vision blurs as she takes me deep, cradling my cock in the warm recesses of her mouth.

Oh, shit. This was a terrible idea. If she keeps that up, I'm going to come.

"I need to be inside you, Piper. Right fucking now."

I pull back and she whimpers, but I pull her to her feet and crush my lips to hers.

"Baby, I want to come inside you."

She nods and I turn to find a condom.

There's one in my wallet, but where are my damn pants?

I spot them draped over the desk and waste no time locating my wallet and the condom within. When I turn back to Piper, she's lying on the bed, spread out like a goddamn present.

Fuck me.

What we're about to do, maybe it's old-fashioned, but it is a gift. That she's willing to share her body with me, that she trusts me to be her first, means something.

I tear open the condom and roll it over my length.

"Are you sure about this?" I have no doubts, but Piper has to be sure as well. It would kill me if she woke up with regrets tomorrow.

"Yes. I want this, Brady. I want you."

My heart swells with pride as I approach the bed, and when Piper spreads her legs for me, revealing her slick pink pussy, I know she wants this as much as I do.

I lower myself onto the bed and our eyes meet as I settle myself between her thighs.

Emotion overtakes me and I can't find the words to express how I'm feeling, so I lower my mouth to hers.

Piper meets me halfway.

The kiss starts off slow and sultry, but when I deepen it, my tongue mating with hers in a chaotic dance, she begins to move beneath me. Her hips roll as she grinds against my cock, and the tip nudges at her entrance.

At least, I think it's her entrance.

Shit. Am I in the wrong position? Without the aid of my hands, it's hard to be sure and since I have zero experience...

Do not fuck this up, asshole.

Sweat beads along my brow and I adjust my position, angling my hips forward.

I want her first time to be memorable for the right reasons, and this ain't it.

Panic floods my chest, and Piper must sense my worry, because she spreads her legs wide—thank you pole class—and slips a hand between our bodies, guiding me into position.

The tip of my cock slides in, and we both stiffen.

This is it.

I'm going to have sex with the woman I love.

I drop another kiss on her lips. "Let's take it slow."

She nods and I sink into her inch by painstaking inch. Her pussy is hot and wet and tight and the need to bury myself to the hilt is almost impossible to resist.

Pleasure radiates up my spine, and Piper gasps, digging her nails into my back when I'm fully seated within her.

I freeze. "Are you okay?"

"Yes." She bites her lip. "I just need a second to adjust, but it's a good hurt."

Is that even a thing?

It must be because her eyes glaze over and she rocks her hips beneath me. It's slow, painstakingly so, and yeah, now I know the meaning of *hurts so good*.

My body aches to move, to go balls deep, but I let her set the pace. When she mewls beneath me, her fingers trailing down my back to grip my ass, I let her guide me, too.

It's the only way I'll get to know her body as intimately as I know my own.

I roll my hips, attempting to replicate the hand motion she showed me just minutes ago. "How does this feel?"

"Very nice." Her eyes drift shut, and a smile pulls at the corner of her mouth. "Do that again."

I repeat the motion and she angles her hips to meet me.

"Oh." Her cry comes out as a breathy moan and then our hips are crashing together again, instinct taking over. By silent agreement, we increase the pace, both of us desperate for the next wave of pleasure as we chase release.

Beneath me, Piper's blonde hair is fanned out on the pillow and the look of pure bliss on her face is like nothing I've seen before.

"That's right, darlin'. Take what you need from me. I want to feel you come all over my cock."

She moans and this time, when our bodies meet, she grinds her pelvis against mine.

I flash back to her last orgasm. To the moment she requested my mouth on her clit, and on my next thrust, I roll my hips, angling for the bundle of nerves that will push her over the edge.

"Yes," she pants, sweat glistening on her forehead. "Don't stop, Brady."

It's not even an option. She feels too damn good.

Every thrust sends me spiraling higher, closer to release, and when Piper cries out, my name on her lips, her tight channel gripping my cock, I fly right over the edge with her.

My orgasm is a supernova. Pleasure explodes from the base of my spine, sending shockwaves through every cell in my body, and it's all I can do not to roar in satisfaction.

I hold Piper close as we ride out the aftershocks and when the last wave of sensation has subsided, I lower my forehead to hers.

"That was incredible." I've never experienced anything so intense in my life.

Piper grins up at me. "Do you think it will always be this good between us?"

"I don't know, but if it's even half as good, I'll be a happy man."

I excuse myself to dispose of the condom and when I return to bed, Piper's curled up under the covers. Before I can ask, she throws them back, beckoning me to join her. I climb into bed and she fits her naked body to mine, head resting on my chest and one leg draped over my thigh.

We fit together perfectly and it's easy to imagine falling asleep like this every night for the rest of my life. Her hair tickles my cheek, but I don't brush it away. She smells like sex and flowers and the combination is working for her.

"Do all the elements of your tattoo hold special meaning?"

Surprise washes over me. Of all the things she might've said in this moment, it's the least expected. Not that I mind.

After what we've just shared, there's nothing I wouldn't tell her.

"My mother keeps a rose garden on the farm, so I got them to remind me of her when we're apart." Which I guess could sound weird for a twenty-one-year-old guy. "She's been my rock over the years and, as a single mom, she sacrificed a lot to make sure I had everything I needed growing up. I think she felt like she had to make up for my dad walking out, like she had to fill both roles."

Piper's quiet for a long moment and doubt creeps in.

Should I have kept that part to myself? To hear Piper tell it, her mother didn't have a maternal bone in her body and here I am bragging about the lengths my mother went to in order to make my life easier.

"That's a really sweet way to honor her." Piper strokes my chest absently. "She sounds like an amazing woman."

"She is." I leave it at that, though I want to suggest she can decide for herself someday. "The clock is to honor my grandfather and to remind me that our time on this earth is finite."

She nods slowly. "It's a reminder to make the most of every day."

"Exactly."

"What about the compass?"

"It reminds me of where I come from and where I'm going." I drop a kiss on her temple. "I never want to lose sight of what's important."

"It's beautiful." She traces the shape of it with her finger. "I can't believe you added the lilies."

There's a note of awe in her voice, proving I didn't make myself clear earlier.

"I told you. I'm crazy about you. There's no one else for me and there never will be." I tip her chin up, meeting her gaze. "However long it takes you to get to the same place, I'll be right here by your side, waiting."

28

PIPER

WILDCAT STADIUM IS UNHINGED.

I've never seen so many people gathered in one place. The fact that many of them are drinking makes it doubly fascinating. Most people are wearing some combination of blue and white Wildcat gear and the number of foam Wildcat paws is staggering.

I take my seat next to Jenna on the metal bleacher. "Is it always like this?"

"This is nothing." She waves dismissively. "It's even worse during white out games."

"This is really your first football game?" Kylie/Rylee asks, leaning forward to peer around Jenna.

I need to figure out her actual name, but it's too embarrassing to ask at this point.

"I'm not big into sports, but I wanted to show my support and see Brady play."

"They're official now," Jenna explains, grinning so hard the temporary Wildcat tattoo on her cheek crinkles.

"Nice," Alexis offers from the end of the row.

I don't bother responding. If this is her attempt to make up for the shade she was throwing a few weeks ago, she's going to have to try harder because I'm definitely not over it.

"You picked the perfect game." Jenna nudges me, oblivious to the tension. "Michigan is one of our biggest rivals, so it'll be an intense game."

We chat about classes as we wait for kickoff, and it's a nice dose of normalcy in what's turning out to be a chaotic semester.

When the team finally comes running out of the tunnel, the crowd goes berserk, screaming and stomping as the Wildcat roar echoes through the stadium.

The announcer rattles off the starting lineup, but I've only got eyes for Brady.

He looks damn fine in uniform, the pads emphasizing his large stature and broad shoulders.

"Remind me again why I never got into sports?"

Jenna laughs. "Girl, you've got it bad."

"If you're talking about lust, then yes, I've got it bad."

Her eyes go wide and she squeals, which, in this crowd, is no big deal. "Oh, my god. You're sleeping with him."

"Shh! You don't have to announce it to the entire section."

"I can't believe you didn't tell me." She juts out her bottom lip. "Now you'll have to give me details to make up for it."

I laugh in spite of myself. "You wish."

"I really do." She hooks her arm through mine and rests her head on my shoulder. "I have so many questions."

I'm saved from responding when we're asked to stand for the national anthem. After, Waverly wins the coin toss, and they elect to receive the ball.

I lean forward, straining to see better when the offense takes the field, Brady among them. He lines up to the left of the center and when the ball is thrown, he springs into action, lunging forward to attack—is that even the right word?—Michigan's defense.

Damn. Who knew watching two men wrestle for dominance could be so hot?

Brady may be soft-spoken and gentle in real life, but he's a beast on the field—and in the bedroom.

Football keeps him busy, but he slept over a few times this week, though technically, there wasn't much sleep involved. The man is insatiable, and I freaking love it. He might be inexperienced, but he's a quick study, and he's willing to learn. He even watched me film a short clip for my channel two nights ago. It helped him get more comfortable with the idea of camming, though he'll never be a fan.

He's got too much caveman DNA for that.

If he had his way, he'd probably toss me over his shoulder and never let me leave the bed.

It's actually kind of nice.

Brady isn't like the men who were in and out of my life growing up. He'll stick because he's loyal and patient and just an all-around good person.

Unlike Mike McConnell.

Surrounded by one hundred thousand screaming Wildcat fans, I'd almost forgotten I'm being blackmailed.

Almost.

Mike hasn't approached me since I paid him and I'm hoping to keep it that way. Five thousand dollars cut my savings in half, but I'll be okay.

I have to be.

The crowd cheers and I join in, shoving all thoughts of Mike McConnell and blackmail from my mind.

"Did you see that?" Jenna screeches, bouncing on her toes.

"How the one guy grabbed the ball from the other guy?"

"That's it." Jenna flips her hair over her shoulder. "If you're going to be a WAG—wives and girlfriends—you at least need to learn basic terminology."

I don't bother reminding her Brady isn't going pro or that these lessons won't benefit me long term. I'm having too much fun, getting caught up in the crowd's energy.

Jenna takes it upon herself to give me a full education and by the fourth quarter, I think I'm starting to get it.

"I told you this was going to be an intense game." Jenna takes a gulp of the beer she grabbed at halftime. "Maybe a little too intense."

Waverly is up by three, but it's been a damn close game and with only three minutes left on the clock, the tension in the stadium is at an all-time high.

The Wildcat offense takes the field and I'm so focused on Brady, I lose track of the ball after it's snapped.

A collective groan goes up from the crowd and I scan the field, searching for the source of disappointment.

"Austin Reid gets picked off with just over two minutes on the clock," the announcer says, his booming voice echoing through the stadium as the crowd boos.

"Dammit!" Jenna yells. "Can we get a flag on the play or what?"

I'm no expert, but I get what she's saying. Waverly has a three-point lead, but if Michigan scores on this drive, the Wildcats can kiss their championship dreams goodbye.

Brady told me they have to go undefeated for the rest of the season to even have a shot.

"I can't look." Jenna buries her face in my shoulder as the Waverly defense takes the field.

I don't want to watch either, but it's like a train wreck and I can't tear my gaze away.

Michigan picks up a first down on the second attempt and

Jenna decides it's better to watch since she can't unhear the announcer.

A chant goes up from the crowd. It starts out as D-fence, but quickly becomes all out chaos, a cacophony of horns and thumps and good old-fashioned screams.

"They're trying to drown out the play call," Jenna shouts, picking up on my confusion. "If the fans are loud enough, there's a chance Michigan will draw a false start or some of their guys won't hear the play."

"Damn." I cover my ears, but the relief is minimal.

"Waverly has one of the loudest stadiums in the country!"

I can't say I'm surprised, since my eardrums feel like they're bleeding.

Down on the field, Coach Collins is hollering at one of the linemen and pointing to a spot a few feet away. His clipboard goes up and one of his coordinators grabs it.

Probably to make sure he doesn't clock the ref.

Waverly's defense holds Michigan on the next two plays, but Jenna's nerves must be contagious, because now my stomach is doing the tango.

"Third and long," she says, gripping my arm. "We need a stop here. If the D lets them get within field goal range, this game will go to overtime."

"So free football?"

She rolls her eyes. "No one wants free football when the game is on the line."

The crowd gets even louder, which I didn't think was possible, and the stadium vibrates beneath my feet.

Michigan snaps the ball and one of the Waverly guys bolts across the line of scrimmage, tackling the quarterback. He goes down like a sack of potatoes and the stadium erupts. The Waverly Wildcat sprints down the sideline, raising its arms to get the crowd pumped up as the players on the field reset.

"They're going to go for it!" Jenna exclaims, and thanks to her coaching, I know she means they're going for the fourth down. If it doesn't convert, Waverly gets the ball back, which is the best-case scenario.

I cross my fingers and we huddle together, waiting for the next play.

The ball is snapped and the QB drops back.

He must not find a receiver, because he attempts to run the ball and gets tackled at the line of scrimmage.

I leap to my feet, screaming and clapping. Jenna, Kylie/Rylee, and Alexis are right behind me. We scream ourselves hoarse and when the offense takes the field, I pull out my phone to text Brady. He deserves a treat for a job well done and I've got just the thing in mind.

Me: Come over after the game. I'll be ready and waiting.

29

BRADY

PIPER ANSWERS the door in a white robe, her blonde hair falling over her shoulders in loose waves.

Shit. Did I read her message wrong? I thought she was inviting me over for sex, but the robe definitely isn't giving *come hither* vibes.

Dumbass.

Whatever. Sex or no sex, I would've come, if only to spend time with her. Today's game was brutal and I could use a relaxing night in.

She closes the door and when she turns back to face me, she unties her robe. It falls open to reveal a black leather corset and the tiniest pair of black panties I've ever seen.

"Damn."

My cock springs to attention, tenting the front of my gray sweatpants.

She slips the robe off and drops it to the floor as she does a slow turn, giving me the opportunity to look my fill.

And look I do. Her breasts spill over the front of the corset and her delectable ass is on full display in a flimsy thong.

"Darlin', you look good enough to eat."

I reach for her, but she waggles a finger playfully. "Not yet."

She wiggles her hips and leads the way to the bedroom.

I don't know what she's up to, but as long as she's wearing that corset, I'm down for anything.

When I round the corner, she's standing at the foot of the bed, feet spread wide, with a leather paddle in her hand.

"I'd like to try something new tonight." She slaps the paddle against her palm and it makes a quiet *thwump*. "Are you game?"

"I—" Christ. Am I game? I've never been into kinky shit.

You've never tried kinky shit.

Same difference.

"I've been a very naughty girl and I want you to punish me, Brady."

A lump forms in my throat. I can't hit a woman.

"I can teach you how to do it." She slaps the paddle against her palm again. "I can teach you how to make it hurt so good."

"You like being spanked?"

Her eyelids fall to half-mast. "I like it very much, but I'd like it even better if you were the one swinging the paddle."

"Can you show me?"

She nods and steps closer, holding the paddle out for inspection. It's the same one I found on her bed before. The one with the word Daddy cut into the leather.

"We'll start slow. We don't have to do anything you're not comfortable with, Brady."

"Okay."

"Would you like to hold it?"

Hell, no. I'm terrified of the thing, but if this is what Piper needs from me, I have to at least try it.

I take the paddle hesitantly, and Piper must sense my apprehension because she places a hand over mine.

"There's no reason to be scared. It's a toy, just like a vibrator or a dildo."

Only this one is meant for causing pain.

I slap it against my palm and the sting barely registers.

"Good." Piper smiles up at me. "You're a natural. Always use the flat side, never the edge."

I nod. "Makes sense."

"Impact play can be a lot of fun when done correctly, but it's important that you know where to strike."

She turns to show me the correct location on her ass and thighs, and I sear the knowledge into my brain. I still don't know if I can do this, but I sure as shit don't want to hurt her by mistake.

"We'll need a safe word." At my puzzled expression, she elaborates. "I don't imagine we'll use it since we're just starting out, but it's better to do it right from the start. My safe word is Pineapple. That's how I'll let you know if I'm feeling uncomfortable or if I want to stop, okay?"

"Pineapple?" I chuckle. "Definitely didn't see that coming."

She grins. "They're sweet and juicy, just like me."

"That they are."

She glances at the paddle in my hand. "Would you like to try it on me?"

I grip the handle tight, feeling the weight of it. No way am I going to use this thing on her until I know how it feels and how to use it correctly.

"I think... I think I'd like you to use it on me first."

Her lips curl into a sultry smile. "Do you have a safe word?"

"Cherry."

Without another word, she takes the paddle from my hand and slaps it against her palm in warning. "Brace your hands on the bed."

I do as I'm told, and she slides my pants down to mid-thigh. My dick is stabbing me in the gut and holy shit, is she going to slap my balls with that paddle?

I shudder at the thought.

"Relax, baby." She caresses my ass cheeks, her touch featherlight as she strokes and massages. It's a new, but not unwelcome sensation. "Do you trust me?"

"With my life."

Piper might want a little spice in the bedroom, but I know she'd never intentionally hurt me.

She swings the paddle, but it doesn't crack against my ass. It's more like a gentle slap and after the light touches, it feels...*good.*

Erotic, even.

She does it again, harder and higher this time, and pleasure radiates from the point of impact.

The third strike is harder still, but she chooses a new spot, and my balls tighten in anticipation.

"Should I keep going or would you like to give it a try?" she purrs.

"I'd like to try." I move to straighten, but she places a hand on my lower back, pinning me in place. "I'm not done with you yet."

She massages my flesh where the paddle struck, making it clear this is an important part of the process. When she finally pulls my pants back up, I'm desperate to get my hands on her.

I lower my mouth to hers, kissing her slow and deep, our tongues doing a familiar dance.

When we finally break apart, her lips are red and swollen, but she's smiling. "How do you want me?"

"Every way possible, but I'll settle for your hands on the bed and your ass in the air—for now."

She plants her hands on the bed and the little showoff

spreads her legs wide, all but doing a split across the end. Her ass calls to me and if it weren't for the thin scrap of damp fabric covering her pussy, I'd have the perfect view.

"You have been a naughty girl." I crack the paddle against my palm. "Your panties are already wet. Is that for me, or were you playing before I arrived?"

"Why can't it be both?"

I slap her ass with the paddle, surprising both of us. "Sorry."

"Don't apologize for making me feel good." She turns to look at me over her shoulder. "Do it again."

I bring the paddle down on her ass, more gently this time, and when the flesh reddens, I massage it gently.

"Again," she pleads, wiggling her hips.

I repeat the motion and she whimpers.

"Relax, Brady. I'm a big girl. I can take it." She glances at me over her shoulder and our eyes lock. "I'm not going to break."

On the fourth strike, the paddle cracks against her backside and when I pull it away, the word Daddy is imprinted on her ass.

Fuck. That's actually hot.

"You know, I think I'm going to need one of these with my name on it."

"That can be arranged," she murmurs, rolling her hips.

Her panties are so wet now, they glisten under the light. I lean down and lick her right up the center before I pepper kisses across the tender flesh of her ass. By the time I'm done, she's all but writhing underneath me.

"Don't move." I grab a condom from my wallet, shove my pants down, and roll it over my length. When I return to the bed, Piper's exactly as I left her, face down, ass up, legs spread impossibly wide. "How attached are you to these panties?"

She makes an unintelligible sound and I rip the sides, letting them drop to the floor.

Then I position my cock at her entrance and drive into her.

She whimpers and I start to withdraw, but her pussy clamps down on me and I remember what she said about the good hurt.

"You like that, darlin'?"

She nods, her hair spilling over the comforter.

"Are you ready to be a good girl now?"

She nods again and I begin to move. Tension coils at the base of my spine and as our hips crash together, the sound of slapping flesh fills the room. She's so damn wet I can hear the slippery slide of my cock filling her and it's the most erotic thing I've ever experienced.

My balls tighten and I increase the pace, pushing us both closer to release as Piper slips a hand between her legs and touches herself.

Jesus Christ. The woman is going to kill me.

Sweat beads along my brow and I will myself not to come. To wait for her.

The orgasm strikes hard and fast and my muscles tense as I bury myself so deep in her pussy I don't know where I end and she begins. Piper cries out, my name on her lips as release takes her over the sweet cliff into oblivion.

After, we lay in bed, her head on my chest and her leg draped across mine.

"You know." I wrap a lock of her hair around my fist. "You still haven't shown me the video you made the night we met. I'd like to see it."

"Now?"

"Hell yeah." I slap her ass with my bare hand. "It's going to help get me ready for round two and this time, I want you to ride my face like a good girl."

30

PIPER

THE SUN WARMS my face and I burrow under the covers, my body aching in the best possible way.

Last night was... I don't even have words for it. I wasn't sure how Brady would feel about impact play, but he took to it like a fish to water and he seemed to enjoy himself.

Maybe I'll get him a paddle with his name on it for Christmas.

I reach for him, but his side of the bed is empty.

What the hell?

I bolt upright, panic flooding my system. Did he slip out after I fell asleep?

Shit. He was probably freaked out about the paddle. It was too soon. I should have waited.

There's a thump in the living room and I spring out of bed. I'm down the hall in an instant. I find Brady leaning up against the apartment door, trying to tie his shoe.

"Sorry." He flashes me an apologetic smile. "I was trying not to wake you."

My heart slams against my ribcage.

"You were sneaking out."

Like every guy Nora ever brought home...

"No." He straightens. "I have an errand to run and I wanted to let you sleep in. We were up so late last night and you've been working so hard lately. I figured you deserved it."

I cross my arms over my flimsy t-shirt, searching his face for signs of deception.

"Since you're up, why don't you come with me? There's someone I'd like you to meet."

I dress quickly and then we head out, but Brady refuses to tell me where we're going or why we need to stop for groceries.

"You remember I don't like surprises, right?" I tease, as we make our way down College Ave. It's a brisk morning and I pull my coat tighter around myself as the wind whips by.

"Don't think of it as a surprise." He flashes me a feral grin. "Think of it as a new experience. If I remember correctly, you're very much into those.

No lies detected.

Just the memory of last night has my pussy doing the Mambo.

When we reach the corner of Pullman, Brady stops and looks around.

Then he grabs my hand and leads me across the street to where a homeless man is sitting on a bench, watching traffic.

"Hey, Marty."

The man looks up at us and it takes a few seconds for recognition to dawn, but when it does, a grin spreads over his face. "I didn't realize it was Sunday already."

"Yeah, sorry I'm late. I slept in a little today." He drops the shopping bags on the bench. "I brought you some sandwiches and there's someone I'd like you to meet." He gestures to me. "Marty, this is my girlfriend, Piper."

It's the first time he's used the G-word and my belly flips

hearing it on his lips.

"Piper, this is my buddy, Marty."

Marty's smile widens. "Good for you. It's about time you met a nice girl. Now you can spend your time with her and stop worrying about an old man like me."

Brady chuckles. "I can do both."

His gaze falls to Marty's bare hands, and he pats himself down, feeling his jacket pockets.

"How's the weather been treating you?"

"Lost my damn gloves, but I'll be okay." Marty shrugs. "We've had colder winters."

"Take these." Brady produces a pair of gloves and hands them to the other man. "I've got an extra pair."

Any doubt I had that Brady has the biggest heart of any person I've ever met is officially extinguished. I can't believe I actually thought he was bailing on me this morning.

Now that I know what he was really doing, I feel like an even bigger asshole.

Because while I was burrowing under the covers like a prairie dog, he was planning a supply run for his homeless friend.

The man is a freaking saint.

We chat for a few more minutes and after the guys say their goodbyes, Brady and I walk to The Diner for breakfast.

"How long have you been friends with Marty?"

He rakes a hand through his hair, leaving it sticking up at odd angles. "We met my first year at Waverly. For the last three years, I've been bringing him supplies every Sunday. I can't do as much as I'd like, but the guy is a veteran and he deserves better than what he's got."

"Doesn't he have family or anyone who could take him in?"

Brady shakes his head. "He's struggling with his mental

health. I don't know if his challenges were exacerbated by his time in the military or the result of it, but he's been estranged from his family for as long as I've known him."

"That's really sad."

"Frustrating is what it is." He shoves his hands in the pockets of his jacket. "I've tried to get him into a shelter, but he won't go and the one time he did, he didn't stay."

"You're worried about him."

He nods. "I don't know what's going to happen to him when I'm gone."

I stop mid-stride, placing a hand on his forearm. "I love that you have such a big heart, and it's clear you care about Marty, but it's not your job to protect everyone you meet."

He pulls a face.

"I'm serious, Brady. You're one man. A damn good one, but even you can't fix all the world's problems. Mental health crises and homelessness are community issues." At least, that's what my therapist says. "Have you considered having one of the younger guys on the team check in on him when you graduate?"

He blinks.

Because it's never occurred to him that someone else might shoulder the burden.

Brady's been looking out for his mom and grandmother since he was twelve. It's no surprise that protective streak extends to everyone in his life.

"I can't believe I never thought of that." He scrubs a hand over his face. "It's a great idea. Hell, maybe the guys could even take turns."

"You should talk to them."

"I will." He pulls me close and tucks me under his arm as we approach The Diner. "Right after breakfast. You're going to need your strength for what I have planned later."

31

PIPER

I STARE up at Fenicci's, willing my feet to move. The restaurant is a cozy Italian place with a red and white awning and the old-world charm you rarely see these days.

If you don't get your ass in gear, you're going to be late.

Not a good look for meeting the parents.

Or, rather, the mom and grandmother.

It's Senior Day for the football team and Waverly defeated Maryland, finishing the regular season 11-1. Before the game, all the seniors were escorted onto the field by their families and recognized for their contributions to the team. Brady's mom and grandmother escorted him and they insisted I join them for dinner, but I don't know how I'm supposed to eat when my stomach is tangled in knots.

Not eating won't look half as bad as showing up late...

What about vomiting in my purse? How will that look?

I shudder. I've never had a *meet the parents* moment in my life and I'm woefully unprepared. Growing up with Nora, I didn't exactly get an education in manners.

Just do the damn thing.

I open the door and the scent of garlic and fresh bread wafts out, instantly putting me at ease.

The hostess greets me with a wide smile and when I give her Brady's name, she leads me to a table in the back.

I spot Brady first, and the sight of him soothes my frazzled nerves. He's sitting in a booth with his arm draped over the back. The top button of his shirt is undone and his sleeves are rolled up to reveal his muscular forearms. He's chatting animatedly with his family, but when his eyes meet mine, his entire face lights up.

My heart skips a beat and I nearly trip over a wayward purse strap that's laying in the aisle.

Real smooth, Piper.

He stands to greet me and drops a kiss on my forehead before he turns to the two women sitting on the other side of the booth.

"Piper, this is my mom, Molly Vaughn, and this is my gran, Janice Vaughn."

Brady warned me ahead of time that since his mother and father never married, they all bear his grandmother's last name, which works well for the family business.

"It's so nice to meet you." I offer my hand to his mother and grandmother in turn. "Brady's told me so much about you both."

"Then I assume he told you about our care packages?" Gran asks, smiling broadly as we slide into the booth.

Brady stiffens beside me and when I glance over, his eyes are about to bug out of his head.

"He did, and he even shared the contents with me once or twice."

Gran chuckles, accentuating the laugh lines around her eyes and mouth. "I'll bet he did."

Brady makes a choking noise and I can't help but feel like

I'm on the wrong side of a joke, but Molly looks as confused as I feel.

"The pumpkin chocolate chip cookies were wonderful. I'd love to learn how to bake like that someday."

His mother smiles warmly. "Thank you. It's one of my favorite recipes."

The server comes over to take our drink orders and then we spend a few minutes scanning the menu. Everything sounds delicious and even though my nerves are fading, I still opt for soup and salad, just to be on the safe side. The server returns with our drinks and we place our order.

"So, Piper." Molly swirls her wine as she studies me, and I do the same. Brady is the spitting image of his mother, though she's far more petite and doesn't have a beard. "Brady tells us you're an education major. What age group do you hope to teach?"

It's a simple question and I'm grateful for it. I could talk about education all day, and if we're talking about my major, we're not talking about my family or my crappy upbringing.

"My specialty is elementary education. I love working with children and I feel like that's where I can make the greatest impact."

The conversation is easy and there's never an awkward lapse, even when our food arrives. Brady's mom and grandmother are warm and welcoming. I can see why they remain such a close-knit family, and the familiar tug of envy creeps in as my phone rings.

I curse myself for not putting it on silent. It's in my bag under the table, so maybe if I ignore it, everyone else will, too.

I'm hardly Miss Manners, but even I know it's rude to answer your phone at the dinner table.

Molly sips her wine as she studies her son. "Well, I can't wait to have you home for the holiday break."

"It won't be much of a break if we win the conference championship next week," he cautions. "If we clinch the Big Ten, we'll definitely pull a bowl game."

He doesn't have to say it, but we all know the best bowl games are on New Year's Day, so Coach Collins will want his players back on campus by the twenty-sixth or twenty-seventh.

That's what Brady told me, anyway.

"What are your plans for the holidays, Piper?"

Heat floods my cheeks. I can't tell this woman, who lives in a multigenerational home, that my mother and I aren't on speaking terms and there's no point going home because she'll just spend the day at the bar, anyway.

Talk about a mood killer.

My phone pings with an incoming text and I force a smile. "I'm going to stay on campus this year. I'm student teaching in the spring, so it will give me extra time to prep."

"You're spending Christmas alone?" Gran frowns. "No, that won't do. Come home with Brady and spend the holidays with us at Willow Bend."

My heart squeezes at the generous offer and it's on the tip of my tongue to say yes, but I shake my head instead.

"I couldn't possibly impose on you."

Besides, if Brady wanted me there, he would have asked. I can't just bogart his family holiday. That's not how this works, is it?

My phone pings again because apparently one of my ten contacts has the patience of a toddler.

"Don't be silly." Molly clasps her son's hand on the table. "We'd love to have you, wouldn't we, Brady?"

He grins, revealing that irresistible dimple. "I can't think of a better way to spend the holiday than celebrating with my three best girls."

My heart melts just a little because I know he means every

word, and there's nowhere I'd rather be on Christmas than at his side.

"That settles it then." Gran claps her hands together. "Piper is spending Christmas at Willow Bend."

An enormous smile splits my face, but I couldn't suppress it if I tried. I can't remember the last time I was actually excited about Christmas, and the prospect of spending it with Brady's family is almost too good to be true.

My phone pings—again—and Molly turns to me, brows knit in concern. "That sounds important. Why don't you at least check it?" She smiles encouragingly. "The only time I message Brady like that is when it's an emergency."

I grab my bag from under the table and dig out my phone. The odds of it being an emergency are slim, unless you count Nora going on a bender an emergency, which I don't.

There are three unread text messages, in addition to the missed call.

Unknown: We need to talk

Unknown: Don't ignor me curvygirl

My stomach drops, the excitement from just moments ago evaporating like water in the Sahara.

Unknown: The clock is tocking...

It's Mike. It has to be. How the hell did he get my number?

And more importantly, what does he want?

"Everything okay?" Brady asks quietly.

"Yeah." I force a smile before looking up to meet his stare. "I just need to make a quick call. I'm really sorry, but it won't take long."

I excuse myself from the table and step outside the restaurant. It's bitterly cold and snow flurries float on the wind, but I won't risk being overheard by Brady or his family.

His mom would probably rescind her invitation if she knew the mess I was in.

I pull up my call log and redial the last missed number.

Mike picks up on the first ring. "Iss about time."

Jesus. Is he drunk?

That would certainly explain the texts...

"How did you get my number?"

He snickers. "WildcatPATH. Obviously."

Just when I thought he couldn't sink any lower, he goes and proves me wrong. Because of course he'd abuse his system access.

"What do you want?"

For the last four weeks, he hasn't even acknowledged me in class, so why is he drunk dialing me now?

"I need you to transfer three thousand dollars to my Venmo."

My blood runs cold. "You're unhinged. I already gave you five thousand dollars."

"That was before my laptop crapped out." He snickers. "I've got my eye on a new MacBook and those things aren't cheap."

No shit. It's why I use a PC.

"I don't have the money," I bite out, clenching my phone so hard it's a wonder the screen doesn't crack.

"Bullshit."

"It's true." I haven't been filming as much because I've been busy with Brady, but I can't exactly say that. The last thing I want to do is drag him into my mess. "If you think it's so easy to make money, start your own channel."

Surely there must be a market for rich women who enjoy entitled white dudes with big egos and small dicks...

"Why would I whore myself out when I've got a cash cow at the end of my leash?"

Red-hot fury tears through my veins, but I bite it back.

Antagonizing him will only escalate the situation. I'll have to take the money from my savings. There's no other choice.

"This has to stop." I speak slowly to ensure his alcohol-soaked brain receives the message. "These large payments aren't sustainable. If this keeps up, I won't be able to pay my bills."

"That's hardly my problem. I want my money by Friday or Barnes gets an anonymous email."

He disconnects and I inhale deeply, filling my lungs with icy air. I need to calm down before I return to the table. If Brady senses I'm upset, he'll push until he gets the truth out of me, and I can't allow that to happen.

This is my problem and I'm the one who has to deal with it.

I'll transfer the money from my savings account in the morning and then I'll have to ramp up my cam schedule. It's the only way to stay afloat, and judging by tonight's call, I'm going to be stuck with Mike, at least until I graduate.

32

BRADY

"It's just another mile or so."

Piper nods and carefully steers her old Honda around the last turn in the road. A sign for Willow Bend appears and I do a double take when I see the words *Live Music* and *Santa's Petting Zoo.*

"What the hell?" I crane my neck to get another look, but it's too late.

"What's wrong?" Piper's gaze shifts to me for a beat before returning to the road.

"The sign. Someone changed it."

She shrugs. "Maybe it was time for an update."

Maybe... Or maybe I'm imagining things because I'm so amped about having an entire week to do nothing but spend time with Piper and my family.

Enjoy it while it lasts.

We clinched the Big Ten conference last week and we're headed to Atlanta to face off with Clemson in the CFP semi-finals on New Year's Eve.

We're so close to the championship game I can taste it.

"Is this the turn?" Piper asks, gesturing to the gravel path that leads up to the farm. Colorful lights have been strung along the fence on either side of the road and there's a new welcome sign declaring Willow Bend a Winter Wonderland.

"This is it." Anticipation floods my chest. "You're going to love Willow Bend."

I haven't been home since August and I've missed the fresh air and open space. I roll the window down and inhale deeply. It's chilly, but not nearly as cold as Central Pennsylvania.

Perfect conditions for a stroll across the property.

I can't wait to show Piper the farm. Winter isn't exactly the ideal time to discover all the land has to offer, but something tells me she'll love it, anyway.

We make our way up the drive, which is lined with signs I've never seen before.

Santa's Petting Zoo

Hot Cider & Cocoa

Pictures with Santa

Sleigh Rides

Piper glances at the colorful holiday signs. "I thought your family wasn't involved in agritourism."

"They're not. Or, at least, they weren't when I left for school in August."

We pull up to the house—an old white colonial—and I don't believe my eyes.

There are more Christmas lights than a Walmart seasonal display and greenery covers every available surface.

What the hell is going on? The farm looks nothing like I remember. It's unsettling.

Change is good.

Yeah, unless your childhood home becomes unrecognizable.

"I need to find my mom and Gran."

We park in front of the house and when we let ourselves in

through the kitchen door, we're greeted by the scent of cookies baking in the oven. It's a familiar, comforting scent and I'm immediately brought back to my childhood.

At least some things haven't changed.

Mom pops into the kitchen, lighter than I've seen her in ages. "Brady, I wish you would have called ahead. We would have turned all the Christmas lights on for you."

"There are more?"

She can't be serious. Is she trying to ensure the farm is visible from the moon? If so, mission accomplished.

Mom ignores that and turns to Piper. "It's so nice to see you again, dear."

"Thank you for inviting me." Piper grins. "Your property is gorgeous. Everything was so festive coming up the drive."

"Speaking of which." I spread my arms wide, encompassing...*everything*. "What is going on around here?"

Mom laughs. "We wanted to surprise you, but we didn't realize you'd be getting in so early."

I huff a breath. "Oh, I'm definitely surprised."

She steps in to give me a hug and when she wraps her arms around me like she used to do when I was little, my apprehension fades. "Let me fix a plate of cookies and we can talk."

I sit down at the kitchen table, but Piper hovers near the door.

"I'm going to take a walk, if that's all right, so you can have some privacy."

"Piper, darlin', there's no need for you to take a walk. We don't keep secrets in this house."

Her eyes widen and she worries her lower lip, but when mom offers her a chocolate chip cookie, she relents and joins me at the table. "If you're sure..."

"I'm sure." I rest my hand on top of hers. "I'd just tell you whatever we discuss anyway, so you might as well hear it firsthand."

Mom sits down opposite Piper and me and places the cookies in the center of the table.

"Your grandmother and I wanted to surprise you, but I suppose the cat is out of the bag now."

My palms begin to sweat. "Surprise me with what, exactly?

"We're bringing your vision to life with... What did you call it?" She snaps her fingers. "Agritourism."

For a moment, I'm shocked speechless. "You read my business plan?"

It's impossible to keep the surprise from my voice. I'd all but given up hope mom and Gran would consider additional revenue streams, and now they're just out here making it happen without even telling me?

It's insulting.

"Your Gran and I both read the business plan, and we agreed it was worth the risk, so we created a Winter Wonderland to bring in new guests and give the idea a test run."

I've been so busy with football and school and Piper; I haven't looked at the farm's social media accounts in months. If I had, I probably would've figured out what was going on sooner.

The realization lands like a blow.

For all my talk of stepping up, I've been painfully absent.

"Why didn't you tell me?"

Because they didn't need you. They've got everything under control.

That they purposefully excluded me hurts more than I want to admit. It's been the three of us against the world for the last decade and now I'm being shut out.

She reaches across the table and takes my hand. "We

didn't tell you because we wanted to see if the idea had legs, but more importantly, we wanted you to enjoy your last year at school without the burden of the farm hanging over your head." She smiles, but it's tired. "Running this farm is a big responsibility. It's a lot of stress and a little income. The world has changed and farming isn't as viable as it once was."

"No one gets into farming for the money. They do it because they love it."

"Or because it's all they know," she counters. "I didn't want that for you. I wanted you to go to school so that if you chose this life, it was a choice, not an outdated legacy established by your great-great-grandfather."

My gut clenches. I get what she's saying, but I don't have to like it.

Maybe the farm is all I've ever known, but it's all I ever want to know. I can't imagine doing anything else with my life or raising a family any other way. I love my life.

"We let you take on too much responsibility from a young age, and for that, I'm sorry. We should have let you be a child."

"There's no need to apologize." I rub my palms against my thighs. "I wanted to be involved. I wanted to be the man of the house. To look after you and Gran, just like Pops wanted."

She presses her lips flat. "If he asked that of you, he was wrong. I love my father, but he was stuck in his ways."

I snort and she holds up a hand. "I know, but I'm working on it."

Piper laughs and quickly slaps a hand over her mouth.

Mom isn't the only one set in her ways.

"Point taken," I concede, shooting Piper a wry grin.

"Brady, your Gran and I are so proud of you. When you graduate, if you want to move back to Willow Bend and work the land, we're prepared to make you an equal partner with full responsibility for establishing and managing the agritourism arm of the business."

My pulse quickens and I'm sure I misheard. "Did you say equal partner?"

She grins. "Yes, and I also said you'd be responsible for everything relating to agritourism. Your Gran and I are limping along, but it feels like a young person's business."

"I— Of course it's what I want. It's what I've always wanted."

"Good." She gives a firm nod. "As the current majority owner, I'm going to need you to show your commitment to this expansion by taking on some of your duties immediately."

I lean forward, eager to get started. "Sure. What do you need me to do?"

"Put on the Santa suit and run the photo booth tonight. My regular Santa got grounded for breaking curfew."

Piper snort-laughs and I join in because what the hell.

"Oh, and Piper, dear? I need an elf as well." She pauses, tilting her head thoughtfully. "Unless, of course, you'd rather play Mrs. Claus tonight?"

33

PIPER

"WE'RE GOING TO DO WHAT?"

Brady grins and hooks his thumbs in his belt loops. He's dressed like a freaking lumberjack in a plaid button up, work boots, and a dark knit cap. It's sexy as hell. "We're going to cut down a Christmas tree. It's tradition. We do it every year on Christmas Eve."

I leap out of the bed and launch myself at him. "Give me twenty minutes. No, fifteen. I can be ready in fifteen for sure."

He chuckles. "There's no rush. We've got all day to find it and then we'll decorate it tonight."

How is this even my life right now?

The last few days at Willow Bend have been incredible. Molly has treated me like family from the start, right down to that stunt she pulled with the elf costume. Joke's on her, though. This elf got railed by Santa Claus in the hayloft and loved every second.

It's been so much fun pitching in at the Winter Wonderland and brainstorming ideas with Brady for next year. It's been low stress and low drama and even though

Christmas isn't until tomorrow, I already know it's going to be my best one yet.

Thirty minutes later, my teeth are brushed, my hair is combed, and I'm standing in the middle of a Christmas tree forest inhaling the glorious scent of pine.

"I've never had an actual tree before. How do we choose?" I shove my hands in the pockets of my jacket and turn to Brady. "Are there any special requirements I should know about?"

"Nope. You just pick the best one you can find or, in a pinch, the one that calls to you."

"So just to be clear, you're saying I can pick any tree I want and you'll be cool with it?"

He slips his arms around my waist and pulls me to his chest. "Darlin', if it makes you happy, it makes me happy."

Warmth pools low in my belly and I stretch up on my toes to brush a kiss across his lips. "Let's go find our Christmas tree."

We walk up and down the rows and Brady points out pines and firs and even a spruce, but none of them speak to me.

"We're getting pretty close to the end." He stops to admire a fat little tree with symmetrical branches and deep green needles. "How about this one?"

I study it, scrunching my nose as I check it from every angle. "Nope."

Brady frowns and cocks his head, looking for the imperfection. "What's wrong with it?"

"There's nothing wrong with it, but there's nothing right either, you know?"

He shakes his head, but he's smiling. "I really don't."

"I just want to find the perfect tree for our first Christmas together."

He slips up behind me and circles me with his arms,

guiding me to the next row. "I hate to burst your bubble, but there's no such thing as the perfect tree."

I twist out of his grip and stick my tongue out at him. "You're entitled to your opinion, even if it's wrong."

"Oh, yeah?" There's a predatory glint in his eyes, and when he narrows them, I bolt.

Brady gives chase, but I weave through the trees, doing my best to lose him.

Or stay out of reach.

Or give him a little thrill.

Even I'm not sure what my goal is by the time I reach the edge of the field, chest heaving. I spin around looking for him, but he's nowhere to be seen.

Where the hell did he go? He was right behind me a second ago.

I creep forward, peering down the next row of trees, but there's still no sign of him, so I move to the next row.

By the fourth row, I'm certain he's hiding from me and when I reach the fifth and he jumps out from behind a massive fir, I shriek like a banshee. He grabs me around the waist and lifts me off my feet, spinning me around.

That's when I spot it.

The perfect tree.

"That's it! That's the one."

I point to it and Brady smirks as he sets me back on my feet. "Seriously?"

"Does this look like the face of a trickster?" I demand, pointing to my face. "So it's a little lopsided. It'll be fine."

"Did you see the bald spot?" He points at the empty patch.

"It's nothing that can't be fixed with an ornament or five."

He pulls me close and lowers his forehead to mine. "You always did like an underdog."

"See? You get it." I beam at him. "Perfection is in the eye of the beholder."

"You're damn right it is." He captures my mouth, kissing me hard and deep and when his tongue sweeps over mine, I moan, and he takes that too, swallowing it down as we lose ourselves in the moment.

When we finally come up for air, Brady cuts down the tree with a saw and then we drag it to the truck and load it up.

Molly and Gran are waiting when we get back to the farm and they rush outside to get a first look.

Brady hauls the tree down from the truck and stands it upright in the grass. For a long moment, no one speaks and my anxiety kicks into overdrive.

They hate it. I'll never be invited back for Christmas.

Or if I am, I won't be allowed to choose the tree.

"I like it," Gran finally announces. "It has character."

"It'll fit perfectly in the corner of the living room," Molly adds, clapping her hands together. "Brady, you get the tree set up in the stand and we'll get the ornaments."

He salutes and I trail Molly indoors, grabbing a chocolate chip cookie as I pass through the kitchen.

Brady makes quick work of the tree stand and when we return to the living room, it smells like Christmas. Molly puts on a holiday record and I help her unpack the ornaments. Most of them are homemade, and she tells me the story behind each one.

"Brady made this one in first grade," she says, holding up a snowman that looks to be standing on a milk crate.

"I remember that one," Gran chimes in, laughing. "He was worried Frosty would melt, so he gave him an ice tray to catch all the water for refreezing."

Brady's cheeks flush, but he just picks another ornament and puts it on the tree.

I sidle up behind him and wrap my arms around his waist. "I think it's safe to say your protective streak started early."

He huffs a laugh. "Was there ever any doubt?"

"Not even a little."

It may be frustrating at times, but it's also one of his best qualities. When Brady loves, he loves hard. There's nothing wrong with wanting to keep the people you care about safe from harm, even if they're fictitious.

"Oh, you have to see this one, Piper." Molly offers me a green foam wreath with a picture of Brady in the middle. He's probably only three or four, but he's giving big cheese, showing all his teeth. It's the cutest freaking thing I've ever seen.

Emotion clogs my throat as I hand the ornament back.

"Thank you so much for having me, Ms. Va—Molly. I've had a wonderful time, and it means so much to me to be included in your holiday traditions."

More than she could possibly know since my family never really had any of its own, unless you count spending Christmas at the bar, which I don't.

"Of course. We're so happy to have you here and you're welcome back any time."

I'm not sure how to respond, though I hope I can take her up on that offer someday. I grab another ornament and as I'm placing it on the tree, my phone vibrates in my back pocket.

I pull it out to check the message and when I see Nora's name on the screen, I shut the phone off without reading it.

Nothing is going to ruin my perfect Christmas.

34

PIPER

I save my lesson plan and check the clock in the lower right corner of my screen. It's 4:58 p.m. A whole ten minutes have passed since I last checked the time.

Go me.

It's Sunday afternoon and I'm supposed to be working on lesson plans because I start student teaching next week, but my brain is refusing to focus, so instead, I'm sitting on my couch obsessively checking the clock. The CFP championship game is tomorrow and even though I told Brady I didn't want to go, that I couldn't afford it, I can't stop thinking about his invitation.

It's too late.

Even if I wanted to go, I probably couldn't get a flight. Or a hotel room. Or hell, even a ticket.

It's just nerves making me second-guess my choice. That or I'm missing Brady.

He left for Miami yesterday with the rest of the team and though he didn't say it, he must be nervous.

Hell, I'm nervous for him.

Not only will the Wildcats be playing for millions of

viewers tomorrow night, they're up against a fifteen-year drought.

The pressure they're under is...intense.

Brady's been putting in extra time with Coach Walker ever since he returned from the Peach Bowl, so we haven't seen each other much this week, but he promised that win or lose, things will settle down when he gets back from Miami. With all the extra practice sessions, he's been staying at his place since it's closer to the football building and though I miss having him in my bed, the break has allowed me to record extra sessions for my Fangirl page.

I haven't been able to completely rebuild my savings after paying off Mike McConnell, but I've scraped together enough to cover my expenses for the spring semester. Even if I only record one or two sessions a week until graduation, I should have a small nest egg to keep me afloat until I secure a teaching position.

Assuming it doesn't take more than a few months.

My phone vibrates on the couch next to me and Jenna's name appears on the screen.

I swipe accept and bring it to my ear. "What's up?"

"Are you watching ESPN? They're doing a whole segment on the Wildcats and Brady's up next."

"What channel?" I flip the tv on, giving silent thanks cable is included in the rent.

"Thirty-two. Hurry!"

I punch in the numbers on the remote and a pretty Black sportscaster materializes on-screen. She's standing on the floor of what must be Hard Rock Stadium.

"Ken, I had the pleasure of speaking with Waverly's quiet left tackle earlier today, and here's what he had to say."

The screen cuts to a pre-recorded clip of Brady. He's

dressed in his practice uniform and there's dirt smeared across his right hip, but he looks good.

"Damn, girl. I cannot believe you're sleeping with that man." Jenna sighs loudly. "Have I mentioned how fine he is?"

I laugh and even though she's ogling my boyfriend, I can't be mad about it. "I think you may have mentioned it once or twice."

The sportscaster shoves a microphone in Brady's face and asks him how he's feeling heading into the big game.

"I feel good." He rubs the back of his neck, giving America a dose of the boy next door charm that made me fall so hard. It's usually Austin Reid and Cooper DeLaurentis who get face time, but with the hype leading up to the game, it's no surprise the networks are broadening their coverage. "We've been working hard all season. The team is healthy, and spirits are high. The Bulldogs are going to give us a run for our money, but we're ready."

Brady isn't used to being on camera, but he's hiding it well. There's a nervous flush to his cheeks, but the casual observer would probably write it off as too much sun or exertion from practice.

"Do you have any words for Wildcat Nation or for your family at home?"

"I want to thank the fans for their unwavering support these last four seasons. It's been an incredible ride and though this will be the last game I ever play for Waverly, I'll always be a Wildcat in here." He claps a hand over his heart and I just know there must be women swooning all over campus. "I'd also like to thank my mom and my grandmother for always believing in me and challenging me to show up and give it my all. I wouldn't be where I am today without them." Brady looks straight into the camera, and it's like he's speaking directly to me. "And Piper, darlin', if you're watching, I miss you like crazy and after we win that title, I'll be on the first plane home so we can celebrate together."

Holy. Crap.

This cannot be my life.

I'm having an auditory hallucination. With heart palpitations.

It's far more logical than my sweet, adorable boyfriend promising to win a national title so he can hop the first jet back to me.

Jenna squeals, damn near shattering my eardrum, and I realize that no, this really is my life.

When she finally gets control of herself, she turns her attention back to me. "Remind me again why you aren't in Miami?"

"I can't afford it, and I don't want Brady paying my way."

She snorts. "So, basically money and pride."

It sounds far less noble when she puts it like that. "Yes."

"*Giiirl.*"

The way she drags the word out lets me know I'm in for it. "What?"

"Sometimes you are so clueless it's scary."

"I am not clueless." About most things, anyway.

"Why do you think Brady offered to buy your plane ticket?" Jenna asks, using her patient classroom voice.

"Because I couldn't afford it and he felt bad for me."

"Uh, uh." The way she says it makes it clear she thinks I'm way off base. "You're looking at this all wrong."

"I am not—"

"And before you go getting all defensive," she says, cutting me off. "Can we please acknowledge that he didn't invite you as some sort of favor, but because he wants you there for emotional support?"

"I—" *Could that be true?* Brady's played more games than I

can count, and he's done just fine without me. "Do you really think that's why he invited me?"

She doesn't miss a beat. "I know. High school volleyball player, remember?"

Okay, so Jenna has more experience in this area than me. I was too busy working to be a joiner. Even if I had played a sport, Nora never would have shown up to cheer me on.

"I'm sure he's fine." I am nothing if not stubborn and I refuse to believe I'm really this clueless when it comes to guys. After all, I read my online fans just fine. "His mom and grandmother will be there."

"That's great, hon, but he's in love with you and he wants you there, too."

"Technically, he hasn't actually said he loves me."

He always stops just short of saying the words.

Jenna groans. "He doesn't have to. He's shown you. Hello?" She barely pauses to breathe. "The man got a tattoo for you. He's probably just waiting for you to catch up. If you love him, which I think you do, you need to tell him."

I shake my head, though she can't possibly see it. "I can't."

"You can."

"It's…" What's the easiest way to say coward? "My mom and her myriad of sleazy boyfriends threw the word love around like confetti, but it never lasted."

"Based on what you've told me, they didn't know the meaning of the word," she says gently. "I hate that your mom has screwed up your perception of relationships so badly, but if there's anyone who can help you heal from the trauma, it's Brady. He's a good guy, Piper, and he loves you."

She's right. The man is patient beyond belief and for everything he gives me—love, support, *orgasms*—he asks for nothing in return.

"Sweetie, I'm saying this with love because I know you

don't have a lot of experience with relationships, but get your ass to Miami and tell that man how you feel!"

I pick at a loose thread on the couch, considering. "It's not that simple."

"Yes, it is. You guys can figure out the rest later. Together."

Could it really be that easy?

I've spent the entire fall semester keeping Brady at arm's length and now I'm supposed to just hand over my heart?

You can't give him something he already owns.

It's true. No matter how hard my brain tries to deny it, no matter how many times I tell myself I'm not falling, in the four months we've known each other, Brady's won me over in a million little ways.

"Win or lose, he's going to need you tomorrow," she says, unrelenting. "If you don't go, you're going to regret it."

She's right. I've made a lot of mistakes in my life, but this is one I can still avoid if I act quickly.

I can't use the money I've set aside for this semester's living expenses, but I could use my emergency credit card. If I do a few extra shoots over the next few months, I'll probably be able to pay it down.

Or you'll graduate with no savings and no money for a new apartment.

Fucking Mike McConnell.

I wouldn't be in this position if it weren't for him. In just a few short months, that asshole has bled me dry and forced me to film personalized content I never would have accepted if I wasn't so hard up for cash.

You should have just told Brady what was going on.

No. The TA is my problem. Brady has enough on his mind without me piling on.

"So?" Jenna prods, bringing me back to the conversation. "What are you going to do?"

I know what I will not do, and that's let Brady down.

"I've got to go, Jenna. I need to make travel arrangements."

Even if Brady's mom no longer has an extra ticket, I can go to Miami for moral support.

My bestie squeals. "I knew you'd make the right decision."

Whether it's the right decision or not remains to be seen, but I've made up my mind and I'm going to see this plan through.

35

BRADY

It's Sunday afternoon and we just wrapped up our last practice before the championship game tomorrow. The guys on the team are feeling bullish, despite the fact that Georgia's grabbed two national titles in the last five years and we haven't seen one in over a decade.

"Listen up!" Coach Collins hollers. He's standing at the front of the locker room, surrounded by the rest of the coaching staff, his trusty clipboard in hand. "That was a good practice today. You guys,"—he cuts his gaze to Carter—"and gals have played your hearts out this season. In all my years of coaching, I've never had a more talented, more hardworking team than the one that stands before me today."

Shouts of "*Damn right!*" and "*Hell yeah!*" fill the air, along with the thump of a few helmets.

"You all play tomorrow like you played today, and we'll bring that title home for Wildcat Nation. You've put in the work. Despite what those assholes in Vegas say, we've got what it takes to upset Georgia and send the Dawgs home with their tails between their legs."

This time, the entire locker room fills with shouts and

thumps as the guys around me bang on their helmets and benches. The raucous goes on far longer than it should, but no one's ever accused us of being a restrained group.

"All right." Coach motions for us to bring it down a notch or ten. "Save it for tomorrow. You're going to need all the energy you've got, which is why I want everyone showered and back to their rooms by 8 p.m. No exceptions." He scans the locker room, doing his damnedest to put the fear of God into each of us. "You'll have plenty of time to celebrate after you win the game tomorrow."

"I know that's right!" Smith shouts, pumping his fist in the air.

"I think I speak for the entire coaching staff," Coach Collins says, gesturing to Coach Walker and the others, "when I say I'm proud of what we've accomplished this season, both on and off the field. We overcame injuries." He pauses, and I know I'm not the only one thinking about Spellman's busted leg. "We welcomed new talent." All eyes turn to Carter and she dips her chin in acknowledgement. "We faced a tough loss, and you guys busted your asses on the field and in the classroom to get to this moment. This team has banded together to overcome adversity and we're stronger for it. Tomorrow Georgia's going to see just how strong we are when we step onto that field."

A loud cheer goes up from the team, myself included, and this time, the coaching staff joins in, Coach Walker the loudest of them all.

When the noise dies down, Coach Collins gives us one last look. "Now go get cleaned up, grab some dinner, and get a good night's sleep. Tomorrow's going to be a long day and I don't want to see any of you dragging ass or you'll be—"

"Running laps until we puke!" the team responds in unison.

Coach shakes his head and mutters something that sounds like "Fucking kids," but the corner of his mouth twitches as he stalks out of the room.

The rest of the coaching staff follows, as does Carter, leaving the rest of us to shower and change.

I strip off my jersey on autopilot, Piper occupying my thoughts just like she has every other spare minute of this trip. I missed her so damn bad during the semi-final game in Atlanta. It sucks that she can't be here for the championship game either.

Money's tight, I get that, but I figured with all the extra cam sessions she's been doing, she might have the spare cash.

Hell, I would've happily paid for the trip from my savings just to have her by my side, but her damn pride wouldn't let her accept. The woman is independent as fuck. It's a blessing and a curse.

This week definitely goes in the curse column.

I've barely seen her since Christmas and even though it's only been two weeks, it feels like an eternity. The only upside is that after I hang up my cleats tomorrow, my schedule will be wide open.

I toss my jersey on the bench and I'm working on my pads when Parker rolls up with a shit-eating grin. "We need to talk."

"About?" I wiggle out of my pads and drop them on the bench, noticing for the first time that all of my roommates are staring at me.

Parker holds up a small sheet of paper, but I can't get a good look at it because his hands are covering the entire thing.

"Hey, Brady!" he reads, doing his best imitation of a female voice. "We really miss you at pole class."

Oh, fuck.

I dive for my bag. The side zipper is open, and I close my eyes, cursing my carelessness.

"Please come back and give us another chance," Parker trills. "Your Fireman spin was getting so good!"

Coop and Reid burst out laughing and flames erupt on my bare chest, spreading up my neck like wildfire.

"It's rude to read other people's mail, asshole."

"How could I resist?" Parker holds the postcard up for the others to see. On the front is a picture of Mai dangling from the pole in some fancy move I couldn't master if I had all the time in the world. "It was just lying on the floor and I wanted to return it to its rightful owner."

"How thoughtful."

I should've thrown the damn thing in the trash, but I was in a hurry, so I shoved it in my bag.

There's a mistake I won't be repeating.

"I need to know more about this pole class," Reid says, peeking over Parker's shoulder to get a better look at the image on the postcard. "Do they train you for exotic dancing or what?"

"Forget the class." Coop smirks. "I want to know if our boy wore booty shorts while he was twirling on the pole." He pauses, giving me a mock serious look. "Is twirling the correct term?"

"As a matter of fact, it's not." I snatch the postcard from Parker and drop it in my bag, careful to secure the zipper properly this time. "And no, I didn't wear booty shorts, fuck you very much."

"Spoilsport. I would've paid good money to see you in a pair of gold lamé hot pants." Coop's eyes go round and he reaches into his locker and withdraws a swatch of metallic gold fabric. "Oh, wait. I did."

He throws the bundle at me and I catch it. Against my better judgment, I hold it up to reveal a pair of—you guessed it—booty shorts.

To his credit, they're a men's style.

Parker nearly falls over laughing and I flip him off.

"I'll give you fifty bucks to try them on," Coop offers.

"Tempting, but I think I'll pass." I hold the shorts out. "If you're so curious, try them on yourself, princess."

"I would, but they're not my size." He grins. "Besides, I'm not a stripper in training."

"For your information, pole isn't just for exotic dancers. It's a sport and you have to be strong as hell to do it."

"Coach would kick your ass if he knew you did that shit." Reid frowns. "Hell, I would have kicked your ass if I'd known about it. It was risky as hell."

No kidding. I don't mention just how close I came to injury.

All's well that ends well.

"I know. That's why I quit."

"Okay, but why did you sign up in the first place?"

"It was the only way I could convince Piper to date me."

"For real?" Reid holds out his fist and I bump it. "Mad respect, brother."

"It was actually kind of fun when I wasn't falling on my face."

"Come on." Coop nudges my shoulder. "You can't say shit like that and not show us something. Give us one move and I swear I'll never bring it up again."

He's full of crap and we both know it.

I'm never going to hear the end of it, but whatever. I'm not ashamed of the lengths I went to in order to score a date with Piper.

"Fine." I toss the shorts in my bag. "You want to see some moves? Give me some music."

Coop pulls out his phone and while he brings up an app, I

walk to the center of the locker room where there's space to move.

A few heads turn my way, but I ignore them.

"Okay!" Coop howls. "Here we go."

The opening notes of *Pony* fill the locker room.

"Really, asshole?"

"What?" He shrugs. "It was good enough for Magic Mike."

I give him the finger and drop into a sitting position with my legs stretched in front of me. I wiggle them mermaid style and as Ginuwine croons about looking for a partner, I transition into a knee spin, which is hell on the carpeted floor. When I lose my momentum, I roll onto my back, fanning my legs the way Mai taught me. My movements aren't nearly as fluid as hers, and there's a real possibility I'm going to split my pants, but I give it my all.

Anything worth doing is worth doing right.

That's what my grandfather always said.

The old man would probably keel over if he could see me now.

So would Piper. She's never going to believe I did this.

A loud cheer goes up from my boys and it occurs to me that one of these assholes is probably filming me, but I'm in it now, the music taking hold.

I pop my hips and thrust into the air, earning a round of applause before I roll onto my knees and arch my back into a bridge.

The music dies and I climb to my feet amid hoots and hollers from the entire team.

"Our boy has skills!" Coop shouts. "Did you see that shit?"

To me he says, "It really would've been better with the shorts, though."

"Give it a rest, DeLaurentis. I'm not wearing the shorts."

Not for him, anyway. I might wear them for Piper.

He shrugs. "Have it your way."

"The real question is this," Reid says loudly. "Are you going to break out those moves after we beat Georgia's ass tomorrow?"

Another raucous cheer goes up from around the locker room and when the noise dies down, all eyes are on me.

For the first time, it hits me that after tomorrow, these guys won't be my teammates anymore. Most of us will never play football again, and even the ones who are lucky enough to get drafted aren't likely to play together.

It's a bittersweet realization.

I always knew this day would come, but I never stopped to consider how I'd feel when it arrived.

"Well?" Reid asks, that million-dollar smile aimed in my direction.

What the hell.

"If we clinch the title tomorrow, I'll give you a show you'll never forget."

36

PIPER

"GET OUT OF THE WAY!"

The cab driver leans on the horn and forces his way into the next lane. I clutch the door handle more tightly, praying I'm not about to become a cautionary tale.

"It's been like this all week." He gestures to the snarling traffic with both hands, and my heart skips a beat. "I'll be glad when this championship game is over."

I give silent thanks I'm not currently wearing Waverly gear. *No need to poke the bear.*

I check the time on my phone. "How much longer do you think it'll take to get to the hotel?"

"If it weren't for this mess, we'd be there already." He drums his fingers on the steering wheel. "Maybe another fifteen or twenty minutes."

Dammit. I'd hoped to surprise Brady at the team hotel, but I'm going to be cutting it close.

Too close.

There weren't many flight options and the early departure was twice as much as the afternoon one, so I decided to chance it, which was clearly the wrong decision.

Where are the last-minute getaway deals when you need one?

I pull out my phone and text Jenna.

Me: Made it to Miami in one piece. Not sure I'll be able to say the same for the hotel...

Three little dots appear on the screen.

Jenna: Should I be worried?

Me: No. Just a losing round of cabbie roulette. I'm sure it'll be fine.

Probably.

Jenna: Have fun at the game and take lots of pictures!

Jenna: Don't forget to tell Brady how you feel!

I shake my head and slip the phone back into my bag. If I don't catch Brady at the hotel, I'll just have to text him. I want to surprise him, but I also want him to know I'm here for him.

Preferably before he steps foot on the field to play the most important game of his college career.

The driver slams on the brakes and my seatbelt locks tight, sparing me from smashing my face on the seatback in front of me.

Who gave this man a driver's license?

Yes, I'm in a hurry, but I'm not trying to show up with whiplash.

I peer out the window, taking in the sea of red taillights before us. The light is green, but the intersection is gridlocked and no one seems to be moving.

Shit. Shit. Shit.

Why did I wait until the last possible minute to come to my senses?

Because you're stubborn AF.

Facts. If it weren't for Jenna, I'd probably still be sitting on my couch missing Brady, oblivious to the fact that he needed me in Miami.

Thankfully, Ms. Vaughn—*Molly*—still had my ticket.

When I called her last night, she told me she had a feeling I'd change my mind.

Mother's intuition.

I must have thanked her a thousand times. We made arrangements to meet at the stadium, but at this rate, I'm going to miss the entire game.

I close my eyes and focus on my breathing. Getting worked up won't make the taxi go any faster and, frankly, this ride is best enjoyed without visuals.

It's not often real life is worse than my anxiety induced fears, but here we are.

When we finally pull up to the hotel—a massive, white stucco mid-rise with all the amenities—I swipe my credit card, grab my overnight bag, and bolt for the lobby.

It's mass chaos when I enter.

There are people everywhere, most of them wearing Wildcat blue and white or the bold red of the Bulldogs. I weave through the sea of bodies, and when I spot the line for reception, which is twelve deep, my stomach drops.

It'll still be a surprise if you call him from the lobby.

The hotel staff probably wouldn't give me his room number, anyway.

I abandon reception and make my way toward the bank of elevators, hoping to find a quiet spot to call Brady. The hotel bar is full to bursting when I pass, forcing patrons to spill over into the lobby with drinks in hand.

That explains so much.

Drunk people are never half as quiet as they think they are.

I duck into an alcove and I'm about to reach for my phone when I spot a familiar face.

Anger flares red-hot in the pit of my stomach and before I

can think better of it, I'm stalking toward Mike McConnell, every inch of my body vibrating with fury.

The asshole is throwing back an overpriced beer like he doesn't have a care in the world.

Because he didn't have to use his emergency credit card to pay for this trip.

Confronting Mike is probably a bad idea, but I have no fucks left to give.

It's been a long-ass day. I'm tired, and because of him, I'm scrambling to be at Brady's side when he needs me most.

I march right up to Mike's group, which is a total sausage fest, and tap him on the shoulder.

He turns to face me and it takes a full five seconds for him to react.

When recognition finally sets in, his eyes go wide and a stupid smirk appears on his thin lips.

What I wouldn't give to smack that look right off his face.

Of course, then I'd probably be arrested, and I'd never get a job in education.

"What the hell are you doing?" I plant my hands on my hips so I don't succumb to the urge to wring his scrawny neck.

"What does it look like?" He pulls a face. "I came to see Waverly break their losing streak, just like everyone else."

"Uh, oh." The dark-haired guy to Mike's right snickers. "Looks like Mikey's got lady trouble."

"What else is new?" The blond on his left rolls his eyes and takes a pull on his beer. "Maybe you two could take it somewhere else? No offense, but I don't need your drama killing my buzz."

Drama? I'll give him drama.

The entire group reeks of alcohol, but it's not like I have to worry about my safety since the lobby is teaming with witnesses.

"Are you shitting me right now? You're—"

"Let's not make a scene." Mike thrusts his beer into his buddy's hand and then he grabs my biceps and drags me away from the group, jaw clenched.

"Get your hands off me." I jerk free of his grip, stopping just shy of the elevators. "Afraid your friends will find out you're a complete piece of shit?"

Who am I kidding? They probably already know.

"You have some nerve," I hiss. "You're bleeding me dry and this is how you're spending my hard-earned money?"

I gesture wide, encompassing the expansive marble lobby of the four-star hotel.

A hotel I can't even afford to stay at because Mike's blackmail scheme has drained my savings account.

"It's how I'm spending *my* money," he retorts, narrowing his glassy eyes.

"Right. Because you worked *so* hard to earn it."

Does he have any idea how many hours I put in to hone my craft, build my following, and create the content that paid for this trip?

No, and he doesn't care.

"You said you needed the money for school, but that was just an excuse, wasn't it? A way to justify your sick scheme when the truth is, you're a selfish-bastard."

My words barely penetrate his alcohol-soaked brain.

"What difference does it make how I use the money? Seems like you're doing just fine to me. Fangirl must pay better than I thought." He pauses, and I can almost see the wheels turning in his disgusting head. "Maybe it's time we discuss a regular payment schedule for the spring semester."

Fuck. That.

"I'm not giving you another dime." I slash my hand through the air to emphasize my point. "I'm done."

"I decide when we're done." He leans in close, his sour breath filling the space between us. "Unless, of course, you'd like me to schedule a little reveal for Dr. Barnes."

My stomach twists at the mention of my advisor, but apparently anger is stronger than fear in the heat of the moment.

"What part of broke don't you understand? My savings are gone, and I maxed out my credit card just to be here today." I glare daggers at him, wishing the heat of my stare could melt the flesh from his bones. "I can't give you what I don't have."

"Come on, Piper." He cocks his head and an oily smile spreads across his face. "We both know there are other ways you could pay for my silence."

Bile stings the back of my throat, trapping my words.

"I've seen your channel." He leans in close, bracing his left arm against the wall beside my head as he cups my chin with his right hand. "I know exactly what you can do with this body." He drags his thumb across my lower lip and revulsion crawls across my skin. "I wouldn't mind having my own dirty little slut on speed dial."

37

BRADY

It's go time.

I sling my bag over my shoulder and follow Parker into the hall, pulling the door to our hotel room shut behind us. Reid and Coop are waiting, and as we make our way to the elevators, we're joined by a dozen other Waverly players.

The bus to the stadium leaves in five minutes and Coach made it crystal clear that if we aren't on it, there will be hell to pay.

"Fuck." Parker shoves his fingers through his short hair. "Am I the only one who's nervous as hell?"

"Nah," says Smith. "I've had the shits all day."

"Dude." Coop shoots him a disgusted look. "TMI."

"Just be glad you're not his roommate," Williams chimes in, not bothering to look up from his phone as he taps out a message.

"Anyone know where we're partying tonight?" Parker asks. "I want to give Sutton a heads up."

My chest tightens and I tune out as Reid rattles off a few places he's vetted.

No matter how badly I'd like to celebrate with Piper

tonight, it's not going to happen. By the time the game ends and we get cleaned up, it'll be after midnight, and I can't catch a flight out until morning.

It sucks, but with the season ending, things will be easier when I get back to campus.

Unfortunately, the knowledge doesn't make it any easier to stave off jealousy when my roommates mention their own girlfriends, all of whom are here in Miami. After months of sneaking around, my boys have finally gone official and I've never seen them happier.

We huddle up at the elevators and Reid calls the first car.

Being friends with the team captain has its perks.

It's a quick ride and when the doors slide open to reveal the lobby, no one moves.

The place is a madhouse.

When we came back from lunch, the lobby was a graveyard, but now, a horde of blue and red clad fans fills the space as they indulge in pre-game libations.

"Shit just got real," Coop deadpans.

Reid rolls his shoulders, stoic as ever. "We go straight to the bus. No chitchat. No autographs. No interviews."

We all agree and follow our team captain as he cuts a path through the crowd.

I make it all of five yards before I spot a woman who's the spitting image of Piper.

The fuck?

I do a double take, and sure enough, that's my girl pressed up against the marble wall with some asshole touching her face.

What the hell is going on? She's not even supposed to be here.

Who is that prick laying hands on my girl?

Anger blooms in my chest, and I don't think twice about

abandoning the promise I made to my team captain just seconds ago.

I cross to where my girl is pinned up against the wall, and it's all I can do not to shove the asshole who's getting up in her face.

Piper spots me and her blue eyes go wide. For the first time, I can't read her expression. Can't tell if it's fear or panic or relief that's got her looking like she wants to disappear into the marble wall.

"What's going on here?" I drop my bag and use my size to force a wedge between Piper and the creep harassing her.

Piper's shoulders slump, but she remains pressed to the wall, an overnight bag dangling from her hand.

"We were just having a little chat," the creep replies smoothly. "Isn't that right?"

I turn to my girl, searching her face. Her lower lip trembles and it nearly breaks me.

She's always so strong, always thinks she has to handle everything on her own.

Whatever's upset her must be a bad fucking deal.

My mind immediately goes to the worst and I flex my hands at my sides. "Did he hurt you?"

I swear to Christ if he harmed a single hair on her gorgeous head, I'm going to break his face.

Piper exhales, chest heaving. "It's not what you think."

"That's probably a good thing." I glare at the asshole, who has the good sense to keep his mouth shut. "Why don't you tell me what's going on, darlin'?"

"I—" She clasps her hands together and when her eyes meet mine, a silent apology passes between us. Whatever she has to say, I'm not going to like it. "Mike is a TA in the education department. He found out about my Fangirl channel and he's been blackmailing me all year."

The words come out in a rush and I'm sure I've misheard because. What. The. Actual. Fuck?

"You wanna run that by me again?" I shift my weight, widening my stance. "Because I thought you just said this asshole is blackmailing you."

She ducks her head. "You...heard right."

"And this has been going on for months?"

Why would she hide something like this from me?

For the same reason she hid her Fangirl channel.

Dammit. She still doesn't trust me.

That, or she thought she needed to handle it on her own.

Whatever the reason, being shut out leaves a sour taste in my mouth. Even worse is the knowledge that this asshole took advantage of her. He's a TA, for fuck's sake. He knew exactly how she'd react if he threatened her with exposure, and he leveraged his position of authority to get her under his thumb.

Blood rushes through my ears, a frantic hum I can't ignore.

My fingers curl and I force out a breath.

I need to stay calm. The last thing Piper or I need is a scene. There are too many people around. Too many prying eyes.

Too many witnesses.

"How much?" I grit out between clenched teeth.

Piper's brow furrows. "How much what?"

"How much did you pay for his silence?"

The color drains from her face. "It doesn't matter."

The hell it doesn't. If I have my way, the prick will be returning every penny.

I level my gaze at the blackmailing piece of shit. "How much did you take from my girl?"

He glares at me, but I'm not about to back down. "Ten grand."

Jesus fucking Christ.

No wonder she's hurting for cash. She can't possibly keep up with that kind of outlay while covering tuition and living expenses. It's impossible.

This is why she's been filming so much.

It was the only way to protect her secret.

My gut hardens at the irony.

"Here's what's going to happen, Mike." I pitch my voice low, ensuring no one outside our little circle can hear it. "You're going to repay every goddamn cent you took from her or I'm calling the police, and you can bet your ass I will make it my personal mission to ensure you spend time in a cage. You will *never* set foot in a classroom again."

That last bit is going to happen no matter what.

This prick is a predator, and he has no business working with students of any age.

"If I go down, she goes down with me." He jerks his chin at Piper. "Do you really want the entire world to know your girlfriend is a dirty fucking camwhore? You might as well—"

Black spots dot my vision and the next thing I know, my fist is connecting with his jaw.

He stumbles back, crashing into a guy wearing a Georgia polo. The UGA fan drops his beer and the glass shatters on the floor just as the blackmailing piece of shit goes down.

Every head in the vicinity turns our way, but I only have eyes for Piper as all hell breaks loose.

She claps a hand over her mouth, a look of horror passing over her face, and then my boys are crowding around and Coach Collins is going ballistic.

"What the hell is going on here?" He whips off his ball cap and quickly places it back on his head when he realizes people are filming. "Have you all lost your damn minds?"

Fuck.

This is going to be online in minutes.

Maybe seconds.

With just hours until kickoff, it's bound to go viral.

Please don't let the broadcast networks pick it up.

The team has worked too hard to have their accomplishments overshadowed by my dumb ass.

"You okay?" Parker whispers, resting a hand on my biceps.

I nod slowly. "I'm good."

Hotel security materializes, their black suits and radios a dead giveaway.

"What happened here?" the taller guard, a Black guy with a piercing stare and a shaved head, asks.

"He hit me!" Mike yells, climbing slowly to his feet. His jaw is bright red, clear evidence to support his claim. "There were witnesses." The asshole has been blackmailing my girlfriend and talking shit about her, and yet he still has the audacity to look outraged. "I want to press charges."

That escalated quickly.

The security guard turns to me. "Sir, I'm going to need you to come with me."

"What? No." Piper rushes to stand between the guard and me. "You don't understand. He was defending me."

"It's okay, darlin'." I squeeze her shoulders and drop a kiss on top of her head, before I cut my gaze at her TA. "I have no regrets."

Hell, I'd do it again. No disparages my girl like that and gets away with it.

She whirls to face me, panic etched in the soft lines of her face. "What about the game?"

"It's just a game, Piper." I take her hands in mine and bring them to my lips, brushing a soft kiss against them. "I love you. You're what matters."

Her cheeks go pink and for a second, I think she's going to return the sentiment. Our thoughts are clearly in two different places though, because she just shakes her head. "Your mom and grandma came all this way…"

"They'll understand."

The guard clears his throat. "Sir, I need you to come with me now."

I nod and release Piper's hands as Coach Collins lays into my teammates, his face the color of a cherry.

"Get your asses on the bus! We've got a game to play." He shoots me a dark look and I swear my balls shrivel up. "I'll deal with Vaughn."

Coach Walker appears at his side and whispers something inaudible. When he's done, Coach Collins throws up his hands. "Fine. You deal with this mess, but you better be on the sideline before kickoff."

"I'll get Vaughn sorted out," Coach Walker promises, giving no guarantee about kickoff. "Do me a favor and tell Davis to be ready. It looks like we're going to need him."

Fucking fuck.

Davis is the second-string left tackle. The kid is a decent ballplayer, but he's only a sophomore and he hasn't seen nearly enough game play.

For the first time, the impact of my actions truly hits me.

I may have saved Piper, but I screwed my teammates.

38

PIPER

THE SECURITY GUARDS haul Brady away like a criminal, and there's nothing I can say or do to stop them. This whole mess is my fault. It never would have happened if I'd just kept my mouth shut, but no, I had to lose my shit and confront Mike McConnell just hours before kickoff.

If only you had a time-turner, you could fix it.

If only.

Nausea roils in my belly.

If it weren't for me, none of this would have happened.

I'm the one who kept secrets. I'm the one who couldn't walk away when I saw Mike pounding a beer in the lobby. Now Brady's going to pay the price.

It's bad enough he's going to miss the game—win or lose, he'll beat himself up for letting the team down—but assault charges? That's serious.

Those charges will follow him for the rest of his life, all because of me.

Wallowing in self-pity won't help Brady.

No kidding, but I don't know what to do.

Maybe I should call his mom. Despite what he said, I'm

sure she'd want to know. We were supposed to meet at the stadium, but there's no way I'm going to watch the game while Brady is about to be arrested and charged with assault. I'm sure Molly would feel the same way if she knew what was going on.

I'm mulling it over when a hotel employee in a sharp black suit comes rushing over, her heels clicking on the marble floor.

She goes straight to Mike's aid and I look at him for the first time since Brady smashed his face in. His jaw is swollen, the flesh a mottled shade of red and purple. He's going to be sporting one hell of a bruise come morning, but there's no permanent damage.

"Hello, Mister?"

"McConnell," he says, gingerly touching his jaw.

"Mr. McConnell, my name is Sierra Rodriguez and I'm the front desk manager. If you'll come with me, I can get you some ice, or, if you prefer, we can call an ambulance?"

My blood runs cold. Surely he doesn't want an ambulance. It would be a gross exaggeration of the situation.

Yes, and it would also garner more sympathy for him as the victim.

He shakes his head and winces in pain. "That won't be necessary. I'm sure an icepack will be fine."

I exhale. It's a minor victory, but I'll take it.

Sierra leads him across the lobby and I follow, hitching my bag up on my shoulder.

If she knew what an asshole he was, she wouldn't be so accommodating.

She takes him to a small office behind the concierge desk, and when she leaves to get ice, I slip inside.

I created this mess. I have to be the one to put an end to it.

Mike's hunched over a small desk and if getting punched in the face has diminished his ego, he doesn't let it show.

"What the hell do you want?" he snarls.

God, he is such a prick. How Jenna ever thought he was cute is beyond me.

"What I want is for none of this to have ever happened." God knows I didn't want to be blackmailed. "Since that isn't on the table, I'll settle for you agreeing to not press charges against Brady."

"Why would I ever agree to that?" He points to his swollen jaw. "He assaulted me. That's a crime."

Pot meet kettle.

"So is blackmail, but that didn't stop you, did it?"

He has the decency to look mildly chagrined. "That was different."

I don't bother asking how. There's no way I'm going to agree with his screwed-up logic and it really doesn't matter at this point. Brady made a snap decision—to defend me—and I will not let him spend the rest of his life paying for it.

"I'm in a bit of a time crunch, so I'm going to make this easy for you." I glance out the door to ensure Sierra is nowhere in sight. "If you press charges, I'm going to do exactly as Brady suggested and file a police report for blackmail. Then I'm going to march right over to Dr. Barnes' office and tell her all about your secondary income."

"You wouldn't dare." He sneers. "If you expose me, you expose yourself, then all of this was for nothing."

Maybe that punch scrambled his brains, after all.

"If you think I'm going to sit by and let Brady catch charges to protect my secret, you're delusional." I level him with a hard stare. "You may be comfortable ruining people's futures, but I'm not."

I couldn't live with myself if I sat idly by while Brady faces assault charges on my behalf. If there's any shot of protecting him, I'll take it and to hell with the consequences.

He leans back in the desk chair, studying me. "Fine. Go to Barnes. It'll be your word against mine."

"It's cute that you think that, but you're not as smart as you think you are." I smirk. "I paid you with Venmo. I've got receipts, asshole."

Every electronic transfer leaves a digital trail. Mike can try to twist things around, but no one's going to believe I paid him ten grand to fix my grade in a pass/fail class.

When I come clean about my Fangirl account, Barnes will have to believe me.

"That's the funny thing about blackmail. It only works if the person you're blackmailing has something to hide."

"So, what?" He throws his arms wide. "Suddenly you're cool with people knowing you're an adult entertainer and you're just abandoning a career in education?"

I'm not abandoning anything—or anyone. Least of all Brady.

Maybe I won't be able to teach in a formal capacity, but I can still help kids from disadvantaged backgrounds. I'll volunteer. Offer free tutoring.

It's cliché as hell, but where there's a will, there's a way.

I just have to find it.

"What can I say?" I flash him a bright smile. "You've helped me realize my priorities."

He snorts. "From where I'm sitting, they look pretty screwed up."

"I don't give a shit what you think." I brace my palms on the desk and lower my face so we're eye-to-eye. "Keep the cash and drop the charges."

It's a sweetheart deal and we both know it, but will he be smart enough to accept?

39

BRADY

MY HAND IS THROBBING like a motherfucker as the security team leads us into a small office full of video monitors. It's not the kind of place meant for a crowd and with the two guards, Coach Walker, and me, it's a tight squeeze.

The taller guard, the one who looks like he might've played college ball himself, sits behind the desk and gestures for Coach Walker and me to take the seats opposite. I drop my bag on the floor as the shorter guard takes up a position by the door.

"My name is Malik Robinson, and I'm the director of security for the hotel." He folds his hands on the desk, but I just stare at him. How the hell did it come to this? "Are you a guest at the hotel?"

I nod. "Yes, sir."

I may be up to my eyeballs in it, but I can still show respect.

"Room number?"

"Four thirty-eight."

He turns to his computer and punches a few keys. "Name?"

"Brady Vaughn."

"I see you're here with Waverly University." He pulls his gaze from the screen, looking me over. "I assume you play ball?"

"Yes, sir."

He grins, and it completely changes his demeanor. "I played for the Gators, but that was a long time ago." He leans back in his chair and I get the sense he's trying to build some kind of rapport. "Want to tell me what happened out there?"

Not particularly.

"It was a private matter."

I don't care who this guy is or where he played football. I'm not about to tell them why I punched that creep. Piper's been through enough, and I will not pull her into this mess.

Malik turns back to the monitors, clearly expecting this response. He taps out a few commands and Piper and Mike McConnell appear on-screen.

My blood heats at the sight of that creep cornering my girl and my fingers curl around the arms of the chair. As frustrated as I am that she didn't tell me about the blackmail, I understand it. Our upbringings were not the same, and she's only ever had herself to rely on.

The scene plays out all over again on screen and I watch as my fist connects with Mike's jaw.

It's just as satisfying the second time around.

Beside me, Coach Walker is silent.

I can only imagine what he's thinking right now. The guy has had my back from day one at Waverly and this isn't the kind of behavior he can condone.

Malik freezes the scene as Mike climbs to his feet on-screen. "The police are on their way. We'll have to turn this video over to them as evidence."

Shit. I'm going to be arrested.

My gut hardens at the realization and all it implies.

This is far bigger than missing today's game. Bigger than letting my team and coaches down. My mom is going to find out about this and she's going to be so disappointed.

Hell, she might have to bail me out of jail.

Fuck. I'm going to have a mug shot.

Gran will probably put it on next year's Christmas card.

It doesn't matter. What's done is done and I can't bring myself to regret it.

The way Mike was talking about Piper... The names he called her...

My grip tightens on the arm of the chair. "I'm prepared to face the consequences of my actions."

Coach Walker clears his throat. "Is this really necessary? Brady is a good kid. He's never been in trouble before. I'm sure there are extenuating circumstances. If he could just explain—"

"It's out of my hands," Malik says firmly. "The other party wants to press charges and hotel policy requires us to notify the police of any criminal activity that takes place on the property."

Criminal activity.

Christ. That phrase takes on a whole new meaning.

There's a knock at the door and the second guard peers out, whispering with the newcomer. When he turns back to us, his face is unreadable, but he jerks his head toward the hall and both guards step out of the room, closing the door behind them.

Coach Walker turns to me, brow creased with worry. "Want me to call your mom?"

"No." I scrub a hand over my face. "She'll find out soon enough."

I'd prefer she not see me taken away in handcuffs.

"Son, I can't help you if you don't help yourself. What the hell just happened back there?"

"Does it matter? They've got me dead to rights."

I can't exactly deny it was my fist cracking Mike's jaw.

My knuckles throb in confirmation.

"You're the last person I expect this shit from." He huffs out a frustrated breath. "Langley? Sure. But you?"

Guilt ravages my insides. I've let him down.

Add it to the list.

I'm disappointing a lot of people today, but I can't bring myself to be sorry. I will never stand by while someone hurts Piper, physically or emotionally. And, yeah, there was probably a better solution than punching the guy, but I lost my head.

Never again.

I'm not sorry, but I'm not cool with violence. I don't plan to make a habit of punching everyone who pisses me off in the future.

Coach Walker shifts his chair so he's facing me straight on. "If you're in trouble, I can help, but I need you to tell me what's going on."

I grin in spite of myself. "I appreciate the offer, Coach, but I think this is outside your area of expertise." What I need is a lawyer. I glance at the clock on the wall. Kickoff is in ninety minutes. "Shouldn't you be at the stadium?"

"Brady, I love the game, but I love my players more. You kids are like family to me." He squeezes my shoulder. "I'll be here as long as you need me."

My throat tightens and I nod. "Thanks, Coach."

"That said, it would've been nice if you could have picked a different day to be arrested," he grumbles. "Coach Collins is going to kick both our asses."

We sit in silence for what feels like an eternity.

Finally, the door swings open and the security director returns.

"The police have arrived."

Every muscle in my body tenses. This is really happening. I'm going to be cuffed and marched out through the lobby for all the world to see.

"The victim has decided not to press charges after all." Relief floods my system and I slump into my chair. "He told my men it was a misunderstanding. You're free to go, Mr. Vaughn."

He doesn't have to tell me twice. My ass is out of that chair in an instant.

I just dodged a bullet. I have no clue why Mike changed his mind, and I'm not sure I care. It's a gift, and I'm grateful beyond words to receive it as I turn to Coach Walker. "What do you say we go win ourselves a national championship?"

40

PIPER

THE LOBBY HAS CLEARED OUT, but the quiet does nothing to settle my nerves or my racing heart. I'm perched on the edge of a plush couch, uncertain what to do next. Mike agreed not to press charges, but will that be enough for the police, or will Brady still be in trouble? A place like this must have security cameras and there were a zillion witnesses.

Even if he's released, will he be allowed to play today or will he be kicked off the team?

Coach Collins isn't known for being warm and squishy. According to Jenna, the man is a known hardass.

Shit. My stupid mistakes are going to cause Brady to miss the game and the Wildcats are going to lose, and it's going to be all my fault.

Imagine how Brady feels.

Impossible. What I'm feeling can't be a tenth of what he and the other guys on the team go through daily with the expectations of Wildcat Nation pressing down.

It's suffocating.

I scan the lobby. I need to do something. Find Brady, call his mom, or at least—

Brady emerges from a corridor near the elevators and my heart sings. I'm on my feet in an instant, rushing toward him. When he spots me, he spreads his arms wide. I leap into his embrace, wrapping myself around him like a monkey on a tree.

He buries his face in my hair and I inhale his familiar outdoorsy scent as my heart finally settles into a normal rhythm.

"I was so scared," I murmur, squeezing him tight.

"It's okay, darlin'. I've got you."

Coach Walker clears his throat and Brady releases me.

"The bus is long gone. I'm going to find us a ride." He glances at me and then back at Brady. "You've got two minutes. Then I expect you outside and ready to go."

Brady nods, his relief apparent. "Yes, sir."

The coach stalks toward the front desk and then Brady's cupping my face, his eyes locked on mine. "What are you doing here?"

I grin. "Surprising you."

He brushes a kiss across my lips. "I was surprised all right." He pauses, looking me over. "Are you okay? I could kill that fucker for putting his hands on you."

"I'm okay. He didn't hurt me."

He grunts as if unconvinced. "I wish you'd told me what was going on sooner. I could've helped." He shoves his fingers through his hair. "Or, at the very least, I could've helped share the burden. If not financially, then emotionally."

My heart swells, but the declaration is nothing less than I'd expect from him.

"You're right. I should have told you." I force myself to meet his eyes. "I was ashamed, and I thought I could handle it. At first it was just money, but today..."

I shudder.

"No one has a right to put their hands on you like that, Piper."

He's fighting for control. It's evident in the way he holds himself, hands clenched at his sides. Today was a tough day for both of us, and it's not over yet.

"Just say the word and I'll break every one of his goddamn fingers." He grins and it's positively feral. "Better yet, I'll rip his arms off and beat him to death with them."

I laugh at the imagery because we both know that despite his protective streak, Brady doesn't have it in him. He's not a violent guy. In the four months I've known him, I've never seen him lose his cool. Today was a fluke. A perfect storm of stress and pressure and Mike pushing him past the tipping point with his vile words.

"I appreciate the sentiment, but I can fight my own battles, big guy."

"I know you can, but you shouldn't have to." He takes my hands in his, cradling them. "Let me in, Piper. What we have is amazing, but we could be so much more if you'd let me be there for you in all the ways that matter."

This is it. The reason I came to Miami.

My palms begin to sweat and the urge to bolt is like a siren song, calling me home, but I stand my ground, holding tight to Brady's massive hands.

"I love that you want to protect me, and I love that you have such a big heart. You've shown it to me in so many ways over the last few months and despite everything I've done to push you away, to keep you at arm's length and protect my heart, I've fallen for you."

His breath hitches and I'm not sure he's breathing as he stares down at me, that familiar longing in his eyes, one that won't be eased with sex or meaningless platitudes. "I love you, Brady, and I want to be with you in every way that matters."

"Say it again," he pleads, releasing my hands and cupping my face.

Emotion clogs my throat, but the words slip easily from my lips because I trust Brady. I trust him with my body and my heart. He will never hurt me, not intentionally. What we have is so far removed from the relationships I saw growing up that I don't know how I could have ever made a comparison.

"I love you."

"I love you, too, Piper Lilian Reynolds." He grins. "You have no idea how long I've waited to say those words."

He crushes his lips to mine, kissing me slow and deep. It's like every kiss that's come before, but also new and different, a deeper connection that tugs at my heartstrings and brings tears to my eyes because Brady loves me. And I love him.

I don't know how long we go on like that, but I know two minutes have come and gone because Coach Walker returns, cussing a blue streak.

Brady reluctantly releases me, but the tender look on his face promises we'll continue this later.

"I talked to one of the hotel drivers. He said traffic is a nightmare and it'll be damn near impossible to get to the stadium before kickoff." He mutters another expletive and I get a mental image of Coach Collins waving his clipboard on the sidelines. *Birds of a feather.* "It's only seven miles, but it could take hours to navigate with road closures and gridlocked traffic."

My heart sinks. There has to be a way. We're so close...

41

BRADY

Piper checks her bag at the front desk and we follow Coach Walker to the porte cochere out in front of the hotel. Cars clog the entrance, a mix of taxis, rentals, and a single police cruiser that's parked in the fire lane.

If the hotel is this jammed up, imagine the stadium.

My gut clenches. I may have avoided charges, but the universe is clearly making me pay for losing my shit earlier. I can't even be mad about it—it's no less than I deserve—but for a minute there, I thought I'd be able to come through for the team.

For Coach Walker.

For the fans.

Piper takes my hand, lacing her fingers through mine.

She squeezes gently and my frustration is immediately replaced with the warm glow of affection.

I still can't believe she came.

This whole day feels like a fever dream, but here she is, at my side, and she loves me. Her words echo in my head, where they'll be living rent free for the foreseeable future.

Whatever happens today, it's going to be okay.

I've got my family, my friends, and the love of an incredible woman.

Coach leads us to a black sedan near the front of the line, but before we can climb in, a police officer waves us down.

"Hold up!" he calls, jogging toward us with a hand on his belt.

Just fucking great. What now?

Has Mike changed his mind? Is this another one of his sick games? The douchebag clearly has no aversion to blackmail, so I wouldn't put anything past him at this point.

Piper looks up at me with worry in her eyes. It's clear she's thinking the same thing.

Coach Walker steps in front of me, shoulders rigid. "Can I help you, officer?"

"I was actually hoping to help you." He grins. "I'm a Waverly alumnus and I'd like to do my part to support Wildcat Nation today."

I guess it's true what they say: There are only six degrees of separation between Waverly alumni.

"I'm a big fan of the football program," he continues. "What you all have done this year is incredible. I mean, I never thought I'd see the day Coach Collins would put a woman on the team, but the Wildcats have never looked better. I'm rooting for you, and so are a lot of the folks back at the station. It'd be pretty damn cool to see my alma mater make history and break that dry spell."

Coach Walker nods and I can almost hear him begging the officer to get to the point.

"Anyway." The officer gestures to the cruiser parked in the fire lane. "On behalf of the Miami-Dade PD, I'd like to offer you a courtesy ride to the stadium."

Coach Walker glances at the black sedan, which is still

blocked in, and then at the green and white car with a slim light bar fixed to the roof.

"Let's do it, Officer?"

"Melton. Jim Melton." He extends his hand and Coach Walker shakes it.

"We appreciate this ride more than you know."

Truer words.

We follow Officer Melton to his car and when he opens the back door, I stop short.

The backseat is basically a cage. Not only is there a divider between the front and back, there's also one between the seats in the rear.

Coach Walker notices my stare and shrugs. "Consider it punishment for rash behavior."

"One ride in this baby and you'll never want to cross the law again." Officer Melton chuckles and gestures to Coach Walker. "You're welcome to ride up front with me."

Piper and I exchange a look, but she climbs in on the driver's side, so I circle around the passenger side and do the same.

It's a tight fit. This car clearly wasn't designed with a man my size in mind. And forget about my duffel bag.

Officer Melton does a seatbelt check and then we're pulling out onto the main road, where traffic is moving like molasses.

My gut coils tight, nerves taking root, but there's nothing I can do except sit back and enjoy the ride. Which is actually impossible when Piper and I are separated by plexiglass like freaking cons while Coach Walker and Officer Melton are up front making small talk like two biddies at afternoon tea.

Officer Walker explains that he moved south after college to be closer to his wife's family. They're raising two little

Wildcats and I'm shocked he doesn't bust out his phone and start showing Coach pictures.

I sigh and Piper taps the glass between us, shooting me a look I'm pretty sure means, *Like you have room to talk.*

I shoot her one back that says, *Yeah, but we weren't in a hurry when I showed you baby chick pics.*

At least, that's what it's supposed to say. I'm not sure she takes my meaning, but she presses her palm to the scratched glass and I do the same, splaying my fingers to align with hers.

"It's going to be okay," she mouths.

"I know."

My phone vibrates and I contort myself like a pretzel trying to fish it out of my pocket.

There's a new message on the group chat with my roommates.

Reid: What the hell is going on, Vaughn?

A better question would be why the hell are they texting me when they should be suiting up, but I tap out a hasty reply.

Me: You wouldn't believe me if I told you.

No way am I getting into it over text. I don't need that shit getting leaked into the world. Besides, Piper's secrets are her own.

Parker: You okay?

Me: Yeah. I'm good.

Or as good as I can be, considering the circumstances.

My knee bounces as I watch the clock, every minute that ticks by another nail in the coffin.

Coop: I always thought you'd look good in orange. Can I see your mugshot?

*Me: *middle finger emoji**

Coop: Is that a no? Because I'm pretty sure I can get it from public records. I'm going to put that shit on a t-shirt and wear it with pride.

He's obviously messing with me. Coop may be a jackass at times, but he's smart enough to know I wouldn't be texting if I'd been arrested.

Reid: Are you going to make it in time for kickoff?

I glance out the window as we pass another closed road. Red taillights stretch as far as the eye can see and the stadium is nowhere in sight.

Me: It's not looking good.

42

———

PIPER

"We're about six blocks out," Officer Melton announces.

I have to give the guy credit. Despite the tension in the car, he's remained cool and collected, chatting about his wife and kids.

Maybe he's trying to ease the strain.

Impossible. There's no de-escalating in this vehicle.

Every second that ticks by feels like an hour.

We're never going to make it on time. The sun has set and the team is probably already on the field warming up. Both Brady and Coach Walker look like they're ready to climb out a window and make a run for it.

The crowds are insane, and it's clear Wildcat Nation turned out to support the team, tickets be damned. Fans spill out of bars and restaurants and every parking lot we pass is full to bursting with tailgaters.

I can't get over how many roads are closed. I'm no civil engineer, but wouldn't it make more sense to have them all open to improve the flow of traffic?

Officer Melton's radio crackles to life. "This is car five-seven-thee-two-alpha," he says. "I'm doing a time-sensitive escort to Hard Rock Stadium. Can we get an assist with the road closures?"

He cites our location and direction and the radio goes silent. A few seconds later, a disembodied voice comes back with a set of instructions, and Officer Melton acknowledges.

"I can't go lights and sirens," he explains, "but if we can get around a few of these closures, I should be able to get y'all to the players' entrance."

I grab my phone and text Brady's mom.

Me: Running late. So sorry. Be there soon.

I clench the phone in my hand, anxiety pressing down on my chest like a lead weight as I watch for her reply. Three little dots appear on the screen and I brace for impact.

Molly: No worries. We'll be here waiting when you arrive. See you soon, dear.

That's it. Just...see you soon.

Molly has no idea how close Brady came to being arrested or that he hasn't reached the stadium, and yet she doesn't point out I'm late as hell or berate me because she's going to miss kickoff for the most important game of her son's life.

A game she traveled one thousand miles to watch.

The woman has the patience of a saint.

Or maybe my thoughts have just been so poisoned by my toxic mother that I don't know what good parenting looks like.

The realization stings, but that's a problem for another day.

I glance over at Brady, and his knee is going a mile a minute.

He looks ridiculous crammed into the tiny cell on his side of the car, his large body pressed up against the plexiglass that separates us. It reminds me of the night we met, when he was smashed into the backseat of the tiny Uber.

We've come a long way since then.

The car makes a sharp turn and I look out to see a pair of uniformed officers moving a temporary roadblock. They swing the sawhorse around, letting Officer Melton pass before putting it back in place.

The road is clear, and he presses down on the accelerator for what feels like the first time on this entire drive. The engine roars and the car shoots forward.

Five minutes later, he pulls up to the stadium, an impressive glass and steel complex with a square sunshade and four white spires reaching for the sky. We locate the players' entrance and Coach Walker leaps out of the car before it's come to a complete stop. Brady attempts to follow, but his door doesn't open.

"Prisoner locks," Officer Melton explains as Coach Walker yanks his door open.

The officer climbs out and opens my door and then we're all shouting our thanks at once, heaping praise upon Officer Melton.

"Get in there and kick some Bulldog ass," he says, resting his arms on the roof of the car. "I've already got my championship tee on preorder."

"Yes, sir." Brady flashes him an appreciative grin before turning to me. "I've gotta go."

"Of course. Don't worry about me." I stretch up on my toes and give him a quick kiss. "Go suit up. I'll see you inside."

He turns to go and I slap him on the ass, earning a quiet chuckle.

I watch as he jogs to the entrance, Coach Walker on his heels. Once they pass through security, I turn and run in the opposite direction, searching for my gate.

It's a mild night, and the temperature hovers in the mid-sixties, but I'm not built for running, nor am I dressed for it.

The underwire in my bra digs into my right boob with every freaking step.

By the time I reach my gate and locate Brady's family, I'm winded and sweat has pooled between my breasts.

Molly and Gran are both decked out head-to-toe in Wildcat gear and Gran's wielding a giant foam paw with *Fear the paw!* printed on it.

Brady's mom takes one look at me and goes full mother hen.

"What happened to you?" she demands, eyes wide with concern. "Do you need a minute to rest?"

I shake my head, panting, but she's not having it.

"Catch your breath, dear. We've got plenty of time."

The national anthem, which drifts from the stadium, would suggest otherwise.

I suck air into my lungs and exhale. "I'm good. Let's go inside and find our seats."

"If you're sure..."

"Leave the girl be," Gran admonishes, pulling a blue and white foam paw from her bag. "I got one for you, too."

She holds the paw out and gratitude warms my chest as I take the gift.

It's a small thing, but it means the world because I know right down to the tips of my toes that this is a sign of acceptance.

Somehow, I've actually won over Brady's close-knit family.

"Thank you."

"No, thank you, Piper." She touches my arm. "Brady's happier than I've ever seen him, and that's a gift beyond measure."

Tears sting my eyes and I don't know if it's her words or the culmination of the day's events, but I can't hold them back. One after another, they slide down my cheeks and without a word, both women move in to hug me. Which only makes me cry harder.

This isn't the time to get up in your feelings...

No kidding, but it's not like I can help it. This day has been a rollercoaster of highs and lows, and it's still not over.

When my tears finally dry up, Molly offers me a tissue from her bag. "We're pretty good listeners, if you want to talk."

"Thanks." I swipe at the tear tracks on my cheeks. "But we should probably go find our seats. Brady needs us right now."

More than she could possibly know...

43

BRADY

By the time I dress and stretch, Waverly is down by seven.

The Bulldogs scored on the opening drive. When we got the ball, Davis missed a block and Reid got sacked for a loss of six yards. As if that wasn't bad enough, our offense was three and out.

It was a total shit show and my dumb ass had to watch it on-screen from the locker room.

I can't fault Davis. The kid is probably a bundle of nerves.

Nothing like being told you're starting ninety minutes before kickoff.

In a championship game, nonetheless.

It's hard to believe this is the last time I'll lace up my cleats, but there's no time to dwell on it. I grab my helmet and jog to the field, unwilling to delay another second.

Football is a game of inches and a single play can determine the outcome.

I need to be on the field with my team, doing my part to make sure this game doesn't become an embarrassment.

Fuck that.

So what if we're down by seven? It's one score. We can make it up. This is still anyone's game.

The air is charged when I step out of the tunnel. The lights are bright, the fans are loud, and the game is hard-hitting. A replay on the jumbotron shows Daniels, our defensive captain, strip the ball from one of Georgia's receivers.

It's a damn good play and a deafening cheer goes up from the crowd as Langley recovers the ball on screen.

When I report to the sideline, our offense has already taken the field.

"You warmed up?" Coach Walker asks, studying Georgia's defense.

"Yes, sir." I bounce on the balls of my feet. I'm eager to get in the game, but Walker won't sub in the middle of a drive.

Not when we have momentum.

The ball is snapped and Reid drops back, looking downfield.

Davis has his man and the coverage from the O-line is solid.

Coop cuts to the outside, puts on speed, and Reid fires a bullet down the sideline for a twenty-yard gain.

"Hell, yeah!" I shout, punching my fist in the air.

That's how you win football games: *one down at a time.*

Our offense picks up ground on the next two drives, and Davis seems to have shaken his nerves, but they can't break the twenty. It's frustrating as hell to watch, but Georgia isn't the top-ranked team in the country for nothing.

On the fourth down, Coach calls for Special Teams.

Carter jogs onto the field, the tail of her braid bouncing with each step. She can make twenty yards in her sleep, especially on a night like tonight where there's no wind.

Perfect conditions.

The offense clears the field and my boys join me on the sideline.

"It's about damn time," Parker says, grinning as he claps me on the back.

"Sorry. I got here as soon as I could."

"Don't sweat it." Reid drags the back of his hand across his forehead, which is already dripping. "You and Piper good?"

"Better than ever, believe it or not."

He shrugs. "That's all that matters."

Reid is a natural born leader and I'm not sure he even realizes it. Here we are playing the most intense game of our lives, there are scouts everywhere, and he's worried about me and my girl.

We watch in silence as Carter takes her position on the field.

The ball is snapped and James catches it, planting it on the ground just as Carter winds up. Her leg swings forward, her foot connecting with a *thwump,* and then the ball sails through the upright.

The crowd goes nuts and just like that, we're on the board.

Coop turns to Reid, smirking. "Are you really going to let your girl show you up like that?"

"It's not a competition," Reid says in a tone that suggests they've already had this conversation at least once.

"The hell it's not." Coop glances over his shoulder, confirming Coach is out of earshot. "Everything is a competition."

"Facts." Parker snickers. "I heard they're taking bets on more than just the spread in Vegas."

"The only thing I'm worried about right now is our next drive."

"I hear that." Coop shakes his hair like a wet dog, sending

sweat flying. "The Georgia cornerback is fast as hell. He's gonna make me work tonight."

I snort. "Maybe you should've spent a little more time on leg day."

He looks down at his biceps and the muscles ripple as he flexes. "Nah, I'm good."

Our defense holds the line and Georgia's forced to punt.

I strap on my helmet and when the return team calls for a fair catch, I take the field with the rest of the O-line, ready to work.

THREE HOURS LATER, I'm sweating balls, my right elbow is torn up, and we're trailing the Dawgs by three. The game has been a dogfight, no pun intended, and as the clock winds down, our dream of winning a national championship slips further from reach.

"Come on," I whisper, willing our D to make a big play.

The momentum has been in Georgia's favor since the start of the third quarter and they're running our defense ragged.

"Daniels and his boys need to buck the fuck up," Coop says, squirting water into his mouth from one of the team bottles. "I've seen turtles with more energy."

I give him the side-eye. "Were their names Leonardo, Donatello, Michelangelo, and Raphael?"

Parker snickers. "You walked right into—"

A roar goes up from the crowd, drowning out the rest of the sentence. Adrenaline floods my system as one of our safeties picks off the Georgia QB inside the red zone. He runs it back twenty-five yards before he's tackled, giving us great field position with nearly two minutes on the clock.

"That's what I'm talking about!" Coop shouts, thumping his helmet.

Reid's jaw is set as he looks at each of us. "Let's bring this thing home."

The noise in the stadium has reached a fever pitch by the time we take our positions on the line of scrimmage. Fortunately, we're used to it. Waverly's known to have one of the loudest stadiums in the country. The Georgia fans can scream themselves hoarse trying to drown out the play call, but it won't work.

I stare across the line at the defensive end, sweat dripping from my brow.

This is it. Everything we've worked for all season. Hell, the last four seasons. It's all going to come down to this last possession.

We have to score or it's over.

The ball is snapped and I charge forward. The defensive end is built like a Mack Truck, but we're pretty evenly matched and when we collide, it's a clash of titans.

He attempts to spin past me, but I hold tight to his pads, making sure I stay on the inside so I don't get called for holding. It's a running play and though I can't see what's happening downfield, I don't relent until I hear the whistle.

We gain eight yards and line up to do it all over.

Reid calls another running play and we pick up the first down, stopping the game clock as we cross the fifty-yard line.

My right hand is throbbing when I return to the line of scrimmage and I want to kick my own ass for throwing a punch before such an important game.

At least you didn't break it.

I can't think about that right now. I need to focus on the next play.

We drive down the field, but when we get inside the twenty, our progress stalls—again.

Georgia's defense is tough, but they're running out of steam. I line up across from the Bulldogs defensive end, who, like me, is sweating bullets. He spits in the grass, and when his eyes meet mine, they're brimming with aggression. "You play with the big dogs, you gonna get bit."

I ignore the taunt and everything that comes after. I've faced bigger, meaner guys on the field and I'm not about to get drawn into a penalty over a little shit talk.

The ball is snapped and the DE explodes off the line. I make the block—barely—but the Dawgs hit us with additional rushers and we can't hold them. The pocket collapses and Reid scrambles before he's forced to throw the ball away.

Fuck.

We're second and ten when we reset.

I roll my shoulders, trying to ease the tension that's got me coiled tighter than a rattlesnake.

It's another passing play, but the receiver can't hold on to the ball and it's ruled incomplete.

"I need you to buy me a little more time," Reid says as we reset. "These fuckers are really bringing the pressure and they're double-teaming Coop."

No surprise there. He's our best receiver and a top draft contender.

"We'll hold them," I assure him, speaking for the entire O-line.

Reid calls a new play, and this time, he finds Parker for a gain of nine.

It's not enough to stop the clock.

We're one yard short of the first down and at this rate, time will expire before we can score.

Reid calls a timeout and hauls ass to the sideline where he huddles with Coach Collins and Coach Walker.

Win or lose, this will all be over in thirty seconds.

Just thirty seconds until I step off the field for the last time. Thirty seconds that were years in the making, with countless hours spent memorizing playbooks, strength training, and running rep after rep to become the best.

Years of blood, sweat, and tears and it's all come down to this moment.

The fans seem to sense it as well. They're on their feet, stomping and cheering as they bring down the house.

We all gather round, waiting for Reid to return with the next play.

"I'm going to need an ice bath when this is over," Parker says, rubbing his shoulder. "Those assholes nearly took my arm off with that last hit."

"At least you can get your hands on the ball. The double coverage is killing me." Coop's gaze slides to the sideline where Carter is kicking into a net, warming up her leg. "What do you think Coach is going to do?"

He could opt for a field goal. If we tie it up, we can go into OT and live to fight another day, but we only need one yard to stop the clock again. If we're quick, there would still be time for another play, maybe two.

"He'll go for it," I say. "He's as hungry as we are for that title."

Reid jogs out to rejoin us and we all put our heads in for the call.

"Who's ready to win a national championship?" He claps his hands together and we all make noises of assent. "We're going Early 94 Y-option." It's one of the new plays. Coach has never called it outside of practice, but he must think we're ready. That, or he's desperate.

"We pull this off and we'll be celebrating like kings tonight."

"I like the sound of that," Smith says, earning a raucous cheer from the group.

We break, and this time, when we line up, the tension at the line of scrimmage is palpable. The Georgia defenders look like they're out for blood, and who can blame them? We all know this game is going to come down to who wants it more.

We're all tired and bruised. The adrenaline we carried onto the field tonight has waned. All we've got left is here and now.

Sweat stings my eyes and the bright lights of the stadium seem to reflect off every surface.

Maybe that's why it takes a beat for the Georgia defense to react to our formation. They're scrambling to adjust, but our center wastes no time snapping the ball.

Reid drops back as the O-line surges forward and Coop cuts through the chaos, stripping his coverage. I crash into the defensive end and latch onto his chest protector, digging my cleats into the soft grass. My biceps burn with exertion, but we need to hold the line.

This play has a high risk of interception given the tight quarters and Reid needs every inch we can give him.

He throws across the middle and a defender reaches up to block the pass.

Fucking fuck. My gut clenches.

The defender gets a hand on the ball and it's tipped, sailing over his head and into the end zone.

Coop leaps into the air, fingertips reaching for the ball. He makes contact with his right hand, before disappearing behind a tangle of bodies that blocks my view.

Did he get it?

My pulse roars between my ears like a freight train as I

wait for the call, and when the crowd goes ballistic, I know.

Cooper DeLaurentis just caught the game-winning touchdown.

Pride floods my chest and the roar that bursts from my lips is nothing short of animalistic.

I rush the sonofabitch—me and half the team—and when I find him at the center of the celebrating crowd, I plant a big sloppy kiss on his forehead.

"You actually did it, you cocky bastard!"

He smirks. "Guess I didn't need another leg day after all."

No, no he did not.

Reid joins us, grinning ear to ear. "You know this is going straight to his head, right?"

"Hell yeah it is!" Coop holds the ball in the air for all to see. "But you know I couldn't have done it alone. That was a sick throw."

"National champions!" Parker shouts, shoving his way through the crowd.

I pull him in for a hug and clap him on the back before turning to congratulate the rest of the O-line. It was a team effort, after all.

Since the extra point doesn't matter, the guys on the sideline rush the field, as does the coaching staff.

Coach Walker is beaming when I find him in the crowd. "Great game, son. I couldn't be prouder if you were my kid."

"Thank you, sir." Tears sting the back of my eyes. "That means more than you know."

Especially after everything I've been through today.

He thumps me on the back. "Go find your girl and celebrate. You deserve it."

It's like the man read my mind.

I need to find Piper.

Fireworks explode overhead and confetti rains down as

the fans rush the field, pouring onto the stadium floor to celebrate. I push through the crowd, making my way toward the bench.

I have no idea if Piper will be there—we didn't exactly have time to make post-game plans—but I'll never find her on the field.

The sideline is overrun with screaming fans and I climb onto the bench, turning slowly as I scan the crowd. I make a full rotation before I spot my girl. She's trying to make her way to me, but the push and pull of the crowd is too much and she's being tossed about like driftwood.

I leap from the bench and shove through the crush of bodies.

The crowd parts like the Red Sea and there she is, right before me.

My heart swells at the sight of her, and I scoop her up in my arms and swing her around.

"Congratulations! I am so proud of you." Her breath is warm on my face and when she cups the back of my neck and pulls me in for a kiss, it's clear she doesn't give a damn about the dirt and sweat that covers every inch of my body. The kiss is hot and wet and it holds the promise of things to come. "I have to admit, you guys had me worried for a minute. I swear, I thought I was going to hyperventilate on that last drive."

"You and me both, darlin'." I bury my face in her hair, inhaling the fresh, clean scent of her. "Thank you for being here. You have no idea how much it means to me to share this moment with you."

She lowers her forehead to mine, a shy smile on her face. "I love you and I will always be here for you."

Damn, I love hearing those words.

"I don't know how I got so lucky, but I will never take you for granted."

44

PIPER

It's well past midnight by the time we hit the club to celebrate, and I make a mental note to thank Jenna for insisting I bring a little black dress, just in case. The guys are riding high as we settle into an oversized VIP booth with bottle service, courtesy of Austin Reid's father. Apparently, he's a big deal in the world of football, so while I feel uncomfortable with the extravagance, Brady assured me there's no point resisting.

I sip my champagne, trying to remember names as I soak up the vibrations of the hip hop song blasting from the speakers.

There's Austin and his girlfriend Kennedy, a tall brunette who's the kicker on the football team. Cooper and his girlfriend Quinn, a tiny redhead and self-proclaimed disaster who's already spilled her champagne. Parker and his girlfriend Sutton, a petite Latina gymnast who doubled as the Waverly Wildcat prior to bowl season. And then there are the single guys: Wyant, Smith, and... Yeah, there's no way I'm going to remember them all.

Especially when people are coming and going. It doesn't help that the bottle girl keeps refilling my glass.

I lean into Brady's large body, pressing my thigh to his. "How does it feel to be a national champion?"

"Not half as good as hearing you say you love me."

My heart flutters because I actually think he means it. "Yeah?"

"Say it again," he murmurs, his lips brushing the shell of my ear.

"You're going to turn me into a broken record."

"Trust me." He squeezes my thigh, his hand a comforting weight in the crowded club. "I won't complain."

"I love you."

He turns my face to his and presses a greedy kiss to my lips, his tongue probing the entrance of my mouth despite our audience.

"Damn, Vaughn! Let the woman come up for air."

Heat floods my cheeks and when we break apart, Brady flashes Cooper his middle finger.

"Leave Brady alone," Quinn says, chastising him. "He's in the honeymoon period, and I think it's sweet."

Coop pulls a face. "We're in the honeymoon period and you don't see me trying to eat your face at a public gathering."

Kennedy snort-laughs and champagne sprays from her mouth.

Reid just shakes his head and hands her a napkin, totally unfazed.

"Maybe you're the one doing it wrong," Sutton muses, planting her elbow on her crossed knees and resting her chin in her hand. "Exhibitionism is a highly underrated aphrodisiac."

Parker raises his glass like he's about to make a toast. "I second that."

The banter goes on endlessly, and I can't help but envy the easy camaraderie. Brady's an only child, but in his teammates, he's found a second family. One he chose for himself.

I'd kill to have what these guys share.

Even when they're ripping on each other, it's clear there's love between them. They'd have each other's backs, no questions asked.

What would that even be like?

Jenna's my closest friend and even she doesn't know all my secrets.

Because you won't tell her.

It's true. The only person stopping me from having what Brady has is me. I've never been good at letting people in, and yes, I know it's a result of my upbringing, but I get enough judgment from the world. Why invite more from the people closest to me?

Brady doesn't judge you.

True, but...

No. No buts. If I want the close relationships Brady has, I'm going to have to stop keeping everyone at arm's length. I have to let them in, just like I've let Brady in, which has turned out to be one of the best decisions I've ever made.

Yes, I was dealt a shit hand in the family department, and no, it won't be easy to let my guard down, but I can make my own family, just like these guys have, starting with Jenna.

Maybe someday Molly and Gran will welcome me into their family, too.

"And then you've got Squatch over there," Coop says, pointing to Brady, "creating a safe nesting environment for the baby bird population."

"I don't care what you say. I'm keeping the beard." Brady grins and strokes it lovingly. "My mom says it makes me look distinguished."

"Dude. She's your mom. She has to say that."

"Piper, please tell Farmer Joe over here that beards are so last season."

He's kidding, but it still sparks an ember of protectiveness in my chest.

"No way." I hook my arm through Brady's and lean into his warmth. "I like the beard and since I'm the one who has to kiss him, my opinion is the only one that matters."

"Facts!" Quinn agrees, raising her glass and sending champagne sloshing into her boyfriend's lap.

"That settles it." Coop rolls his eyes, ignoring the champagne that's just soaked the front of his pants. "It must be love."

"Speaking of love." Smith leans forward to rest his elbows on his knees. "Can we just talk about the fact that all you shady motherfuckers got wifed up this season? One minute y'all are single as hell and then, *boom!* Girlfriends everywhere." He turns to the women. "No disrespect ladies."

"None taken," Kennedy and Quinn return in unison.

"For real, though. Who am I supposed to party with this semester?" Smith flops back on the bench, draping an arm over the back cushion. "Y'all are leaving me high and dry and you haven't even graduated yet."

"I hear Langley's always looking for a drinking buddy," Parker offers with a smirk.

Smith groans. "Fuck that."

"I don't know..." Reid says, trailing off. "It might be time to find yourself a good woman."

"Exactly." Brady squeezes my thigh again. "Spending time with the woman you love is way more satisfying than playing the field."

Smith's brows knit together and he mutters something unintelligible.

"No, they're right." Coop nods sagely. "Think about it. Waverly hasn't won a national championship in fifteen years, but as soon as we all started dating, look what happened."

I can't tell if they're fucking with him or if they really believe it, but the theory completely discounts raw talent and years of training.

"You want a shot at a repeat?" Reid shrugs. "You need to get yourself a partner."

"*Shiiiit*," Smith drawls. "I'm gonna have to go talk to the boys about this."

Coop smirks. "Just don't forget what Coach said."

Smith cocks his head and the other guys all reply in unison. "Wear a damn condom. Anyone who shows up for training camp with a newborn is running extra laps!"

Sutton gasps. "He did not!"

Kennedy snickers. "It was quite the post-game motivational speech."

We all laugh and true to his word, Smith moves to another booth to discuss Coop's girlfriend theory. Judging by the looks his teammates are slinging his way, they're not buying.

"Athletes are superstitious as hell," Brady whispers. "Ten to one, Smith will have a girlfriend before training camp starts in the fall."

"That's...wild." But also, kind of sweet.

"That reminds me." Coop stretches his long legs out in front of him. "I believe you owe us an unforgettable show, Vaughn. Time to pay up."

"I was kind of hoping you'd forgotten about that." Brady sighs and climbs to his feet. "But I'm a man of my word."

I arch a brow in question, but he just drops a kiss on the top of my head and lopes off toward the DJ booth.

"He promised us a show if we won the game today," Parker explains.

"What kind of show?"

He shrugs. "Your guess is as good as mine."

A few minutes later, the opening notes of *Naughty Girl* drift from the speakers and a spotlight directs our attention to the bar.

"Holy. Shit." Brady is standing on the bar, back arched, as he leans against a silver pole that extends from the scarred countertop to the ceiling. "He's not..."

"Oh, he is," Parker howls, pumping his fist in the air. "Get it, big boy!"

Queen Bey starts singing and Brady slides down the pole into a crouch. Then he pops his hips, and the crowd goes nuts.

I whistle as he crawls across the bar, shaking his head as if whipping his hair, and I can't help but laugh because he's mimicking a routine I did for him a few weeks ago. If I had any doubt he was enthralled, it's been erased.

He climbs unsteadily to his feet and takes two long steps that aren't quite a run before jumping onto the pole and executing a chair spin. His hand position is actually pretty good and when he finishes the move, he transitions into a back arch. It's really more of a dip, but it doesn't matter because by the time he throws a few body rolls and finishes the routine with a fan kick, half the club is on their feet, cheering him on.

The song ends, and he jumps down to high fives and back slaps.

"That was hot." Sutton turns to me, eyes wide. "Did you know he could do that?"

I nod because I have no words.

"I. Am. Dead," Quinn exclaims, fanning herself. She turns to Coop. "Have you been holding out on me?"

He smirks. "No, but I have other talents."

Brady returns, red-cheeked but looking quite proud of himself.

I wiggle my brows suggestively. "Nice moves."

"Damn." Reid shakes his head, oblivious to the fact that Brady only has eyes for me. "I thought I had it tough in ballet, but that shit looks hard."

Brady shrugs, but holds my gaze. "You want to get out of here?"

He extends his hand and I take, letting him pull me to my feet. "Are you sure you don't want to stay to celebrate with the guys?"

"No one will miss me." He leans down to whisper in my ear. "Besides, the only person I want to celebrate with is you, and I'd prefer to do it naked."

45

BRADY

THE INSTANT THE DOOR CLOSES, I grab my girl and push her up against the wall, pressing my body to hers. I'm so hard it hurts, and the tension at the base of my spine has become a maddening, desperate need.

"You look so good in that dress." I cup the back of her neck, tangling my fingers in her silky hair as I kiss her hard and deep. She tastes like champagne and sunshine and I can't get enough of it. "I haven't been able to think about anything but fucking you in it since you put it on."

"Yeah?" She spins out of my grip, planting her hands against the wall before turning to look back at me over her shoulder. "What's stopping you?"

Not a damn thing.

I yank the dress up around her hips and hiss out a breath.

"You're not wearing underwear."

She laughs, the deep sexy one that vibrates through every cell in my body. "They didn't really go with the dress."

"You mean to tell me you've been walking around all night with a bare pussy and you didn't tell me?"

The corner of her mouth twitches. "What would you have done if you'd known?"

"This." I drop to my knees, admiring the curve of her voluptuous ass. It's sweet and round and when I drag a finger down her crack, she shivers.

I love seeing her body on display like this, and though I'm desperate to bury myself inside her, the taste of her pussy is a temptation I can't resist. I cup her ass cheeks and gently massage them as I move her into position, nudging her feet apart with my knees.

I've got a perfect view of her hot, pink flesh and I'm ready to feast.

My tongue glides up her center, and she moans my name as I circle her clit.

"That's right, darlin'. You know exactly who's eating that gorgeous pussy, don't you?"

"Yes."

I give her another lick and she wriggles her hips, angling for more pressure.

"You taste so good, like berries and cream."

"Please," she pants. "I need more."

Maybe it makes me an asshole, but I love it when she begs. Love knowing she's as desperate for me as I am for her. It calls to some instinctual part of me that wants nothing more than to please her.

I devour her, licking and sucking and when she's writhing against my face, her whimpers a steady plea for release, I fuck her with my tongue. She comes loud and hard and the entire floor can probably hear her cries, but I don't stop until the last wave of pleasure has subsided.

"You learned a new trick," she mumbles as I climb to my feet and unbuckle my belt.

"Thought you'd like it."

"You thought right."

I press a kiss to the back of her neck. "This is going to be hard and fast."

She nods and I fish a Magnum out of my pocket. I make quick work of my pants and roll the condom over my length before I position myself at her opening.

Christ. She's so wet my cock glides right past her entrance.

I grab her hips and tip them forward before I plunge into her, seating myself to the hilt.

"*Fuuuck.*"

Pleasure radiates up my spine and, in this moment, nothing else matters. The world could cease to exist, but as long as I've got Piper, I've got everything I need. She feels so good, her channel gripping me extra-tight after her recent orgasm.

I begin to move, each thrust quicker and harder than the last.

My balls slap her ass and the sound calls to the neanderthal in me, heightening my arousal as I slam into her over and over, chasing my own release.

"I'm almost there, darlin'. I'm going to need you to come for me."

She shakes her head, the blonde hair tickling my cheek. "I don't think I can."

Like hell.

I lick my fingers and reach around, finding her clit. The tiny bundle of nerves is swollen with arousal and I work her with abandon, increasing the pressure as I push us both toward climax.

"Come on, baby. I know you've got one more orgasm for me," I whisper, nipping at her ear. "You're such a good girl. Show me how good you can be, Piper."

Her head falls back against my shoulder and I pepper

openmouthed kisses across her shoulder as she bites down on her lower lip.

Christ. I'm so close. I need her to come.

The tension at the base of my spine detonates, sending me barreling over the edge into oblivion just as Piper's inner walls clampdown on my cock, milking every last drop from me as she gives herself over to pleasure.

We ride out the aftershocks together and when her knees buckle, I scoop her up and carry her to the bed.

She looks up at me with a soft smile, her pupils blown wide, and my chest tightens. "That was...wow."

"Darlin', I'm just getting started."

46

—————

PIPER

R ETURNING to campus feels anticlimactic after the Wildcats win in Miami. There are parades and parties and the guys on the team received a well-deserved hero's welcome, but I've spent the last few days trying to figure out how to move forward.

Not with Brady, but with myself.

There's a part of me that wants to bury my head in the sand and pretend Mike McConnell doesn't exist. After all, I'm not in Dr. Barnes' class this semester, and after I turned the tables on his blackmail scheme, I doubt he'd have the balls to contact me again.

But I just can't let it go.

I pull out my phone and text Brady as I approach the education building.

Me: Heading into my meeting with Dr. Barnes. Wish me luck.

He's in class, but that doesn't stop him from replying immediately. I don't expect it, but I have to admit it's nice. Not because I want him at my beck and call, but because it's comforting to know I'm a priority.

Brady: I'd wish you luck, but you don't need it. You've got this.

I smile and slip the phone into my pocket.

If only I had his confidence...

When I get to the education department, the administrator waves me straight through to Dr. Barnes. Her office door is open and my heart damn near beats out of my chest as I knock to announce my presence.

"Ms. Reynolds, come in." She gestures to the chairs opposite her desk and a sense of déjà vu sweeps over me. "I assume you're here to talk about the letter of recommendation you requested?"

The question catches me off-guard, and I falter.

I've been so focused on the situation with Mike that I'd forgotten all about Barnes' promise.

"Actually, there's another matter I'd like to discuss with you."

She folds her hands on the desk, waiting for me to continue.

"I—" My throat goes dry and my hands begin to shake.

I knew this would be hard, but I didn't fully grasp just how difficult it would be to sit across the desk from Dr. Barnes' and reveal all the details that could bring my world crashing down.

It's not too late to bail...

I could walk away now. Pretend none of it ever happened. But I couldn't live with myself, knowing Mike was free to continue exploiting his students.

"I've been working as a camgirl to pay for my education."

Nice lead up. Way to ease her into the conversation slowly.

Pretty sure there's no easy way to tell your advisor you're a sex worker.

"I film adult content and stream it as part of a subscription service."

Barnes' lips go flat, but she remains silent, so I press on.

"Mike McConnell found out about my channel and

threatened me with exposure." I lift my chin. Cowering will only reinforce the stigma around sex work and I'm not here for that. "He blackmailed me and I paid ten thousand dollars for his silence because I was afraid of the impact on my future if anyone at the college, or even a prospective employer, found out."

The professor's face gives nothing away. "I see."

That's her response? No 'That's terrible,' or 'I'll see he's punished,' or even 'What were you thinking?'

"You realize this information could jeopardize your student teaching position?"

"Yes." That doesn't mean I have to like it. "I don't want to lose my spot, but I am aware of the school's position."

I'm careful to not say I respect or understand it since neither would be true.

"And yet," Barnes says, drumming her fingers on the desktop. "You still scheduled this appointment. Why?"

Frustration wells up from the pit of my stomach, but I swallow it down.

Waverly's policies are archaic and any school that refuses to hire a teacher because of what they do in their personal time probably isn't a school I'd want to work for, anyway.

"I'm a damn good teacher." I straighten my spine. "I deserve to finish my degree, but I couldn't live with myself if I let a predator loose in the profession I love. If coming forward means I lose my student teaching position, so be it. I'll find another way to fulfill my dream of helping children in need."

Dr. Barnes studies me for a long time and it's a struggle not to fidget as her dark eyes bore into mine.

"Do you have proof of your allegations against Mr. McConnell?"

I pull a memory stick out of my pocket and place it on the desk. "There are records of the financial transactions on this flash drive. Most of our discussions were face-to-face, but I also included transcripts of the few texts he sent me."

Barnes takes the drive and rolls it between her fingers. "I'll need to review the files, but if what you say is true, Mr. McConnell will be dealt with accordingly."

Relief washes over me. The TAs reign of terror is over. I don't know if he was blackmailing anyone else, but I'd be shocked if he doesn't have other victims. He was way too confident for someone lacking experience.

"Thank you."

"Don't thank me for doing my job, Ms. Reynolds. I don't condone abuse of power, and I certainly don't condone blackmailing students." She arches a brow, giving me a speculative look. "It was brave of you to come forward."

"I should have come forward months ago," I admit, wringing my hands. "To be honest, I was afraid of what you'd say. You've always been so vocal about making good choices and being hyper-vigilant about our online activity."

"You know." Barnes leans back in her chair and crosses her arms. "It wasn't so long ago that I was sitting where you are. Oh, sure, we didn't have smartphones and streaming services, but I remember what it was like to be young and hopeful, convinced you can change the world."

Ha. "I'd happily settle for gainful employment and a steady paycheck."

She chuckles and it might be the first time I've ever seen her laugh.

"It might surprise you to hear this, but the reason I'm so passionate about professional conduct is that I made some pretty serious mistakes when I was your age." The admission lands like a blow. Dr. Barnes? *Miss Always-put-your-best-foot-forward-and-for-God's-sake-don't-give-the-admin-a-reason-to-fire-your-ass* is preaching from a place of experience? "It took me a long time to bounce back and I don't want to see any of you kids experience what I went through."

She doesn't offer to elaborate and I don't ask. Whatever mistakes she made are her own and dredging them up won't change the message.

"I wouldn't be where I am today if another educator hadn't been willing to give me a second chance. I was lucky, but these days, with social media, the past rarely stays in the past. The internet is forever, Miss Reynolds."

Despite her admission, the words carry the weight of a warning. "I understand."

"Good." She holds up the flash drive. "I'm going to need a written statement to take to the dean."

Panic squeezes my chest like a vise and I open my mouth to argue, but then I remember my vow: *Whatever it takes.*

"I'll email you a statement by the end of the week."

If it's going to be put on file, I want to take my time. Not only for accuracy, but to ensure I'm comfortable with the final draft.

"We'll need a record of his actions to pursue expulsion, but between you and me, I never liked him much, anyway." She offers me a wry smile. "He was always just a little too self-righteous, if you know what I mean."

Do I ever.

"Now." Dr. Barnes turns to her computer and brings up my student record in WildcatPATH, the student information system. When she turns back to me, she's all business. "We still have one rather important matter to discuss, and that's your student teaching position."

I wipe my palms on my thighs, promising myself that whatever happens, I'll be okay with it. After all, what other choice do I have?

47

———

BRADY

I PACE back and forth in front of the College of Education, my breath forming a white cloud as students file past for class change. Several people call out to me, congratulating me on the win over Georgia.

It's been like this all week. Some guys on the team relish it, sporting championship gear everywhere they go, but I prefer to fade into the background. Especially now, when football is the furthest thing from my mind.

A cold January breeze whips through the quad, but it does nothing to distract me from the thoughts ravaging my brain.

What is taking so long?

Piper's meeting with her advisor is going far longer than I expected. That can't be good.

Are they stripping her of her student teaching position? She's supposed to start next week.

My chest tightens, a mix of nerves and outrage. I shove my hands into the pockets of my jacket. She's worked too damn hard to lose this opportunity because of some asshole.

It won't just be her student teaching position she loses...

I banish the thought. It's a defeatist attitude. Maybe she

can find a student teaching position somewhere else. Or she can volunteer. I have no clue how certification works, but they're always saying on the news how there's a shortage of teachers. Surely she won't be locked out permanently because of some sexy videos.

It's not like she's planning to show them to her students.

The door to the building swings open and I do a double take as Piper steps out into the sunshine, a smile on her face.

That has to be a good sign, right?

"How did it go?" I ask, jogging up the stairs to meet her.

Her brows shoot up and she glances around, as if she might be in the wrong place. "What are you doing here? You're supposed to be in class."

"I skipped." Before she can say anything, I throw my hands up in self-defense. "I couldn't leave my girl hanging when she needs me."

I jog back down the stairs and grab my supplies, a bouquet of lilies and a hot chocolate from Daily Grind, the campus coffee shop.

She huffs a laugh and her breath crystallizes in the air. "What is all this?"

"I know you're a strong woman and you can handle whatever the education department throws at you, but I wanted to be here for you, just in case you needed to talk."

"That's very sweet." She stretches up on her toes and plants a chaste kiss on my lips before taking the cocoa. "Have I told you that you're the perfect boyfriend?"

"I think you just did. So?" I ask, nervous energy roiling in my gut. "How did it go?"

"Better than expected." Her smile falters. "Barnes promised to let me student teach, and she's going to write me a letter of recommendation for my job search."

Relief floods my chest. "That's great news."

Better than even I could have hoped for. It must be a tremendous weight off Piper's mind, too.

"It is." She nods slowly, her smile faltering. "But I have to write a statement about what happened."

Christ. That's not going to be easy. I hate that she has to give that asshole anymore of her time and headspace. "How do you feel about it?"

"Good, actually." She dips her chin, almost like she's convincing herself. "If I want Mike to be held accountable, I have to tell my story."

If he weren't such a manipulative piece of shit, there'd be no story to tell, but I don't say that because it's not helpful, even if it's true.

"I'm a damn good teacher, regardless of how I paid for school, and I'm not ashamed of my cam work, but..."

She worries her bottom lip between her teeth.

"But what? Whatever it is, you can tell me, Piper."

She sucks in a deep breath and exhales, the words following in a rush. "I'm going to give up camming."

"They can't make you do that. They have no legal—"

"No one is making me do anything. I've had some time to think it over these last few days, and my conversation with Dr. Barnes solidified my decision."

The news is unexpected, and even though I'm still not a fan of sharing Piper with other men in any context, I'm even less thrilled with the possibility that she's being forced to give up something she enjoys because of someone else's outdated, misogynistic view of sexuality.

You've come a long way in the last four months.

I really have. Piper opened my eyes to the joy of sex and I will never close them again. What we have is incredible and I wouldn't trade it for the world. I love exploring her body and trying new things with her and if the close-minded pricks of the world think it's shameful or dirty, it's their loss.

"Are you sure this is what you want? Because if you want to keep camming, we'll figure this out."

She nods. "I'm sure. I have enough money to scrape by for the rest of the semester and I don't want to take any more chances. Once I finish student teaching and get my certification, I'll be interviewing for a permanent position. It's just not worth the risk." She grins and slips an arm around my waist. "Besides, I don't need any more zaddies coming onto me. There's only one guy I want to dance for these days."

My cock stirs at the admission. "Yeah?"

"Yeah."

I wiggle my brows and squeeze her ass with my free hand. "Then what do you say we go back to my place and you can show me your moves?"

She laughs and the light, joyous sound of it is music to my ears.

I lower my mouth to hers, capturing her lower lip between my teeth before going all in with the kiss, giving and taking in the easy rhythm that comes so naturally with her.

We've only got a few months left until graduation and though we haven't talked about the future, I hope Piper will consider getting certified to teach in West Virginia. I can't walk away from the farm any more than I could walk away from her and the thought of having to choose feels like trying to split my heart in two.

But for now, I'm content to make the most of the time we have left at Waverly. I'm one lucky bastard and it doesn't matter how much time passes—it could be fifty minutes or fifty years—I will never stop loving this woman. There will never be a day where I'm not protecting Piper.

EPILOGUE
ONE YEAR LATER…

BRADY

There's no way in hell it's going to fit.

It's going to be way too tight, and I don't want to accidentally tear anything.

Piper swears she ordered the white Easter Bunny costume from the big and tall store, but something tells me getting it on is going to be like trying to fit ten pounds of grain in a five-pound sack.

Where there's a will, there's a way.

And my girl has determination to spare.

Not that I'm complaining. Spring has always been my favorite season at Willow Bend, and I'm thrilled to be sharing it with Piper. There's nothing like experiencing the renewal of life firsthand as the flowers bloom and we welcome new chicks, calves, and kids to the farm.

This year we're doubling down on the kids.

Not only do we have a new baby goat named Reese's—you can guess who named him—we've also added some springtime activities for the local children. We're doing hay rides and egg hunts, and we even set up a petting zoo with Gran's menagerie.

So naturally we're doing pics with the Easter Bunny, too.

I probably should have made Piper dress up since it was her idea, but she pitched it while going down on me. In that moment, with her lips wrapped around my cock, I probably would've agreed to hand over my soul if it meant release.

"The kids are ready when you are."

I turn to find Piper at the mouth of the stall where I'm supposed to be dressing. She's wearing a pink sundress and her hair falls in loose waves over her shoulders. She's as pretty as a picture, and my heart swells with love as I take in her bright eyes and flushed cheeks.

"I'm going to need some help." I gesture to the costume. "There's no way this is a one-person job."

Hell, I don't even know where to start.

She grins and sashays toward me, hips swaying. "All right, let's get you dressed."

Once she's within reach, I slip an arm around her waist and pull her close. "You know, it would be way more fun to get undressed."

She twists out of my grip, her skirt twirling around her thighs. "Don't even think about it. The kids are waiting for you." She grabs the costume and holds it out to me. "You don't want to disappoint them, do you?"

Of course not, but even more so, I don't want to disappoint her.

I take the costume and when I find the zipper on the front, I'm certain it came from one of those fly-by-night web stores. Still, I keep my mouth shut because it's making her happy.

Piper helps me step into the costume, and when my boot gets stuck in the narrow leg, she works the furry nightmare over my shoe, somehow avoiding getting the damn thing filthy.

I watch her as she squats before me. She's adjusted well to life on the farm and though she hasn't found a teaching position yet, it's just a matter of time. She's been working as a substitute and helping at Willow Bend in her spare time. We've settled into an easy routine and I couldn't ask for more.

Life is good.

I've got the love of an amazing woman, a loving family, and the simple life I've always wanted. That Piper's bonded with my mom and Gran is just icing on the cake.

For me anyway. For her, I think it runs even deeper.

It's the first real family she's had and I'm so thankful I can share it with her.

I step into the second leg and she pulls the costume up, holding out the sleeves so I can shove my arms in. As predicted, it's a tight squeeze. The damn thing barely reaches my shoulders and I'm pretty sure I've got the mother of all wedgies as she zips me up.

"How do I look?" I ask, extending my arms to the side.

She giggles and I'm pretty sure she's laughing at me, not with me.

"You look good." That she barely manages to keep a straight face tells me everything I need to know. "You just need the finishing touches."

She adds the gloves and shoe covers, but when she comes at me with the giant rabbit's head, it takes every bit of my will to let her put it on my head. It's hot and dark and...

"How long do I have to wear this?"

"Until all the kids have gotten their pictures." She pats my stomach. "Don't forget, no talking. The Easter Bunny is silent."

Right. "Because that isn't creepy at all."

"Shh!"

I let her take my hand and lead me out of the barn because there's nothing I wouldn't do for this woman, including making a complete jackass of myself.

~

PIPER

BRADY IS SUCH A GOOD SPORT. He might have played Santa without reservation, but as I lead him to the bench I've set up for pictures, it's clear he's not a fan of the Easter Bunny.

Good thing he doesn't have to talk.

I can only imagine what he'd say to the kids. No, that's not true. He's good with them and even if he's not feeling the fur suit, he'd never say or do anything to ruin the illusion. He's a great man and someday, he'll make a great husband and father.

But that day is in the distant future.

For now, I'm happy with the way things are, and I think he is, too. Living on the farm with his mom and Gran is...really freaking nice.

At first, I was worried I'd feel like an outsider or be in the way, but they welcomed me like family on day one. I've never been made to feel like an inconvenience or a burden and they're teaching me all kinds of things I've never learned, like how to cook and bake and cultivate a flower garden. Gran even taught me how to change the oil in my car and rotate my tires.

I'm anxious to find a full-time teaching position, and I've been interviewing like crazy, but they've helped me fill my days when I'm not subbing and I'm starting to feel like a fully formed adult.

The kids are lined up as we approach the photo area and

when they spot the Easter Bunny, a ripple of excitement goes through the line. Several of the kids wave aggressively.

Brady waves back and once we get him settled on the bench, I invite the first child in line to go up and sit with him for a picture.

I'm behind the lens today, so I've got a great view of Brady's interactions with the kids. Though he can't talk, he uses his hands to communicate with them, his outsized gestures comical in contrast to their tiny statures.

He really is a natural.

My heart flutters and it's impossible to wipe the grin off my face as I snap one pic after the next.

The way I love this man defies words. Hell, it defies logic.

I never knew I could feel so much or love so deeply, but every day with Brady is better than the last. Sure, we have the occasional spat over what to eat for dinner or what movie to watch or why he left a rank sock on the floor, but it's all small stuff.

He's there for me when it matters and I know that with him at my side, I really can accomplish anything.

A little girl in a purple dress inches toward the photo booth, her mom gently encouraging her to step up. The poor thing can't be more than three, and the look on her face says she isn't having it. Brady waves and she takes another step forward, but when he pats the bench next to him, she bursts into tears.

"It's okay." I squat down to eye-level. "You don't have to sit with him if you don't want to. The Easter Bunny knows some children are shy."

She eyes me warily as her mom wrings her hands.

"I'm so sorry. The same thing happened at Christmas, but I thought maybe she'd do better with the Easter Bunny."

"It's okay. Happens all the time." Not here on the farm, but I'm sure it happens somewhere.

Nora didn't take me for holiday pictures growing up, but I have a feeling if she'd put my three-year-old ass on the bench with a giant white rabbit, I probably would've freaked the eff out, too.

"If you'd like," I say, turning back to the girl, "you can stand in front of the Easter Bunny and get a picture without sitting on his lap or talking to him."

Her brow furrows as she considers, and I point to a pot of pink tulips.

"If you stand right there, we can get a nice picture for mommy."

She agrees and her mom flashes me a grateful smile as I snap the pic.

By the time we wrap up for the day, Brady's seen well over one hundred children and with only two criers in the group, I'm calling it a success.

I lead him back to the barn and true to character, he doesn't say a word, just waves as we pass the children in the petting zoo.

We enter the barn and Brady makes a beeline for the stall where he dressed as I close the door behind us. Can't have any kids seeing the Easter Bunny disrobe, now can we?

He peels off his gloves and drops them in the costume box as I pull out my phone and check the home screen.

One new email.

My heart leaps into my throat the way it does every time I receive an email lately.

It's probably just a sale notice, but I tap the email icon, adrenaline coursing through my veins.

My eyes go directly to the sender. *Monroe County Schools.*

I interviewed there three weeks ago, and I thought it went well, but it's so hard to tell and I heard nothing afterward.

Just open it up and see what it says.

I tap the message and hastily skim through the opening paragraph.

We are pleased to offer you a position teaching third grade...

A thrill races up my spine and a loud squeal bursts from my lips.

"I got the job!" I flip my phone around so Brady can see the screen. "In Monroe County."

His face lights up, or I assume it does. I can't actually see it because he's still wearing the Easter Bunny head. "Congratulations, darlin'. I'm so proud of you. I'm going to take you out to celebrate tonight."

The juxtaposition of his deep gravelly voice coming out of that costume is...*everything.*

Heat floods my core and I squeeze my thighs together in anticipation. "Why wait when we can celebrate right now?"

He tries to remove the rabbit's head, but I grab his hand.

"The costume stays on." He lowers his hand and I unzip the costume before setting to work on his jeans. I shove them down and his cock springs free, poking me in the belly. "I've always had a thing for the strong, silent type."

He pushes me up against the wall and then his hand is between my legs, stroking me through the thin cotton of my dress.

I tip my head back, reveling in his touch as tiny bursts of pleasure zing straight to my brain.

"Yes," I murmur, running my hands over the soft fur of his suit. "This is exactly how I want to celebrate."

Despite my words, Brady must decide it's not enough because he lifts my skirt and strips off my panties. He stuffs them in the pocket of his jeans and I silently bid them farewell.

He did the same thing the first time we hooked up and, in my lust-fueled state, I can't bring myself to care. If he wants my panties, he can have them.

I'll happily go commando if it means I get orgasms on demand.

He cups my ass cheeks and boosts me into the air, using his body to pin me against the wall as he positions himself at my entrance.

I know without asking that it's going to be quick and messy.

I'm on the pill and we still use condoms most of the time, but there are moments like this when he rides me bare. I freaking love it. Being skin to skin with him and feeling him come inside me with nothing to separate us is the ultimate high.

"Fill me up, Easter Bunny."

I grip his shoulders as he thrusts into me, seating himself to the hilt. Blistering heat flares between my legs and I roll my hips, urging him on. He pulls back and the slow glide is a delicious torture that leaves my pussy clenching at the loss of fullness. When he slams back into me, his thumb pressed to my clit, my brain goes fuzzy from the rush of endorphins.

Holy shit. This is really happening. I'm getting railed by the Easter Bunny.

And damn if I'm not loving every second.

Our bodies crash together as we chase release and maybe it's the risk of getting caught, but I get there in record time, the tension between my legs coiling tighter with each thrust. The orgasm takes me with force, an explosion of sensation shattering me to bits as Brady stiffens, his release coming just as fast and hard.

When the last waves of pleasure subside, Brady lowers me to the ground and straightens my dress.

I press a kiss to his lips. "Always such a gentleman."

He smirks, revealing the dimple I love so much. "Darlin', there was nothing gentlemanly about what we just did."

I laugh. "You won't hear me complaining."

In fact, you won't hear me complaining about much these days. My heart is full to bursting and I know that whatever the future holds, Brady will be at my side, loving me with every fiber of his being, the same way I love him.

Thank you for reading Protecting Piper! For more of Piper and Brady's story, visit www.jenniferbonds.com to download the Bonus Epilogue for a must-read glimpse of their future!

Visit www.jenniferbonds.com to check out Jen's other series!

ALSO BY JENNIFER BONDS

Waverly Wildcats

Holding Harper

Claiming Carter

Catching Quinn

Scoring Sutton

Protecting Piper

The Harts

Miles and Miles of You

Not Today, Cupid

Royally Engaged

A Royal Disaster

Royal Trouble

A Royal Mistake

The Risky Business Series

Once Upon a Dare

Once Upon a Power Play

Seducing the Fireman

ABOUT THE AUTHOR

Jennifer Bonds writes sizzling contemporary romance with sassy heroines, sexy heroes, and a whole lot of mischief. She's a sucker for enemies-to-lovers stories, laugh-out-loud banter, over-the-top grand gestures, and counts herself lucky to spend her days writing swoonworthy romance thanks to the support of amazing readers like you!

Jen lives in Pennsylvania, where her overactive imagination and weakness for reality TV keep life interesting. She's lucky enough to live with her own real-life hero, two adorable (and sometimes crazy) children, and one rambunctious K9. Loves Buffy, Mexican food, a solid Netflix binge, the Winchester brothers, cupcakes, and all things zombie. Sings off-key.

To connect with Jen, visit www.jenniferbonds.com to sign up for her newsletter and be the first to know about new releases, giveaways, and exclusive content! You can also find her on Facebook, Instagram, and TikTok @jbondswrites.